C000027131

Cover design: Shauna Mairéad

Editor: Zainab M (Heart Full of Reads Editing Services)

❋ Created with Vellum

This book is dedicated to all the messy haired, book reading, day dreaming, anti-hero loving, lost souls.

AUTHOR NOTE

NOTE: Shauna Mairéad writes in British English. Therefore, spelling and grammar may differ from American English.

Pronunciation chart:
Rohan (ROW-EN)
Saoirse (SIR-SHA)
Éanna (AY-NA)
Beibhinn (BEVAN)
Fiadh (FIA)
Áodhan (AY-DON)
Donnacha (DONE-NA-KA)
Lorcan (LOR-CAN)
Roisin (ROW-SHEEN)

Delectable Lies playlist (available on Spotify)

*Delectable Lies is book one in the **Kings of Killybegs** series.*

This is a dark romance, mature new adult (17+), and contains dubious situations that some readers might find offensive.

This book is part of a series and is **NOT** standalone, so expect a cliffhanger ending.

For a more in depth list of Trigger Warnings, you can click the link or find them on my Instagram @shaunamarieadauthor

Saoirse

"WAKE UP, SAOIRSE. WE NEED TO GO. NOW."

My mother tugs the bottom corner of my duvet, forcing a deep growl to rumble from my throat. I grip the covers tighter, unwilling to expose myself to the fluorescent light dangling from the low ceilings of our rundown, two-bed townhouse.

"I'm sleeping. Come back, never."

"Saoirse, I don't have time for your dramatics. We need to leave. Now."

My lungs deflate as a frustrated breath huffs from my nostrils.

"Please, Saoirse." She drops the empty grey duffel bag onto the foot of my bed. "Just pack the essentials. We can replace the rest."

As I draw the duvet cover back, defiance pulls at my brow line, narrowing my amber eyes. "What's the urgency? It's after midnight. Can't this impromptu move wait until the morning? Isn't there some way to switch your flight mode off? At least until the sun rises."

Ignoring my cranky arse, she heads for my dresser, pulling out clothes and underwear and stuffing them into the bag. "If you could rein in your attitude, that would be great." Her stern, clipped tone catches me off-guard, making me wonder what in God's name has her so on edge. Tonight is not the first time we've upped and left in a hurry, but we never run in the middle of the night. And never without our belongings.

I scan her fragile frame, noting the panic haunting her every move. Then, suddenly, my careless attitude shifts to worry, dread, and fear.

"What's going on?" I pry, although I have a feeling I already know. Whatever past my mother is scurrying from has finally caught up to us.

After averting her gaze towards the door, she avoids my question with a demand of her own. "Do as I say, Saor. We need to get going."

"Will we return?" It's a stupid question. I've occupied twenty-three houses in over twelve counties and attended eleven schools in seventeen years. But unfortunately, I was foolish enough to think this time was different, that maybe, just-fucking-maybe, we'd found a town I could call home forever.

For too long, I clung to that ludicrous pipe dream, allowing myself to settle, plant roots and make friends, believing or just plain hoping this place would be the one to stick.

I was wrong. Some things — or in this case, some people — never change. I don't know why I thought my mother was an exception. I should have known better. When the going gets tough, Éanna Ryan gets going. I only wish she'd tell me what has her running so fast; because I'm struggling to keep up.

Deciding there is no point in fighting, I swing my legs out of bed. My feet collide with the aged wooden floorboards. The heavy thud accentuates my anger and rattles my bones. "You need to tell me why." My eyes lock with hers, needing something, *anything* to justify why I should leave my life behind. *Again.*

"I'm sick of this. Every few months, it's the same old-as-time story. You get spooked and then run, taking me and the life I've built with you. I'm tired, Mam. Is it too much to want real lifelong friends and some stability? It's my final year of school. I *need* roots."

Her hands grip my shoulders, holding me steady and

squeezing so tight she's sure to leave finger marks on my flesh.

The soft orange glow bleeds through my bedroom window from the streetlights, illuminating her chestnut hair and the tired lines around her grey eyes. "I know, darling. I promise you'll get all that and more. But right now, I need you to pack your bag. No questions asked." Her words are breathless and airy, lined with a quiver of fear and heavy desperation. My defiance melts away as defeat fills my lungs. My shoulders sag, and I close my eyes. "Okay."

Once again, she wants me to stuff my feelings at the bottom of my duffle, hiding them beneath whatever measly belongings I'll bring with me. I need to believe my mam has a good reason for up-rooting me halfway through my final year of school. As soon as we get to where we're going, she better tell me what those reasons are. After all, she promised me.

Not that her promises mean much these days.

My teeth chew the inside of my cheek as I nod, unable to fight her when she looks so terrified.

"Okay," I echo, knowing that protesting will get me nowhere. It never does. "But once we get to wherever you're taking me, you tell me everything. It's time I learn why I've been running from a demon that's not mine."

Our eyes collide, and I see something I haven't seen before — a hunger, an unquenchable need to keep me safe.

Then, Mam brushes the hair from my face with a swipe of her hands. "Do you know why I called you Saoirse?"

When I don't respond, she continues, a small smile curled at the corners of her mouth. "Saoirse means freedom. My intention was never to lock you up. It was to give you a life where you could fly. Soon, sweetheart; soon, you will soar."

She pulls me closer, cradling my head in the crook of her neck. "Now, please. Pack your things and meet me downstairs in ten minutes. Not a second longer."

Right before she turns to leave, the unmistakable sound of glass shattering echoes from downstairs, freezing us both in place.

"*Fuck!*" Her eyes close as she captures her curse behind her clenched teeth. "They're here."

"Who's here?"

My mother's grip tightens as she draws me closer. Finally, her voice drops barely above a whisper. "I need you to listen carefully. There's no time for questions. Do what I tell you to, okay?"

Fear floods my solar plexus, hitching my breath and stealing my ability to form words, so I nod instead.

My mother exhales an explosive breath. "Go to my room and find the mahogany box hidden underneath the creaky floorboard in my wardrobe. Once you have that box..." The look on her face devastates me — wide, wet, round eyes; pursed, chapped lips; and a deep crinkle above her brow. She's terrified, but she's holding it together, barely for me.

With teary eyes, she swallows. "Once you have that box," she repeats, "*run!*"

My head shudders, rocking from side to side, refusing to leave her behind. "No."

"Éanna, I know you're here. Come out, come out, wherever you are."

I swallow. Whoever is downstairs is coming, and he means business from the sound of his hoarse, gravelly, somewhat sarcastic baritone.

My mother's eyes tighten, closing for a brief second as a plan formulates behind her crescent lids. "Go," she whispers, thrusting my duffel bag against my chest. "Don't leave without the box. The answers to all your questions are inside it, Saoirse. Once you have it, run. Everything you need will be inside that box."

Tears dance along my lashes. "What about you?"

She leans forward, and her lips press against my forehead. Her breath hitches as if she's drawing my scent through her nose. My body trembles at the finality; it feels too much like goodbye. "Never feed your fears, Saoirse. Because if you do, they will eat you alive."

"Éanna. You can't keep running." The male sneers, his voice louder, closer than before. "You know he'll always find you."

I want to ask who he is, but the bottom step creaks, and I know my time is running out. I need to go, and I need to go now.

My mother senses my fear, but she forces my rigid body towards the door. "Run, Saoirse, and don't you dare stop."

I take one last look at my mother's terrified face, and I do the last thing I want to do... I leave her behind.

Careful not to make any sound, I scurry across the hallway and into my mother's bedroom. Silently closing the door behind me, I click the lock and rush towards the built-in wardrobe. I tear at the floorboards, ripping them up one by one. Until finally, the old wooden box is visible.

Behind the door, my mother's screams rip through me, and vomit barrels up my throat, burning my oesophagus.

"Fuck you. You'll never take my baby from me. Over my dead body." Although muffled by the closed door, her words ring loud and clear. "Run, Saoirse. Keep running."

I unzip my bag in a flurry and shove the box inside, not stopping to look at the intricate detail carved onto the lid.

I rush towards the window, push it open, and climb

out onto the utility room roof. The chilly night air steals my breath, filling my lungs with a razor-sharp bite. Looking down, my fear of heights causes my head to spin. Sure, it's only one story, and I could probably jump it with no significant injuries. *Fuck.*

Cold sweat seeps from my pores, and I can't seem to control the goosebumps that have taken over every inch of my body. Then, when the bedroom door bursts open and a chorus of footsteps enters the room, I hurry out of view, moulding my body against the cold, gritty brick.

"Find her," the same voice I heard earlier roars with venom. "I'll deal with Éanna."

"Don't worry, boss man." A new, slick, velvety bravado licks my skin, raising the goosebumps along my arms. If I had to guess, this one is nearer, right next to the open window. "She's closer than you think."

I clutch my bag tighter to my chest and inhale, trying desperately to steady my erratic breaths. Then, without permission, my eyes flick towards the open window, and there he is, a black balaclava concealing his face. "Hello, Saoirse."

His hollow eyes pierce my skin, the colour of moss-covered acorns, just bright enough to shine through the shadows lingering in the moonlight. A shiver of fear races down my spine. In those earthy hues is a soulless man, the kind demons hide from. Yet, somehow, they draw me in, and I can't find the strength to look away.

Suddenly, he folds his body, climbing out the window and stepping closer to me. My survival instincts kick in, and just as he reaches for me, I do the only thing I can.

I rush to the edge and jump.

Saoirse

My bare feet hit the ground with so much force the rattle of my bones reverberates through me, clattering my teeth and disorienting me. Dizziness fogs my head, dulled by the sharp pain ricocheting up my leg.

Teeth clenched, I bite down and push back the excruciating pain in my right ankle. Trying to focus on my surroundings, I blink, but the sound of twisted laughter has me peering over my shoulder and towards the rooftop.

"Did you *really* think that was a good move?"

Standing tall, the mystery man leans next to the open window with his arms folded across his chest, immobilising me with his watchful gaze.

My mind screams at me, begging me to run as fast as possible, but my physical form stays frozen, assessing his too-cool demeanour. He makes no move towards me. Instead, he stands there as though he has all the time in the world.

First, he extracts something from his pocket — a small silver box. Then, he flips it open with ease, pulling out what I presume is a cigarette, slowly raising it to the circular hole cut from his ski mask, where his wicked smile resides.

Finally, he sparks his lighter, and the flames highlight those unusual eyes, keeping me paralysed.

I drink him in, watching as he inhales before blowing out a cloud of smoke. The white fog floats through the air, and the musky, woody scent travels in the breeze, tickling my nostrils.

Not a cigarette.

I rack my memory for any recognition of the mysterious man. He is tall, maybe six-one or six-two, slender but not skinny — judging solely on his skin-tight, long-sleeved black tee that moulds to his broad, bulging shoulders and defined biceps. Then, finally, my greedy gaze falls south, over his distressed black jeans and the black Prada combat boots adorning his feet. Whoever this guy is, he screams arrogance, wealth, and power, none of which is familiar to me.

"You have three seconds, love."

His velvety sneer has me crashing back to reality and

clutching my bag tighter to my chest. I peer around, searching for an escape — left, towards the main road, well-lit but nowhere to hide, or head right, into the thick woodland, secluded but easy to get lost.

"Two." He edges closer, readying himself to pounce from the roof.

I swallow, my gaze flicking between both options, neither of which is ideal.

He drops his blunt and then stomps on it with his designer boots. "Time's up."

I waste no more time and take off running into the unknown. The wet leaves cling to the soles of my feet as I sprint across the back garden. The frigid air burns my lungs as I push myself to move faster.

Footsteps pound behind me, and I know if I don't hurry, this game of cat and mouse will end far sooner than I'm ready for. I grip the strap of my bag, holding on to it for dear life. Whatever happens, I know I need that box and whatever it contains.

As the frosty bite in the air rushes past me, it pinches my cheeks. The throbbing in my ankle worsens, but I don't stop. I can't stop.

The fence comes into view, and I hang right, where the wooden boards have rotted, leaving a small gap I can squeeze through. My heart thumps in my eardrums, matching the faltering thud of my feet against the dew-covered grass.

Menacing laughter cuts through the white noise fogging my brain, a haunting sound that shivers through my core. "Running will only get you so far, love. You have something that belongs to us, and I won't stop chasing you until I have it."

I drop to my knees, pushing through the evergreen shrubs blocking my path to freedom. The branches tear at my exposed arms, decorating my skin with hundreds of tiny red scratches, but I don't allow it to slow me down. Finally, once the gap is exposed, I rip the bag from my shoulder and shove it through the hole in the fence, at last squeezing myself through it.

The streetlights fade, leaving me to depend on nothing but the light of the moon peeking through the thick woodland. I haul the bag over my shoulder and take off with little to no visibility, depending only on my other senses. Raising my hands, I use them to guide me through the night. My ears prick as the sound of the forest comes to life — leaves rustling in the breeze, owls hooting overhead, the sound of my heavy footsteps slugging through the waterlogged mud…and *him*.

"You can't run forever, love. Eventually, you'll run out of steam. Of course, you could try to hide, but I'll still find you. I know this forest inside out. After all, I've been watching you from it for weeks now."

His voice bleeds through the night, and somehow it appears to be coming from every direction. Something about his tone and how it licks over my skin ignites fear and terror, yet it excites me. Maybe it's the thrill of the chase or the impending high of danger it brings, but whatever it is, it's both petrifying and exhilarating.

The treeline thins, opening into a small — yet still enclosed by trees — clearing, and I struggle to keep moving. My feet are torn to shreds, wounded by the fallen debris. My pace slows as I struggle to push forward. I look over my shoulder, seeking him out, whoever *he* may be.

My skin pricks with awareness, and even though I can't see him, I know he's close enough, watching me from behind the thick forest. I can feel those hypnotic eyes on me, scorching my insides.

I stop and scream into the night, "What do you want from me? I have nothing."

His shadowy figure steps out from behind a large oak tree, but his eyes aren't on me. Instead, they're downcast to his boots. "You made me dirty my new boots."

My natural defence mechanism kicks in, and the sarcastic comment flies from my lips before I can stop it. "You're worried about your fuckin' boots?"

He slinks closer, and the moonlight glimmers against

the object dangling from his gloved grip, and I swallow the nervous energy trapped in the base of my throat.

His wrist twists, spinning the double-edged knife with ease. "Not worried, love. Annoyed might be more fitting."

I edge back, but my spine greets an algae-covered trunk. "Who are you?"

He advances, enclosing me in. I'm trapped, exposed to him and his motive with nowhere to go.

Three more steps, and he moulds his chest to mine. "I think I'm the hero." His lips curl to one side. "You think I'm the villain." His tongue slides across his perfect white teeth, taunting me with how unfazed he seems.

"Which one is it?"

The blade of his knife slides along the curve of my neck, dancing over my skin, but not enough to leave a permanent mark.

"I suppose it's a matter of perspective."

I draw in a breath, which I regret when his intoxicating scent penetrates my nose — fresh, masculine, powerful, and downright sinful.

"Creed Aventus."

His words break through my scent-induced fog. "Huh?"

"The name of my cologne. You seemed to take a good whiff, so I thought I'd tell you why I smell utterly un-fuck-ing-touchable."

Frustrated by how easily he crawls beneath my skin, I push against his solid chest.

"Now, now. No need to be so aggressive."

"Says the guy holding me hostage with a knife," I mutter, not meant for his ears, but our proximity does me no favours.

"Listen, love. This" — he gestures between us with the tip of his knife — "doesn't need to be difficult. Just give me the USB, and I'll be on my merry way."

Confusion settles on my brow line, and I narrow my eyes at him. "What the hell are you talking about?"

"The box you took," he clarifies. "Something I need is in that box. So, either you give it to me, and I let you keep the rest of the junk in there." The tip of his knife trails down my throat, over the flimsy material of my tank top, through the valley of my breast, and over the tiny swell of my stomach. Until finally, it meets the waistband of my pyjama bottoms. "Or I take it all."

His twisted smile peeks out from behind his mask-covered face, unnerving me, but I do my best to remain indifferent.

"How did you—"

"I saw you. I was in the room when you stormed in, Saoirse."

"Then why didn't you stop me?"

His knife presses against my lower stomach, the pressure just enough to pierce my skin. "Two reasons. One, I didn't think you'd jump. And two, if you did, I'd enjoy chasing you."

I swallow, clenching my stomach muscles beneath his blade.

"Just the USB?" I know I shouldn't even contemplate handing it over to him, but what choice do I have? If I want to get out of this fucking forest without losing all the answers to a lifetime of questions, much less alive, I need to give him what he wants.

His wicked gaze focuses on my eyes. "What will it be, love?"

Closing my eyes, I suck in a fortifying breath. "Fine, but that's all you're getting."

He steps back, just enough to allow me to reach into my duffle. Once my fingers glide across the mahogany, I pull it out and flip the lid. The nameless guy holds his phone towards the box, shining a light for me to see the contents inside. The faint smell of old worn paper, musk, and dust assaults my nose. My eyes scan the documents, notes, and old photographs as I search for the USB he's demanding.

"There." He points to the solid gold Celtic knot keychain I've seen a million times. "That's it."

"No. That is a family heirloom, not a USB." I shake my head, realising a little too late that this is why my mother told me to take the box. This keychain has been in my family for generations. They have passed it down to the eldest member of the Ryan family on the day they turn eighteen, which is only a couple of weeks away for me.

"Naïve little Saoirse. Did your mother teach you anything? Most of the time, all is not what it seems." He plucks the keychain from the box and then twists the bottom like a Rubik's cube. The base comes away, and right there, beneath the gold casing, is what he said — a USB.

I reach for it, but he holds it high above his head, far out of my reach.

"Ah ah ah."

"Give it back."

"A deal's a deal."

His hollow eyes drop to the box clutched against my chest, and he scans the intricate design carved on the lid. "Time for you to disappear before I change my mind. But don't worry. I'll see you real soon, love."

A slow, smug smile curls at the corners of his lips. Then he pivots on his heel and struts away, leaving me stranded in the forest with more fucking questions and even fewer answers.

What the fuck just happened?

I can't help it. My eyes follow him as he retreats

towards the house, more than likely holding the one thing I need to piece all this shit together.

My rapid breaths pound my eardrums, a fast-paced tango mirroring the rise and fall of my breasts. Once he's out of sight, I close my eyes and gulp in a lungful of the frosty night air. The burn rushes through my chest, trapping itself inside my lungs, but it's soothed by the rush of relief coursing through my veins.

I don't know what I was expecting from my hunter, but a snippy, careless attitude, paired with sarcastic goading, was definitely not it. He could have left me for dead, taking everything I possess with him...worse, he could have killed me. I could see it in his eyes. The flicker of darkness swirling beneath their depths.

Ruthless, cunning, and downright intoxicating — a lethal combination.

That man, whoever he was, could have murdered me with his bare hands, and he would have slept like a baby after the deed. So, the question is: why didn't he?

The urge to follow him gnaws at me, but my mother's words force me to retreat.

Never feed your fears, Saoirse. Because if you do, they will eat you alive.

Promise me; whatever happens, you will not turn back.

Run, Saoirse, and don't you dare stop.

The night wraps around me like ivy vines, strangling

my ability to breathe. More confused than ever, my mind races. Why tell me to disappear when it seems the goal was to find me?

I need answers, but I sure as shit won't find them standing barefoot in the middle of the woods in this one-horse town. My focus shifts to the box clutched against my chest.

Flipping the lid for a second time tonight, I search for any sort of information I can use. A worn photo catches my eye. I don't recognise the young couple or the building they're standing in front of, but something inside me screams at me to look harder. Defeat eventually seeps in, but before I toss the photograph back, I flip it over. In my mother's distinct cursive handwriting, there's a note with an address attached.

Saoirse, if you are reading this, find the couple in this photo — Oliver and Fiadh Devereux.

3 Raglan Street,

Kingscourt,

Killybegs.

You'll be safe there, for now.

And, Saoirse, remember...Trust can only be earned, not given freely.

Mam. X

Guess, I know my next destination. "Killybegs, here I come."

Rohan

"Where the fuck is she?"

I kick back in my seat, plonk my feet on the edge of my father's desk, and place my hands behind my head.

Watching Gabriel King have one of his colossal meltdowns is one of my favourite pastimes. Especially when the veins protrude on his forehead, as they are now. "You had one job, Rohan. One."

He paces back and forth, frustration evident at the way he's gripped his hair in his hands. "Can you do nothing right? And for fuck's sake, take your feet off my desk. Show some fuckin' respect, son."

"She got away. Once she took off into the forest behind her house, I lost her."

Okay, that's a blatant lie, but what my ole man doesn't know won't hurt him.

Sure, I followed her into the woods, and I intended to tie her up and drag her back here, per my father's request, but then I saw the box she clutched as though it were her only lifeline. The Ryan family crest, amongst others, was delicately engraved into the ancient old redwood top, and I knew I didn't have to kidnap the heir to the Ryan family because pretty little Saoirse would find her way home all on her own.

It's not what my father asked, but I'm not exactly known for following orders. I have my own motives for the missing, and most definitely clueless, gangland princess, and letting her come to me could work out better for my bigger plan.

I bite down on my bottom lip, muffling the laughter teasing the tip of my tongue, but I do as I'm told and remove my feet from his precious desk. Even I know when not to push Gabriel's buttons.

"What's so important about this bitch, anyway?" I ask as I turn to face him, playing innocent. "I get that she's a Ryan, but keeping her away from here would be the better choice, no? The Ryan seat is free for the takin'. Especially if little Saoirse stays hidden."

My father drops to his hunkers before me; his eyes, a mirror image of my own, scalding my skin. "There's more than that at play here, Rohan. And contrary to what you think, you do not know everything, so do what you're fuckin' asked to do next time."

"How the fuck am I to know there's more at stake when you won't tell me shit?"

Oh, how easy the lies fall from my lips when they're all I've been fed my entire life.

One swift and lethal movement, and his hand curls around my throat, squeezing so fucking tight, he cuts off my airflow. "Listen here, son. You may hold the King surname, but you're not in charge. You're nothing more than a foot soldier, and until you stop fuckin' up and start doing what you are told to do, it will stay that way. Understood?"

I nod, unable to formulate words as his hand crushes my windpipe.

Finally, he loosens his grip and then stands to full height, peering at me with fierce eyes. "You better hope Saoirse Ryan doesn't step foot in Killybegs because if Oliver Devereux gets to her before we do, we're fucked. Now get out of my office. I need to clean up the mess you made before everyone finds out what a colossal fuckup my son is."

I stand, then raise my hand to my head, saluting my arsehole father. "Yes, sir. I've got shit to do, anyway."

Little does he know, Saoirse Ryan is already on route

to his kingdom, and I'm going to have one hell of a time helping her tear it fucking down.

Your reign is almost over, ole man, and I'm going to fucking enjoy taking it from you.

WHERE THE FUCK IS SHE?

Ironically, that's the same question my father asked me two days ago when I returned, *empty fucking handed,* as he so eloquently put it.

Three nights ago, when I stood in the woods with the long-lost princess, it was painfully apparent she was, and most likely still is, unaware of her mother's past and the legacy she left behind. It was all over her annoyingly alluring face.

Saoirse didn't know who we were or why we were there…because if she did, I can guarantee she wouldn't have hesitated when she jumped off the roof.

She would have run and never looked back.

She might think I let her go, but Saoirse hasn't seen the last of me, and once she arrives at my playground — which should be any minute now — I'm going to enjoy teaching her how to play my games.

"It's been days, man. You sure she's coming?" Aodhán's voice quips through my Air Pods. "What does she look like? She could walk right by me, and I wouldn't notice her."

"Trust me," I reply. "Saoirse Ryan is not someone who goes unnoticed."

From the front seat of my gunmetal grey Lamborghini Aventador SVJ, I peer across the street towards the bus station. I spot Aodhán waiting by the doorway to arrivals, ready and bouncing on the balls of his feet, trying his damndest to keep warm on this piss-cold Irish day.

Passengers flood off the bus, and my best friend — and right-hand man — scans every face, searching for a girl he has not seen before. I can tell the second he spots her. His shoulders stiffen, and his back goes rigid.

Jackpot, love, I knew you'd find your way.

"Fuck me," he moans. "Please tell me that's not her?"

Head bowed, her long tresses of black velvet fall forward, curtaining her face. Her shoulders are round, caved into her chest as she clings to herself, but her frightened composure doesn't steal from her beauty. It enhances it.

I know Aodhán sees it too, the kind of beauty men start wars over.

Saoirse Ryan is trouble, or as my father says: bad for business — just like her mother was all those years ago when the last generation took over as the Kings of Killybegs.

I believe she's quite the opposite, especially if I can make her fall for me.

Unbeknownst to her, Saoirse holds the key to this empire. That much I'm sure of —my father wouldn't be this threatened if she didn't possess what it takes to ruin his plans. I know she's the match I need to ignite to watch my father go up in flames, and that's precisely why I let her go. She needs to come to me, and thankfully, I'm a patient man when it comes to getting what I deserve. The Killybegs empire will be mine, and Saoirse is the first step in making that a reality.

I need to be careful, though, because as much as I hate to admit it, nobody has ever looked at me the way Saoirse did that night. A wild, hypnotic blend of curiosity, excitement, fear, and lust rolled into a beautiful parcel of burnt oranges and rustic brown hues. It was those fucking eyes that made me halt and stop my pursuit. The same eyes that, if I let them, I know I'd lose my blackened soul to their depths.

Together, we'd be toxic, but I crave her, nonetheless.

I can't let that happen, though.

Lust is for the weak, and love is for the poor — the only lesson my father taught me that holds any fucking substance.

Inserting myself into Saoirse's life has one purpose, but

if I get to fuck her while I screw her over, all the better for me.

"Rí, is it her?" Aodhán repeats, breaking through my fog.

"Yeah, it's her."

Finally, she lifts her head, peering left and right before reaching into her pocket and pulling out something that resembles a piece of paper.

My eyes never leave her as she glances from her hands towards the people bustling around the busy bus station and back again.

"What's our next move?"

"Walk towards her. She looks lost. See if she needs help."

"Are you fuckin' serious? Do I look like a tour guide?"

"Stop being a little bitch, Aodhán, and do what you are told."

"For someone who detests his father so much, you're sounding *a lot* like him."

"Fuck you." I start my engine and press down on the accelerator, ready to put my next step into motion.

"Hey," Aodhán protests. "Where the fuck are you going?"

"Devereux's. Now, go…help the princess find her way. And Aodhán…"

"Yes, your lordship," he teases as he strolls across the terminal towards his target.

"If you so much as flirt with her, I'll rip your ball sack off and feed it to the pigs. Understood?"

"Loud and clear, arsehole. Loud and fuckin' clear."

Saoirse

As I stand in the centre of the bus terminal, wondering what direction I need to take, I pull my phone from my back pocket and dial my mother's number. But like every other time I've called her over the past seventy-two hours, it goes directly to her already-full voicemail.

I don't know why I keep calling her. I already know she's never going to answer.

That first night, even though every part of my body screamed at me to go back to the house to save her, I didn't.

Instead, I did as she asked, and I stayed away. I took the money from the box, rented a room in the nearest motel, and cleaned myself up as I waited to hear from her. The hours were endless. Seconds felt like days as I sat waiting on her call, only it never came.

By the second afternoon, I was going out of my mind with worry.

My stomach lurched in my lungs, rising further with every second of untameable concern and anxiety. But stupidly, I thought they'd got what they came for, so maybe, *just-fucking-maybe*, they'd let my mam go.

When the hours turned to days, dread flooded every cell in my body, so I did the one thing she asked me not to.

I went back because I had to know for sure. I couldn't bear the unknown.

Only what I found didn't put my mind at rest. It sent me spiralling. Gone was the home I once knew, and in its place, nothing more than a destroyed shell surrounded by extinguished ash. So, out of my mind with worry, I did what any sane seventeen-year-old could. I waited and waited by the phone, hoping, fucking wishing for it to ring. Only it never did.

Then, on day three, the news bulletins announced the town's headlines, and my worst fear became my desperate reality. My mother was gone.

She was in the house when it went up in flames, or they took her. Either way, the sinking feeling in my gut made me believe I'd never see her face again.

With no one to turn to, I knew I couldn't stay in Baile Laragh. I had to leave and find the couple in the photograph. My mother wrote that they'd keep me safe, and fuck knows I need that now more than ever. So, after forcing my grief down, I gathered the few measly belongings I had and took the first bus out of there.

And here I am — Killybegs, the Emerald Isle's hidden gem. Set in the heart of the Dublin/Wicklow mountains, this prestigious town is the home of Ireland's elite and most powerful families. I don't know how my mother knows anyone here because this place is a far cry from the life of poverty we've been living. Yet, here I stand, with nothing more than a photograph to guide me.

"Hey." A deep masculine drawl pulls me from my thoughts. "You look a little overwhelmed. Do you need help?"

My gaze roams over his pristine white Gucci trainers, past the black tracksuit with the Ralph Lauren logo stitched into the breast. Then, finally, I focus on a set of mischievous baby blues.

What's a guy like him doing at a bus station? With clothes that expensive, there's no way Richie Rich uses public transport.

When I don't respond, he lifts his hand and runs it through his thick blonde beach waves.

His lips quip to the side, and he flashes me a wide smile. "Sorry, that was a bit forward," he apologises. "I'm waiting for my little sister, and I saw a pretty girl looking around as if she didn't know where she was. Don't mind me. I'll just…" He steps back and throws his thumb over his shoulder.

Even though I'm in no mood to get hit on in a public transport depot, his cute boy-next-door awkwardness puts a smile on my face, and for the first time in days, I don't feel like the world is caving in on top of me. Of course, it's fleeting but nice all the same.

He turns to leave, taking my small moment of happiness with him.

"Wait," I call out, desperate to cling to the slight reprieve, even if it only lasts a few more seconds.

Peering over his shoulder, the cute stranger shoots me another megawatt smile.

"You wouldn't know how I'd find the Devereux family, would you?" Of course, it's a long shot, but in a town like this, I'm banking that everyone knows everyone around here.

His tongue travels over his bottom lip as he nods. "Out those doors and turn right. When you get to Maeve's ice cream parlour, turn left. Their gym will be the third building to your left."

"Thank you…" I let my words hang there, hoping for the handsome stranger's name.

"Aodhán." He winks, making my cheeks heat when his eyes sparkle with delight.

"Thanks, Aodhán."

He moves backwards, never taking his eyes off mine. "Not a problem…" He pauses, waiting for me to offer my name with a tilt of his chin.

Raising my hand, I brush the fallen strands of hair behind my ear. "Saoirse."

"See you around, Saoirse." Then, with a cheeky wink, he disappears through the arrival doors.

Maybe Killybegs won't be as bad as I thought.

THANKS TO AODHÁN'S DIRECTIONS, I FIND DEVEREUX'S GYM with ease, but I'm hesitant to push through the large, black glass doors because I don't know what answers I'll find behind them.

Who are Oliver and Fiadh Devereux, and why did my mother lead me to them?

Over the years, my mother did not mention anyone from her past. Honestly, she avoided it at all costs.

Who is her family? Where did she grow up? Did she have any friends or siblings?

For all the questions I asked, I never received a straight answer.

Stubborn to the end, my mam's response would always be the same: *Some things should stay buried.* Only now, I'm left to wander this life alone, and all I have is a box full of her memories to guide me.

My chest rises as I draw in a breath. Then, after filling my lungs with false courage, I grip the handle and push the door open.

"I was wondering how long it'd take you to come in. Honestly, there was a moment there I thought you'd turn and flee."

Startled by the unexpected greeting, my eyes flick upwards to the reception area. A girl around my age leans back in her chair with her feet kicked up on the reception desk.

Confused by her statement, I ask, "How'd you know I was out there?"

She points behind me, and I twist my head to peer over my shoulder at the wall full of windows I just walked by. *Were those always there?*

"They're one-sided," she states, validating my confusion. "I can see out, but nobody can see in."

Dropping her feet to the floor, she pushes herself from her chair and rounds the desk. "So, are you a fighter?" Her eyes roam over me, assessing me from head to toe and back again. "No offence, but you don't look like one."

"No, I'm not a fighter."

"OKAY! So, if you don't mind me asking, what are you doing in an MMA gym? Is it for the eye candy? Honestly, that's the only reason I work here. Have you seen my view?" She tosses her head to the side towards the complete wall of glass that gives you a three-hundred-and-sixty-degree view of the gym floor full of mostly shirtless men.

I shove my hands into the front pocket of my hoodie. "As impressive as that view is, I'm looking for someone."

"Hmm." She plonks her arse on top of the desk as her eyes light up with interest. "Well," she pries. "Are you going to tell me who, or are you gonna leave me in suspense? Who is he? Did he get you pregnant and run? Oh, wait, lemme guess…he cheated on you with one of the recyclables?"

Her wild and wonderful imagination humours me, and my lips tilt into a smile. "The recyclables?"

"You know, Killybegs' very own mean girls. Everyone knows hard shiny plastic is recyclable."

"Creative." I smile, loving how carefree and wild this girl is. "But thankfully, I'm neither pregnant nor heartbroken." *At least, not by a man, anyway.*

"Well, that's good." She winks. "So, who's this man-child you're trying to locate?"

"Oliver Devereux."

Her eyes widen as her brows jump into her hairline.

"A guy at the bus station said he owns this place."

"He does, but I think his wife might have something to

say about his side piece rocking up to her fine establishment. Just saying."

"Oh, no…I'm not…I've never…"

Her laughter cuts through my panic. "Chill! I was only joking. My dad would never step out on my mam. She'd kick his arse if he even thought about it."

Her dad.

"Whose arse would I kick?"

Turning to the side, I finally catch a side view of the woman whose photograph I've spent the past three days studying. Her eyes stay trained on her daughter, giving me plenty of time to take in her auburn hair. It's still as long as it was back when the old picture was taken, which, if I had to guess, was before I was born. There are some soft lines around her eyes, but other than that, she hasn't aged a day.

"Hi, Ma!" the receptionist greets. "This young woman here was looking for Dad. I was politely telling her he's married to a badass. You know, just in case she was trying to swoop in on him." She winks at her mam, and the easy banter between the two makes me miss my own.

"Beibhinn, what have I told you about messing with the customers?" Finally, the woman turns to face me. "I'm sorry about my daughter, she can be a bit…Saoirse?" Her hands fly towards her mouth, covering her shock. She takes a few steps forward and then grips my cheeks between her palms. "Oh, my lord. Saoirse Ryan. You've got so grown up and so beautiful. You look just like your mam when she was your age."

Frozen in place, I stand as she peers around me.

"I wasn't expecting you both for another few weeks."

"Wait, what?" I question her statement. "We were coming here in a few weeks?"

A deep V mars her brow. "Yes, darling. Éanna wanted to wait until you turned eighteen because of, you know, family reasons."

I want to scream at her that no, I don't know because my mother never told me a goddamn thing about anything. I didn't even know these people existed. I don't, though, because I can't seem to formulate any words after this revelation.

"Where's Éanna, anyway? Is she here with you, or did she head straight to the house?"

I don't know whether it's exhaustion, the weight of untold truths, or just plain grief, but my tears break free out of nowhere, as do my words. "My mam," I cry out, "is gone!"

Saoirse

Unfortunately, my minor meltdown has caught the attention of everyone on the gym floor. Beyond the glass wall, several sets of eyes bore into my skin, causing me to curl up into myself as I will the ground to swallow me whole.

My emotions rarely boil over. Instead, I disguise my feelings behind the mask of sarcasm and indifference. It's a trait I picked up from my mother.

It was always impossible to know what she was really feeling or thinking — an impenetrable vault of concealed thoughts and emotions — but like my mother, I erupt every now and again. Usually, it's in the privacy of my space. Not in front of an audience, but it seems the past few days have finally caught up with me.

Fiadh's hands hold me steady as her eyes peer over my shoulder. "Deep breaths, sweetheart."

Suddenly, her face hardens when her eyes connect to something behind me. Curiosity claws at me, and before I know it, I'm following her line of sight.

Through my tear-hazed eyes, I spy two men sparring in the centre of the fighting cage.

Toe-to-toe and punch for punch, they rail on each other with wrapped knuckles, seemingly oblivious to their surroundings. Sweat beads on their skins, making their patchwork tattoos glisten underneath the bright lighting. They move seamlessly, dodging blow after blow. Something about the duo fascinates me — chaotic destruction wrapped up in two deliciously sinful packages.

Beibhinn chuckles behind her hand. "Great. She's dickmatized already. And here I thought we could be friends."

Shaking her head at her daughter's sarcastic tone, Fiadh looks back at Beibhinn, but I can't tear my eyes away. "When did he arrive?"

I'm not sure which of the two Fiadh refers to, but Beibhinn's reply tells me she knows exactly which one of the Adonis her mother was glaring at. "'About fifteen minutes ago."

Fiadh nods before bringing her attention back to me. Her hand cups my cheek. "We shouldn't talk out here. We'll

go to my office. There's more privacy back there. Bev…"
she directs at her daughter. "Call Roisin, tell her to get the
guest house ready." After taking my hand, Fiadh leads me
towards the opening to the gym floor, but before we head
in, she spins on her heel, almost knocking me over.

"Oh, and keep an eye on him. Let me know the second
he leaves."

Beibhinn nods. "Sure thing, boss."

Finally, Fiadh pushes through the doors. Falling into
step behind her, my eyes dart around the open-plan space.
It's modern, and with the high ceilings, mass concrete
walls, and state-of-the-art gym equipment, I can understand why it seems most of the young male population
work out here.

I know I shouldn't, but my body betrays me by seeking
out the two men in the octagon. The taller of the two has
his back to me. His muscles clench with every movement,
and the tattoos covering his skin dance to the brutal two-
step. As stunning as this man is, his opponent makes
every inch of my skin feel as though it's being licked by
flames.

There's something about how he moves as if he's
floating on the very air he breathes. His black hair is
striking against his pale porcelain skin, highlighting his
haunted vibe. My heart quickens as he bounces around
the cage with a smirk pulling at his lips. His hypnotic

confidence reminds me of the mysterious man who flipped my world on its axis only days before.

Head bowed, he refuses to look my way, even though I silently beg him to prove my wild thoughts wrong.

Is it him?

My body screams yes, and my mind roars at me to run.

"Saoirse?" Fiadh breaks through my thoughts and steals my attention. She stands in the doorway to her office, holding the door open for me to enter.

My feet carry me forward, but not before I sneak one more glance over my shoulder. My heart stops when those hypnotic eyes meet mine, but he's too far away to determine the colour. His tongue traces the seam of his bottom lip as he shoots a wink in my direction. Then, without taking his focus off me, he darts forward, taking his opponent to the mat and holding him there by pinning his neck with his forearm.

"That boy is trouble," Fiadh mutters with a shake of her head.

"Who is he?"

Her response both intrigues and baffles me. "He…is his father's son."

Realising that's all she'll say on the matter, I slip by her and take a seat on the sofa across from her desk.

What's with the people in my life always avoiding my questions with non-answers?

"COFFEE?" FIADH THROWS THE QUESTION OVER HER shoulder as she busies herself with the state-of-the-art coffee maker in the corner of her office.

My nose crinkles. I've never acquired the taste for coffee, not from the lack of trying; it's just…too bitter. "Have you got hot chocolate?"

Her lips curl at the corners, then she bends to the cabinet below and pulls out a box of Butler's hot chocolate bombs. "You really are your mother's daughter, aren't you? Éanna never liked coffee, either. Luckily for you, I stocked up on these when she said she was coming home."

Home…that one word swirls around my head like a tumbleweed, struggling to find its place. Most kids my age can close their eyes and envisage a house full of love and laughter or the warmth of their parents' arms as they wrap them up in a safe hug, somewhere they can run and hide when things become too much or too scary.

A place called home.

I don't have that, not anymore.

Her words make me wonder, though. If this was my mother's home, the place she yearned to be, then why did she stay away for so long, and why did she hide it from me?

"So," I begin, hoping to coax some information from

her. "You must've known my mam very well if you know she hated the taste of coffee."

Walking towards the seating area, Fiadh hands me my hot chocolate and sits in the armchair facing me. "She's my best friend. There are times when I think I know her better than she knows herself."

"When was the last time you two spoke?"

"I've spoken to your mother every Thursday for the past eighteen years. Not once did I miss our weekly check-ins."

My eyes narrow. "How? Surely, I would have seen or heard her talking to someone that frequently."

"You were always at school. When you had days off or holidays, she'd phone once you went to bed."

Why did she have so many secrets?

"How come she never told me about you? About her life here?"

"She has her reasons, Saoirse. All she ever wants is to protect you."

"From what?" I roar. "What could possibly be so terrible that she felt the need to hide her true identity from me."

Fiadh looks down at the ground but doesn't respond.

Irritated, I push myself off the chair and allow my gaze to roam over Fiadh's office, which is surprisingly very feminine for an MMA gym. The same black, one-way glass wall faces the gym floor, giving her the perfect view of what's happening outside her domain. Behind her white and grey, natural-edged marble desk is a wall of rose gold shelving stuffed with books, Devereux's Black Orchid gym merchandise, and some files. Framed photographs take up the entire wall to my left, and before I can stop myself, my feet carry me towards the display. Many of the pictures contain Fiadh and what I can only assume is her husband, Oliver, alongside some fighters, but one photo, in particular, catches my eye. The one with a younger version of my mother standing amongst a group of seven other teenagers around the same age.

Realising Fiadh won't divulge the reasons behind my mother's avoidance, I try something else. "Who are all these people in this picture with you and my mam? Were these her friends, too?"

Fiadh pushes off her chair and crosses the room. A slight smile pulls at her lips when her eyes land on the photo. "We were all friends, once upon a time."

"If you're no longer friends, why keep this photo?"

"To remind me, buried beneath the power of the Killybegs Empire, the version of those people in that photo still exists. Somewhere."

Her features soften as though she recalls fond memories of better, simpler times.

"Can you tell me who they all are?"

Biting down on the inside of her mouth, she contemplates my request. When her eyes finally find mine, her shoulders sag. "Sure."

Using her index finger, she points towards the glass. "That's my brother Luke and his now-wife Maura. Next, we have my husband, Oliver, then me and my sister, Elouise."

If I wasn't standing so close to her, I wouldn't have noticed the slight dip in her voice at the mention of Elouise's name. "Bad blood?" I ask, more than a little curious.

"Something like that." She turns to the image, clearly not wanting to dive into her family drama. "That's Darragh Ryan, your uncle."

"I didn't know I had an uncle."

Fiadh rolls her head back before muttering, "Jesus, Éanna, didn't you tell this girl anything?"

"Clearly not."

"Darragh died almost eighteen years ago. On your birthday, to be exact."

Taking a closer look, I notice the similarities between us. We both have the same dark brown hair and shy smile. "How'd he die?"

Fiadh places her hand on my shoulder and squeezes. "That's a story for another day, darling."

I nod, then run my fingers over the next person in the

photograph. "She looks happy here. I don't think I have ever seen her look so carefree." A lone tear slips free, slowly sliding down my cheek until I catch it at the corner of my lip with the tip of my tongue.

"She was always the wild card of the group, kicking arse and taking names. It's why I love her so much. I know I only met you, but something tells me you're a lot like her."

I know she's trying to comfort me, but her words only make me feel worse. As if I didn't know the real Éanna Ryan.

"Who's he?" My interest piques as my gaze roams over the man beside my mother. Unlike everyone else in the photograph, he's not looking at the camera. Instead, his stare is fixated on the woman in his arms, and it's… strangely possessive.

Fiadh's shoulders rise as she inhales a deep breath, and her words rush out on her exhale. "Gabriel King." There's something about the way his name slithers off her tongue with poisonous disregard, and it stirs my curiosity.

"Is he?" The question lodges in my throat, swelling with uncertainty and blocking my airflow.

Fiadh recognises my struggle. "He's not your father, Saoirse."

"But you know who is?"

"Sadly, no. It was the one thing your mother refused to

tell me. Although I have my suspicions about who your father is, I know you're not a King."

Turning to face her, I wait for her to give me something, *anything* that will help me figure out who I am.

For the second time today, she grips my cheeks between her palms and surveys every inch of my face. "Enough questions for today. Let's get you back to the house so you can get some sleep. You look exhausted, darling. I'm sure the last few days have taken their toll on you. I know you want answers, sweetheart. I promise you, you'll get them, but not until I know you're ready to handle the life the truth will bring."

"When will that be?"

"After we teach you everything you need to become a true Ryan."

Saoirse

THE SUN LOWERS BEHIND THE TREES AS WE DRIVE TOWARDS Devereux manor, and just like the night, exhaustion creeps in, stealing the light, hooding my eyelids, and weighing down my shoulders.

The past few days have been a shit show. Somehow, I'm depending on a stranger for the answers my mother should have given me. A few days ago, if someone were to ask me where I saw my week going, I would never have come close to this bleak reality. Not in a million years.

Yet, here I am. Uncertain of the past my mother kept from me, unaware of what my present holds, and judging solely on Fiadh's less-than-informative words, I am entirely ill-prepared for what the future will bring.

I have no clue on how to navigate whatever comes

next. Especially when Fiadh keeps those cards close to her chest.

"After we teach you everything you need to become a true Ryan."

As I stare out the passenger window, following the thick treeline guiding our way, her words tumble around my head, but I can't grasp the hidden meaning behind them. My mother never talked about her family. I know her parents died when she was a teen, but other than that, I have nothing.

Fuck, I wasn't even aware I had an uncle.

Then we have Fiadh Devereux, my mother's lifelong friend, apparently.

Even though I don't know her, I need to trust her. All I know is that my mother wouldn't have led me here if she had any doubt about keeping me safe. Those men, whoever they were…want something, and I have a gut-wrenching feeling that something is me.

For now, the Devereuxs are all I've got. If that means following them blindly into the dark, I guess that's what I'll have to do, at least until I can begin to place what little pieces of the puzzle I have together.

Pushing down the hyperactive anxiety coursing through my skin, I glance towards Fiadh. Her hands are carefully wrapped around the steering wheel as she navigates us up the winding mountain roads surrounding the town of Killybegs.

The further up the mountain we go, the wider my eyes and the larger the homes become — long, lavish driveways that lead to mansions concealed by mountain rock and greenery.

With a side glance, she shoots me a small smile. "We're almost there."

Finally, large, double wrought iron gates come into view. Right in the centre, where the two gates meet, an oversized coat of arms is lasered into the metal with the words '*Virtutis comes invidia*' engraved above it.

Fiadh follows my line of sight. "The Devereux family crest," she confirms. "All the homes of the syndicate members have a coat of arms at the entrance. Personally, I hate it, but it's tradition."

Nodding, I ask, "What does the saying mean?"

She presses a button on the key fob hanging from her rear-view mirror, and the gates slowly begin to open when she responds, "Virtutis comes invidia. It means envy is the companion of virtue. It's been the Devereux family motto for thousands of years."

With a tip of her chin, she motions for me to look ahead. "After all, envy is not a sin, not if you use it to strive for greatness."

Halfway up what seems like a mile-long drive sits a

huge gate lodge house, but impressive as that is, it's not what has my mouth agape — that honour goes to the three-story monster mansion sitting on the top of the hill.

When Fiadh said house, I wasn't expecting it to be bigger than most fucking resorts. This place is insane.

"Welcome to Devereux Estate, Saoirse. Feel free to make yourself at home. Ar scáth a chéile a mhaireann na daoine." *Under the shelter of each other, people survive.*

After exiting Fiadh's Range Rover, I tug my bag over my shoulder and follow her towards the house.

My feet carry me forward, but my widened eyes dart around the exterior. I've never seen anything like this place. It's a looming giant forged by a mass of glass and stone, set into the rivets of the mountainside. The Devereux manor screams wealth and importance, both excessive and decadent, and I'd be lying if I said it didn't make me slightly uncomfortable. I've never known wealth like this. My mother and I lived a simple life, surviving paycheque to paycheque. I can't help but wonder if this would have been my life if she wasn't always running from her demons.

Following Fiadh's lead, I trail behind her as we climb the imposing outdoor steps towards the front entrance.

Finally, Fiadh pushes through the expansive glass doors once we reach the top, leading us into the spacious open-plan foyer, showcasing a grandeur double black marble staircase with wrought iron rails.

Everything in this house feels familiar, even though I'm sure I've never been here before.

Yet, grandeur as it seems, there is a comforting — almost reminiscent — feel about the place. The strange, unwanted sense of belonging somewhat dulls the uncertainty growing like a bad mould in my gut.

"Let me find Roisin and see if she has the gate lodge ready. The kids spend most of their time out there these days, and I'm sure you'd rather be with people your own age than cooped up in this place with the adults."

"How many kids do you have?" The question rolls off my tongue.

"Two." She smiles. "Beibhinn, whom you've already met, and her twin brother, Liam. He should be around here somewhere."

"Why don't you give me your bag, and you can head out to the garden while I sort out a room for you," Fiadh's voice echoes off the walls as she points towards the large glass doors leading to the pool area.

"Oh, and Saoirse…Don't go too far." She smiles. "Dinner will be ready shortly, and I have a rule that dinner is family time, and now, that includes you."

I nod, hand her my bag, then shove my hands into the front pocket of my hoodie. "Oh, okay."

Her smile widens. "Stop worrying. You'll give yourself wrinkles. My house is your house, sweetheart. Now go make yourself at home." She shoos me towards the garden. "If you need anything, the fridge out there is stocked, and the remote for the tv should be in the centre pocket of the couch. I'll come to get you shortly."

"Thanks, Fiadh."

"What are godmothers for?" She winks, then turns on her heel before I can ask any more about her *'godmother'* comment. I watch as her heels clap against the marble, and once she's out of sight, I head towards the garden, not knowing what else to do with myself.

OH, HOW THE ONE PER CENT LIVE.

Feet cocked up; I laze back on the recliner while adorning one of the soft, chunky knit throws I found in a wicker basket beneath the flat screen tv.

When Fiadh said I could hang out in the garden, I wasn't expecting an outdoor living room with a fully stocked fridge and a giant stone firepit. But, as insane as this house is, this garden area is my new happy place.

With a view of the mountains, this cosy nook is every girl's Pinterest dream. Fuck the room in the gate lodge. I'd happily sleep out here underneath the glow of fairy lights and the moon.

Flicking open the can of Coca-Cola I grabbed from the fridge, I take a gulp, snuggle up, and watch *The Witcher* on Beibhinn's Netflix account.

Hello, Henry Cavill.

I'm ten minutes in when my eyelids begin to close, and the past three days finally catch up to me. Leaning forward, I place the can on the coffee table before lying back and letting myself drift off to the Jaisker, serenading me to sleep.

The blanket I wrapped around me whips off, and in the next breath, a cool night breeze sweeps over my skin, making me shudder.

"Who the fuck are you?" The gravel tone forces my eyes open to find a blurry giant-like silhouette blocking the tv screen.

Willing my eyes to focus, I blink and push myself into a sitting position. When my intruder's face comes into view, I almost swallow my tongue. Beneath his furrowed brow, his striking grey eyes bore into my skin. Annoyance wafts from him, highlighted by his flared nostrils. My eyes home in on the skull-shaped studs pinching either side of his nose before they drop to his plump, pursed lips. Intricate ink peeks out from beneath the round neck of his black tee, travelling up his neck and halting at his razor-sharp jawline.

Mother of God, what is in the water here? This is the third hot-hole I've seen today, but this guy, whoever he is, looks nothing like the guys at the gym.

He's bigger, broader, and the artwork on his skin is a canvas of photorealism tattoos, not misplaced patchwork. Yet, somehow, it makes him seem…I don't know, more dangerous.

"What's wrong, darlin'? Cat got your tongue or some-thin'?" His intrusive stare slides over me again, only this time it lingers on my body a little too long. First, a pierced tongue slides across his bottom lip, then he bites down on his lip, and my entire body heats at his attention. I hate myself for it. This douche is clearly trouble, but I was never very good at avoiding that.

Standing to my full height, I square my shoulder and offer, "Saoirse…Saoirse Ryan."

One brow hikes up, levelling me with a glare that's both humorous and could also burn buildings. "Ah." He sneers. "The long-lost Ryan returns."

"What's that supposed to mean?"

His devious smirk widens. "That's for me to know and you to figure out, darlin'," he punctuates with a wink.

"Liam." Fiadh's voice bleeds from the doorway, cracking the tension between the tattooed God and me.

"Stop harassing our guest. I don't care how old you are, I will put you on your ass, and you know it."

The smile he flashes her is nothing like the devilish grin he gave me; instead, it's softer, loving even. "Yes, ma'am."

Shrugging past me, he halts at my shoulder and levels his mouth to my ear. "Do you taste as good as you look?"

My cheeks heat, but I know he's only trying to get a rise out of me. Dropping my tone to a whisper, I decide to play him at his own game. "That's for me to know and for you to never find out."

"Oh, darlin'...I'm going to have so much fun proving you wrong."

With that, he saunters past his mother and into the house.

Fuck me. This should be fun.

Saoirse

"So, Saoirse, Éanna tells me you're in your final year of school, is that correct?" Oliver Devereux glances up from his plate.

My eyes flash towards his wife, and she quickly reads the question brewing in them.

"Remember those weekly calls I told you about?"

I nod.

"Well, most of the time, your mother talked about you and your achievements."

"You may not know us yet, sweetheart," Oliver states. "But we know all about you and the fine young woman you've become."

I wasn't sure what to expect from the eldest Devereux, but it wasn't the laidback and casually dressed man seated at the head of the table. His grey-blue eyes are almost identical to his son's. Only, his appear less murderous and far friendlier.

Maybe it's the way he dotes on his wife, with nothing but love and adoration, that has me so at ease, or the way he listens to his children with his full attention, as though every word that leaves their mouth is precious.

Whatever it is, Oliver Devereux dulls my anxiety with his mere presence alone.

"Yeah, I am. Although, I don't think I will be going back to school anytime soon. I have to figure out a few things first."

Like where I'm going to live. How I'm going to survive on no income. Oh, and who the fuck those masked men were, not to mention what happened to my mother!

"Nonsense. You need an education, Saoirse. I'm on the *Killybegs Secondary School's* board. I'll see what I can do."

"Sir," I begin, "I don't mean to be rude, but I feel like I have more pressing issues than my education."

He cuts me off before I can protest any further. "Please, call me Oliver. Sir makes me feel old." He wrinkles his nose in distaste. "Considering I'm only turning thirty-nine, I'd like to hang on to my youth for a little longer." His smile is genuine, matching his joking tone and the wink he directs my way. "And as far as your education is concerned, your mother would want you to stay in school. So, until we can figure out what happened to Éanna, you're free to stay here and attend school with Liam and Beibhinn. I won't force it upon you, but I want you to know the option is there."

He's right. My mother always stressed how important it was to finish school and complete my exams, but how could I possibly do that with her gone.

Suddenly, Oliver's words settle in, and rage, as I've never experienced before, explodes from me. "You want to know what happened to my mother? Two men in fucking masks broke into our house. One chased me through the woods, while the other, I *presume*, lit a fucking match, burning down our house and leaving her for dead as it burnt to the ground around her."

I can feel the weight of Liam and Beibhinn's eyes on me, boring into my skin as I push from the table, the chair scraping across the floor with the abrupt movement, but I don't care.

Before I can storm away, Fiadh is by my side, wrapping her arms around me and turning my body to face hers.

"Saoirse, there are things about this life you don't know yet. Trust me, if I felt like you could handle them all, I would spew it all out, but you're not ready. Don't get me wrong; I love your mam with all my heart, but in protecting you, she's made you vulnerable."

"Stop," I cry. "Stop speaking about her in the present

tense. She's gone, and she left me here with nothing but secrets and lies."

"No, sweetheart." Fiadh's eyes soften. "She led you here, to us. People who could protect you at all costs, to the very people you need to figure everything out, just like she always planned."

Her hands glide up my arms, then stop at my shoulders. She pulls back and holds my gaze. "I know Éanna better than most, and until I see her body or proof that she was in that house when it went up in flames, I will hang on to the hope that she is out there. Trust me when I tell you, I am doing everything I can to find out what happened that night, but for now, I need you to trust me."

Squeezing my eyes shut, I hold back the tears burning behind my eyes and nod.

Could she be right? Could my mother be alive? Do they have her, or could she have escaped? If so, why didn't she contact me and let me know she was okay?

On one hand, it's hard to believe she could have defied the odds, but on the other, I want to think she's out there somewhere, trying to find a way back to me.

"Listen, sweetie. I know these past few days have been rough on you, but things will only get more intense from here on out."

"So, enjoy tonight, finish your food, and then Beibhinn will give you a tour of the gate lodge."

Lifting my palm, I pat beneath my waterline, catching the tears trying to escape. "Okay."

"Tomorrow, you will start your training, and on Monday morning, you can start school. Trust me. You'll need that bit of normality to keep you grounded." She pulls me into her chest. "Your answers will come, Saoirse, but only when you're ready to hear them."

I WAKE WITH A STARTLE, COVERED IN A COLD SWEAT AS MY heart rages against my chest, thumping to an erratic beat. Slightly disoriented, I inhale as I blink the sleep from my eyes before sitting up and allowing my gaze to take in the unfamiliar surroundings of charcoal walls with matte black furnishings, arched church-like door frames, and a plush smoky grey carpet.

It takes me a few seconds to register that I'm in my new bedroom at the Devereux twins gate lodge. After dinner, Beibhinn gave me a quick tour, but I was exhausted from the past few days. So, forgoing the party she invited me to attend, I crawled into bed before collapsing. It's a decision I now regret because, in these lonely moments, I remember just how much my life has gone to shit.

Clutching my chest, I take deep, steady breaths as I

scan the room, checking every corner for the masked man who played the leading role in my nightmare. Every night since the forest, he's penetrated my subconscious — psychological warfare caused by flashes of his haunting kaleidoscopic evergreen and rustic brown hues. Only in my sleep, he doesn't set me free; he drags me through the debris, and no matter how hard I try to fight, he doesn't relent. The dream ends with the same warning each night, with him standing above me as water rushes over my limbs, chilling my core. *Mine,* he warns. *You were always meant to be mine.*

My panic rises. *Relax. It was a bad dream, nothing more.*

Pushing the rumpled cover off, I slide from the king-sized bed and force my exhausted boneless body towards the open window. The night breeze rustles the curtains, and an eerie sensation washes over me as I peer out into the night.

Beneath my skin, my blood runs cold as the feeling of someone out there watching me creeps in. Realising my mind is playing tricks on me, I shake the unwanted thought away, slam the window shut and draw the curtains closed.

Fuck, I need to get out of this room, and quick.

When I couldn't sleep as a child, my mam would always make me a large mug of hot chocolate. Needing some comfort, I decided to check if there are any in the kitchen. I tiptoe down the hallway and descend the spiral staircase leading to the lower level. With each step closer to the kitchen, I become more aware of a faint pounding coming from the back of the house. The repetitious thuds feed my curiosity, and before I know it, my idiocy carries me past my desired destination, towards the in-home gym Beibhinn pointed out on our tour earlier.

Much like the main house, the exterior walls are reflective glass, old, aged stone and contradictory heavy metal beams. The beautiful blend of modern meets rustic Celtic Irish architecture is a stunning sight, but when I push through the gym doorway, its beauty doesn't hold a candle to the view before me.

Hands wrapped in white cloth, wearing nothing more than grey sweatpants, Liam pummels the large boxing bag, rattling the thick metal chains that attach it to the iron beams running across the span of the ceiling.

Only a fool would not recognise the enigma who is Liam Devereux. Arrogant confidence radiates from him, paired with a dangerously dishevelled exterior, making it hard for me to look anywhere else but his glistening skin.

Resting my shoulder against the doorframe, I watch him release his anger on to the bag, grunting each time his fists make contact.

Seconds pass, one hit turns into ten until finally, his shoulders drop with a rush of breath.

"You gonna stand there watching me like a deranged little stalker all night, or are you gonna come over here and release whatever it is that has you awake at four-thirty in the morning?"

My lungs tighten at his question, and I freeze. Even though I know it's a ridiculous action. It's not like my lack of airflow and movement will make me invisible. Besides, he already knows I am here.

"What's it gonna be, free bird?"

My eyebrows furrow into a hardened V at his use of the nickname. It seems familiar, like a memory lost to time. Deep within my subconscious, I know I've heard the name before, but where? I scan my mind and come up empty-handed. *Weird.*

"You don't talk much, do you?" He lifts his hand to his mouth as he turns to face me, then using his teeth, he grips the tape securing his hand and tugs. The white cloth unravels before he uses his other hand to unwrap it the rest of the way.

Tracing his fingers, I find his slow, precise movements hypnotic. He repeats the action with his right hand, but his thundercloud eyes stay trained on me this time.

"I talk plenty."

"Oh, so it's only my presence that gets you all starry-eyed and tongue-tied?"

"Did you come out of the womb big-headed? Or perhaps it inflated over time, like your ego."

His tongue travels over his bottom lip, and a seductive smirk curls in the commissure of his mouth. "There it is."

"There *what* is?"

He steps closer, narrowing the distance between us. Each step he takes tightens my stomach, and I find myself holding my breath in my lungs.

When he finally reaches me, he places his pointer finger beneath my chin and tilts my head until my gaze is trapped by his.

"The feisty fighter hiding beneath the sadness in your eyes." He winks. "Question is, are you ready to let her come out to play? After all, you are a queen, and queens protect their kingdom."

Stepping back, I pull away from his touch as his words tumble around my head, my confusion and intrigue blending into one. My brow furrows as I search for the meaning behind his cryptic statement. "What…what do you mean, my kingdom?"

Liam rolls his neck and shoulders, releasing the tight muscles from his workout. "My ma and da think you need to train before they tell you why your mother led you here, but I have a different opinion."

"Yeah, and what's that?"

Liam leans forward, drawing his mouth closer to my

ear by placing his hand on the wall behind my head. "Never send someone to battle when they don't understand the war. You're the key to dethroning a false king, free bird."

He inches closer, and his hot breath brushes against my exposed neck. "I happen to think you need to know what you're fighting for."

"So, tell me." My demand is pathetic, weakened by my airy tone and Liam's closeness.

Pulling back, he sidesteps. "Maybe I will, maybe I won't. You'll have to wait and see."

With that, he walks through the doorway, but not before tossing departing words over his shoulder. "See you at breakfast, free bird."

Rohan

WHAT IS THAT FUCKIN' NOISE?

Burying my face further into the mattress, I tighten my grip on my pillow and shelter my ears from the deafening sound.

"MAKE. IT. STOP!" I grumble, the words muffled by the bedsheets.

"Get the fuck up then." Aodhán laughs as he continues to blast a fucking foghorn next to my head, only solidifying how much of an irritating arsehole he is.

"I'm runnin' on two hours of sleep, and the last thing I need is my so-called cunt of a friend standing next to my bed, torturin' my eardrums."

"Maybe if you weren't out all night stalkin' Killybegs's newest arrival, you wouldn't be so fuckin' grumpy."

"Piss off."

"No can do. Your daddy dearest has called a meetin'."

After tossing the pillow at Aodhán, I roll over onto my back, push myself into a sitting position, and bring my knees to my chest. "Meetin'? About what?"

He drops his torture device onto my bedside locker and reaches into his pocket. "If I had to guess, I'd say it has something to do with the sexy brunette you're stalkin'."

My facial features tighten. "What makes you say that?"

"Just a hunch. Oh, and the fact his message read," Aodhán holds the phone up and attempts a horrible impression of my father's monotone, "we'll be discussing Rohan's astronomical fuckup."

I'm seconds away from wiping the smug, see-what-I-mean look off his face when he adds, "And just so you know, that part is not only in all caps, it's in bold too. You, my friend, are royally fucked."

I flop back and then repeatedly bang my head off the headboard. "Okay, so he knows she's here. Either he has a plan, or he's panicking and scrambling to put one in place." Averting my gaze to the ceiling, I run through possible scenarios. "We go to this meeting and play dumber than a box of rocks."

I'm talking to myself, but Adorn agrees. "He can't know you let her go. He'll fuckin' kill you on site. What about Lorcan? Does he know what happened in the forest?"

"Lorcan knows nothing. As far as he's concerned, Saoirse got away. He's loyal to Gabriel, and we can't risk him blowing this whole thing up before it's even begun." I tell Aodhán what he needs to hear.

"What about Donnacha? He and his dad got summoned too."

Once upon a time, Donnacha Deegan and I were best friends, back before he chose the wrong fucking side.

Unfortunately for him, he still believes he's one of my boys, someone I can trust and confide in, and until I get what I need from him, it will stay that way.

Nobody knows what I uncovered about the eldest Deegan heir, and until I can figure out what to do about the information, nobody will, not even Aodhán. After all, a good player never reveals all his moves at once.

All I'll say is, Donnacha's clueless bastard of a father wormed his way into our world by licking my father's hairy arsehole and throwing money at him, then his whore of a mother sealed the deal by spreading her legs and offering up her cunt as if it was a five star-hotel for my daddy dearest's dick.

The Deegan family doesn't deserve the power the Kings of Killybegs reputation brings, and once I dethrone my father, they'll be the first ones demoted. Good riddance to bad rubbish and all that jizz.

"I'm sure he did. My father always loves to have someone present to applaud his greatness."

"Are you ever gonna tell me what happened between D and you?"

Pulling back the duvet, I grunt, "Are you on your period? Do you need a tampon before you share your feelings?"

"Fuck you, Rí."

"No, thanks. As pretty as you are, Brady, I prefer pussy."

THE SECOND AODHÁN AND I WALTZ INTO MY FATHER'S office, we find him pacing up and down by the window. He's irate, judging by his dishevelled state.

For a man who is always so well put together, with never as much as a lock of hair out of place, he's a chaotic mess. Gone is his pristine appearance, replaced by a rumpled charcoal suit and wayward strands of ink-black hair. His tie hangs loose and crooked as if he's been tearing at it for the better half of the morning. He is unravelling, and fuck me, it's comical.

Scanning the office, my eyes roam past Donnacha and his dickless dad, Kevin Deegan, until finally, they connect with Lorcan Reilly.

He's a big bastard, who wouldn't hesitate to put me on my arse if I disrespected him, or his authority. For the past twenty years, he has run everything with the King name, from the legitimate businesses to the dodgy side deals.

"Sit." His words are quiet, but any fool would recognise the demand in his eyes. Aodhán doesn't hesitate and plonks his arse down on the couch by the door.

"You too, kid."

My jaw tightens, and the sound of my clenched teeth grinds in my ears. Of course, I could call him out for that little nickname, but I won't.

Lorcan knows I have a love/hate relationship with him calling me *kid*, and honestly, I think he only does it to piss me off.

Now, now, Lorcan. Two can play that game.

A smirk tugs at the corner of his mouth. He tips his chin towards the free chair across from his, motioning for me to take my seat.

I raise a brow, keeping the rest of my features unreadable. "I'll stand."

Turning towards my father, I ask, "Are you going to enlighten us on why we were summoned, or are we to take guesses?"

My father halts his pacing, then swiftly turns on his heel. Suddenly, his hands slam onto his desk with a heavy slap, the dense sound cutting through the room, and everyone freezes, including me. Then, the office is silent for seconds. Not so much as a breath is taken.

Finally, he directs his frustration at me. "Listen here, you disrespectful piece of shit. You are the reason we are here. You had one job, and you failed, *miserably*, might I add. Word has gotten back to me that Ms Saoirse Ryan has not only arrived in Killybegs, but she's staying at the Devereux Estate."

Over the years, my father has called me many names — arrogant, self-righteous, and let's not forget — pig-headed. But the beauty of being me is I don't fucking care. I'm known for being a cunning, calculated, untouchable bastard, and one day I will cull him and all his pretentious arselickers and then, I'll replace them with people with a bit more substance.

"Saoirse is in Killybegs?" Lorcan frowns, and I can garen-fucking-tee he'll be pissed I didn't make the effort to mention it sooner. *Oops!*

"Yes. She arrived yesterday afternoon. A fact you should have made me aware of. After all, you are here to be my eyes and ears. Instead, Donnacha" — he points to the smug arsehole kicked back in the chair facing him — "told me he saw her at the gym."

Spineless cunt, running straight to his lordship with every detail.

Okay, so I knew he saw her yesterday, especially when

he noticed how much she pulled my focus from our sparring match, but in my defence, I was banking on him not knowing who she was. If I thought for one second he would recognise her, I would have demanded he keep his rat-mouth shut.

Shoving my hands into my black jean pockets, I rock on the soles of my boots. "As interesting as the princess's arrival is, this seems like a *'you'* problem, old man."

"A me problem? Let me spell this out for you, Rohan, because your thick skull doesn't seem to be comprehending how much of a complete shit show this is." He stalks around the desk, stopping mere centimetres from my face. "If Saoirse Ryan comes to the syndicate looking for her rightful place at the head of the table, they will give it to her. She is a Ryan…heir to the Killybegs throne."

From the corner of my eye, I spy Lorcan shifting in place.

What the fuck is his problem? He's acting shadier than Eminem. Well, I suppose that's to be expected when you lose eyes on your boss's biggest threat.

Gabriel spreads his arms wide, demanding my attention as he gestures to everything around him. "If that happens, all of this, everything we've built, dis-fuckin-appears."

"We could have the boys watch her, make sure she

knows her place," Kevin interjects, making me want to rip his head off and shove it up his son's anus.

My father looks at his watch and then releases a curse. "Fuck. I have to go. There's a shipment due in an hour. Kevin, come with me. Lorcan," he addresses. "Formulate a plan to contain this before I have to take drastic measures."

"Yes, boss."

They head for the door, and once Gabriel's hand rests on the handle, he turns to trap my eyes with his lethal glare. "For once, do as Lorcan asks. Understood?"

I shoot him my best fake smile. "You got it, Daddy."

Once they're gone, I round the desk, plonk myself into my father's chair, and kick my feet onto the desk. "So, boss man. What's the plan? Fuck Saoirse into submission? You know I wouldn't be opposed to tying her cute arse to my bed and making her forget her own name, let alone the kingdom she's about to inherit."

Lorcan's jaw ticks at my crass language, but hey, what can I say? I love getting underneath his skin.

"Saoirse Ryan..." Lorcan spews. Her name rolls off his tongue as he leans forward, his hollow eyes boring into my skin. "...is out of bounds."

Crossing the room, he places his palms flat on the solid oak desk between us. "Keep her close. But under no fucking circumstances do you fuck her. There is no place for a Ryan in a King's bed. Understood?"

Aodhán and Donnacha acknowledge him with a tip of their chins, but I stay silent, unwilling to make the devil's advocate a promise I refuse to keep.

"Rohan?" he questions, eyes murderous as he glares right through me.

"Sorry, boss man. But fucking Saoirse Ryan is exactly what I intend to do."

Saoirse

After Liam left me to my own devices, I begrudgingly hauled myself back to my room, where I spent the rest of the early morning tossing and turning, fighting sleep and the unwanted visions it would bring.

Finally, the morning sun reflects through my window, illuminating the room with its warm, orange glow. Still restless, I push from the bed and head for my duffle bag.

Maybe if I busy myself unpacking the few belongings I managed to take with me, which isn't much — a few clean pairs of underwear, two pairs of leggings, and two ratty old t-shirts — I can get out of my head.

As I open the zipper, my attention strays from my task to the old wooden box perched on top. I haven't opened it since the motel, not wanting to relive the trauma its existence brings. Stupid, I know, especially when I'm aware it holds some of the answers I need.

Suppose now's as good a time as any.

My need for something, anything to explain how I ended up here grows, and I take the box over to the small vanity by the window. Once I'm seated, I run my fingers over the detailed lid.

In the shape of a triangle, three small coats of arms surround one larger one. The one at the top is identical to the crest I saw yesterday on the Devereux's entrance, and the two on the bottom I've never seen before. The larger coat of arms in the centre draws me in. Two lions stand off to either side, holding up the crest, showcasing three gold gryphon heads with the words *Malo Mori quam foedari'* scrolled beneath.

After reaching for my phone, I pull up my google search and type in the quote. Pages and pages of translations appear, but one, in particular, catches my eye, captioned: 'The Ryan Family Crest & Motto.'

Clicking onto the site, an image identical to the main image on the lid appears. I scan the text until I find the quote I'm looking for. Finally, I see it at the bottom of the page.

The Rían (anglicised to Ryan) family motto and Latin phrase 'Malo Mori quam foedari' translates to I would rather die than be disgraced.

It seems my ancestors were a morbid bunch.

Done with my research for now, I place my phone onto the vanity top and carefully lift the lid off the box. The dusty scent catches in my nostrils, reminding me of the old bookshop in my old town.

Breathing it in, I get lost in a nostalgic world created by typed words. Then, for a brief moment, I let my eyes shut, and my mind wanders back to simpler times when my biggest worry was what my mam was cooking for dinner.

However, reality seeps in, leaving me longing for a moment I can't go back to. This, whatever fuckery it is, is my life now. I just pray I'm strong enough to withstand all that comes with the truth my mother sheltered me from.

I reach into my mother's past with another deep breath and pull out a stack of old handwritten notes and photographs. Most hold no significance to me, nameless faces, unknown places, and random numbers scribbled with no meaning. One torn page, yellowed with time, stands out amongst the rest.

Éanna,

A heart as wild as yours needs to be free.

Free from all the ties your last name bound you to.

I need you to know no matter how far you have to run to keep her safe, my love will always follow.

Take care of our girl, and be sure to tell her every day just how much her daddy loves her.

Forever yours, always mine, protecting you from afar.

A lone tear slides down my cheek as I re-read the note repeatedly, searching for any clue about the man behind the words. The man who I know without a doubt is my father.

I questioned my mother for my entire childhood, begging her to tell me who the other half of my DNA belonged to, but she always shot me down. Unintentionally making me believe he didn't want me in his life. I always thought he'd abandoned us, not wanting any part of the life he created with my mam.

Year after year, I would wait by the door on my birthday, hoping for a strange man to come and claim me as his child. Pathetic whims of a tender heart; I know.

When I reached my teens, I gave up, choosing to believe he never cared about us, and whoever he was, he didn't deserve a place in my life.

However, this note couldn't be any more different to the false reality I crafted in my mind. These are not the words of a man who chose to leave his family for selfish reasons. No, they are anything but. A desperate man who let us go, all so my mother could be free of whatever bound her to this place.

"Who are you?" I whisper, even though I know I won't get a reply.

Riffling through the remains of the contents, I search for any information on him, but I come up empty-handed. Finally, frustration kicks in, and I fling the now-barren box across the floor. If he loved my mam and me as much as this note suggests, why didn't he come for us?

"So, my brother is low-key obsessed with you," Beibhinn calls out from her walk-in wardrobe as I sit on the edge of her bed, waiting as she picks out some gym clothes for me to borrow for my first training session.

"Um…what do you mean?" The slight squeak in my voice does nothing to help hide my avoidance.

As much as I hate it, she's not wrong, but she's not entirely correct, either. Over breakfast, Liam's stormy eyes remained on me, watching my every move. I spent the whole meal shifting in my seat and trying to ignore his accessing glare. So much so I can still feel the weight of his scrutiny beneath my skin. Would I call it obsession? Absolutely not.

Hate, want, curiosity, or lust — whatever it was, now is not the time to figure it out. I'm still raw after this morning's trip down my mother's memory lane, and the last thing I need to be doing is diving into the mystery that is Liam.

Sure, I can't deny he was trying to read my mind across the breakfast table, but for what reason?

"He's just trying to figure me out."

Beibhinn steps into the room, her brat-tamer brow raised as her knowing glare calls me out. She tosses a pair of deep purple Gym+Coffee yoga pants and a matching sports bra towards me.

"I'm calling bullshit. Everyone at the table could feel the tension between you two. I'm pretty sure my ma was playing wedding bells in her head. I could hear her brain ticking from across the table — a Ryan and a Devereux, a match made in Killybegs' history," she punctuates with an eye roll.

I don't correct her way-off observation. Mainly because I don't want to discuss my morning breakdown or the fact her brother, who had just met me, could tell there was something wrong with me the moment I stepped foot into the main house. Liam is *too* good at reading my body language. Even last night in the gym, he knew whatever was on my mind was keeping me up at night. When Liam looks at me, he's not looking at my exterior. Instead, he sees past the wall I put up to the emotions I hide inside. It's unnerving.

Beibhinn has mistaken Liam's ability to read me for

something else, and it's easier to let her believe whatever fantasy she's conducting in her head.

"Killybegs' history?" I ask as I change into the clothes she gave me.

"Yeah. Two of the Killybegs Kings together, making pretty, arsehole elite babies who'll one day rule the syndicate and all its peasants." She opens her mouth and then sticks her finger in, pretending to gag as she rummages through her impressive shoe/runner collection.

I laugh at her antics and ask, "Who are the Killybegs Kings?"

"They are the families who run this town, and all of Leinster, really."

"Wait, that's twelve counties."

"Yup. Welcome to the life of the rich and corrupt. Money breeds power, and power breeds fear." She hands me a brand new pair of Nike Air Zoom Pegasus 38. "Try those."

Pulling on the runners, I ask, "Who are the families?"

When I arrived in Killybegs, I knew it was home to the wealthy. What I didn't realise was just how far that wealth ran. If my mam was part of this, why did we spend my childhood on the coattails of poverty? Why did she run from it all? Who was she trying to escape?

At first, I thought it was my father. But now, after reading that note this morning, I'm back at square one.

"Well, there are the Ryans and Devereuxs, obviously." She holds out her hand and starts counting on her fingers. "Then you have the Kings and the Bradys. Those four families are the originals — old money with enough power to rule the Emerald Isle."

Beibhinn takes a seat at her vanity and starts applying her face cream. Through her reflection, her eyes find mine. "In the later years, they brought in four more families, with newer money but enough connections overseas to make them valuable players. They're known as the Bishops and Knights of the Killybegs syndicate — The Reilly, Deegan, Crowe, and Smith families."

"Soooo," I draw out. "You're saying I'm part of some Irish mob family?"

She spins around to face me and tilts her head to the side. "Mob? This isn't some American tv show, Saoirse. The Killybegs Kings are legitimate businessmen."

Finally dressed, I access my reflection in her ceiling-to-floor length mirror. "Why do I get the feeling you're being sarcastic?"

"Have you ever met a legitimate businessman who lives on a multi-million-euro estate?"

My face must say it all because she throws her head back with a laugh. "Welcome to Killybegs, Saoirse. Now, move your peachy arse. Time to turn you into the badass you were born to be."

Saoirse

My HEELS BEAT AGAINST THE TERRAIN, LEGS PROPELLING ME forward as I try to keep up with Liam's lengthy and unnaturally-effortless stride.

Cold air zips past my parted teeth as my lungs pump hard. Each breath stings, roaring at me to slow down, but I don't. Instead, I push forward, forcing my legs to keep moving, unwilling to give in to the crippling defeat burning at the backs of my thighs.

"You doing okay back there?" Liam pivots on the balls of his feet, facing me but still jogging backwards towards our destination of the gym.

How does he look so at ease? Three miles of torture, and he hasn't broken a sweat. Sure, we were running down the mountain, so momentum is supposedly on my side, not that it has helped. But, in my defence, I am not a runner — unless we're talking metaphorically. Then I'm a champ.

My mother made sure I knew how to run at a moment's notice. As for the physical, not so much — a brisk walk is the height of my usual exercise routine. And by usual, I mean once in a blue moon and twice of a bloody sun.

The moral of my rant is I'm pretty sure Liam is trying to kill me. And, if my heart failure is his endgame, he's succeeding.

Ignoring the stitch developing under my left breast, I power through. "G-good. I'm goo-good!"

"Are you sure, free bird? You're looking a bit flushed." His mouth swoops to one side, spreading a sneer across his handsome face, goading me. Sparks of amusement crinkle his eyes as they roam over my exhausted limbs.

He slows to a stop, allowing me to creep closer and narrow the distance between us. Once I reach him, my body folds in half, hands clutching my knees as I permit my starved lungs to draw in a gulp of air. The taste of blood coats my tongue as I run the tip over the roof of my dried mouth. "My insides are bleeding."

A deep laugh rumbles from the depths of his chest. "Bit dramatic, don't you think."

Cranking my neck, I tilt my head up, searching out his eyes, skewering him with a don't-push-me glare.

"Here, take a sip of this." He holds out his water bottle. "The bloody taste is normal. It means your body is doing its job, pumping more oxygen-rich blood to your muscles."

Hoisting myself upright, I ignore my jelly limbs, reach for the bottle, and then bring it to my lips. The rush of cold water dampens my parched tongue before it swirls down my throat, easing the burning sensation scorching my lungs.

"Easy," Liam warns. "Don't overdo it. Small sips, or you'll make yourself sick."

Finally, when I feel somewhat stable, I ask, "What's the point of this, anyway? I thought we were supposed to be training. Correct me if I'm wrong, but how is running supposed to help me?"

"Stamina, speed, agility — there are several reasons, really. But, mainly, it's to warm up your muscles before we begin the real training."

"What?" My eyes widen as I tilt my head to the side. "A warm-up? Meaning there's more."

A contagious laugh explodes from his mouth. "Come on, free bird. We'll walk the rest of the way. Give you a second to catch your breath."

"Fuck you, Liam."

Our eyes engage as his lips cock into a sexy sloped

smile. "I'm free later if you're willing." His wink shoots through my core, setting a billion butterflies free.

"In your dreams, Devereux."

"Every. Fucking. Night."

I'M DYING — BOTH LITERALLY AND FIGURATIVELY. BLACK spots dance behind my lids, and every inch of my body aches as my soul cries out for mercy. Liam was not joking. This morning's run seems like a walk in the park after the excruciating workout he just inflicted on me.

Lying on the flat of my back in the large canvas octagon in the centre of the Devereux's gym, my rib cage rises and falls in a turbulent rhythm as I fight to steady my serrated breaths.

"No more, please." As much as I enjoyed rolling around with a tattooed Adonis, I can't take another second without keeling over.

Looming over me, Liam encourages me. "Come on, one more run through. Time to show me what you're made of, free bird."

"Tell me why I need to know how to defend myself, and I'll think about it."

His eyes crinkle into slits as his attention moves

towards his mother. Who is *not* so subtly watching us from her office doorway.

"I can't say too much."

"Give me something, please. Anything."

Finally, he brushes his hand under his nose like a child with a cold before his hesitant eyes fall back to mine.

"Thieves don't break into empty houses."

"What's that supposed to mean?"

His eyes flutter shut as though he's wrestling with how much he should tell me. Then, finally, he responds, "It means something about who you are is valuable, darlin', and they won't stop until they have it."

I want to ask who they are, but I don't want to push him too far, not yet anyway.

Liam and Beibhinn are the only ones willing to give me any information, and even though it's primarily cryptic, it's better than nothing.

"Question is, *are you willing to protect it at any cost?*"

My hands cover my face, and I groan into my palms. "Fine. Once more, then I'm done."

Finally, I reach up and take his extended hand, but instead of lifting myself up, I use every ounce of strength I have left to tug him forward.

Caught off guard, Liam loses his balance and tumbles down faster than I expected.

Luckily his reflexes kick in, and his open palm hits the

canvas with a vicarious thud, catching himself before completely squishing me. He shifts slightly, positioning his hands so he's holding himself suspended above me.

At our closeness, heat flames my cheeks, and with greedy eyes, I drink him in. There's no denying the want tightening my core or how my skin silently begs to have his hands roaming over every inch. It's been a while since I've had a guy hover above me with want-filled eyes, but none of them holds a candle to the brut of a man before me.

Sure, my ex-boyfriend wasn't a bad looking guy, and the few times we had sex were okay, good even, but never did he ever look at me the way Liam Devereux is right now. Our tangled limbs are entirely non-sexual, but try telling that to the little slut that controls my vagina.

I'm seconds away from exploding, and he's barely touching me.

"If you wanted me on top of you, all you had to do was ask." His crooked grin pulls at the corner of his mouth, shooting another rush of lust up my spine.

A glaze of sweat glistens on his face, highlighting his defined cheekbones and full lips. A hunger like I've never experienced floods through me as our gazes stay chained to each other. The rest of the gym fades to a blur, and all I can see is him as he runs his tongue in a slow trail along his bottom lips.

Aware of my current predicament, a slow, smug grin creeps across his face. His too confident demeanour fuels my fire, and the need to put him on his arse overrides my other senses.

Shifting upwards, I force his arms to a ninety-degree angle above my head. Then thrusting my hips forward, I knock him off balance, just like he taught me to do.

Immediately, I wrap my hands around his waist and mould my torso against his broad chest, clinging to him like a tree.

Keeping my fast pace, I use all my body weight to knock against his elbow while using my right arm to flip him onto his back.

Suddenly, I have the upper hand as my tiny frame straddles his waist. "How was that?" I can't keep the smug smile from twisting on my lips. It's taken me all day to get that one move down, but the look on Liam's face makes all my aching muscles worth it.

"Fuck me."

Leaning forward, I place my palms on his shoulders and hold him down against the canvas.

"Buy me dinner, and I'll think about it."

Rohan

Anger's ferocious teeth bite into my skin, seeping its deadly venom into my bones. His hands are on her, touching her, teasing her, marking her.

There is no way to describe the thorny knot of emotions uncoiling my muscles as I stand on the sideline, staring at the sight before me, completely impuissant.

My teeth bite down on the inside of my cheek as I fight to contain myself from barrelling into the octagon and strangling Devereux to death with my bare-fucking-hands.

Tearing my eyes away from her flushed cheeks, I try to extract this strange tangle of hate from my system.

My arms flash towards the punch bag.

Left, right, left, right; I connect my fists to the leather.

Each hit punctuates the lesson Liam Devereux will soon learn.

Mine.

Mine.

Mine.

Saoirse Ryan belongs to me.

The words resound in my head, echoing as though they're the only mantra I need to justify the murderous scenarios playing out behind my eyes.

Suddenly, the sweet sound of Saoirse's delirious laughter filtrates through the open space, and once again, I find my eyes honed in on her.

Only this time, she's no longer on her feet sparring with that cuntface. No, instead, she's straddling Liam's waist, her fingers needling into the bare flesh of his exposed shoulder blades.

I think not, love. Those hands, your delicate hands, belong to me.

My skin is the only skin you will touch. My body is the only one you'll tease.

Mine.

Mine.

Mine.

My seized jaw cramps as I chomp down my bitterness. This was not how my plan was supposed to go. No, no, no...I did not mean for Saoirse to be blinded by

Liam's pathetic hero complex. I don't care who his family is. I can't let him fuck up my carefully crafted plot.

Sure, a Devereux and a Ryan could bring my father's entire operation to its knees, but that's a situation I gain nothing from, and everyone knows I do nothing for less than full fucking price. So the sooner she realises everything and everyone in her life has a cost, the better off we'll all be.

The Killybegs empire belongs to me, and I'll be dead before I allow some tattooed arsewipe to steal what is rightfully mine from right under my nose. Deranged, maybe slightly, but with good reason. There is more to gain than lose, and Rohan King never loses.

In conclusion, it's time to step up my game because clearly watching her from afar is no longer an option.

Your running days are over, love. It's time to meet the man behind the mask.

As I edge closer, I strain to hear the private conversation, although judging by the sickening body language, it's not something I want to hear.

Finally, their vomit-inducing flirtations grace my eardrums, forcing my gag reflex to work overtime. *Who knew Liam was such a little bitch? Oh, yes, I did.*

Fortunately for Liam, Saoirse clears her throat and pulls herself to her feet before I can swan-dive right off the edge of my morals and land headfirst into what's known as my sociopathic killer territory.

As much as Saoirse's swift departure from Liam's lap may have saved his arse, the reminder still has my stomach pitting into tight coils as anger froths in my mouth.

No more sitting around waiting, watching her from afar. Time to make myself known. I promised her I'd see her soon, and I don't make promises I can't keep.

With a confident swagger, I set my feet in motion, creeping forward like a lion seeking his prey.

Once I reach the octagon, I haul myself up onto the edge of the canvas and lean against the enclosure. Liam shoots me a glance from the corner of his eye, then pushes himself to his feet.

The animosity behind his poison-tipped gaze is unmistakable. But as always, I don't let other people's emotions faze me. So, wasting no time, I enter the octagon, unwanted and undoubtedly uninvited.

Oh, well, the devil never knocks. He just waltzes right in. Consequences be damned.

Honestly, I can't care any less about what the elite prince of Killybegs thinks of my intrusion.

I'm a King. And he just had his grubby hands all over my queen. Correct me if I am wrong, but that's a dangerous move. Not to mention a stupid one.

Alas, Devereux does not know of his wrongdoings, so I let it slide…for now. He's used his one *get out of jail* free card. Next time, he won't pass go.

"What do you want, Rí?" Liam asks, his head sloping slightly to the left as his eyes narrow at the corners.

His cold, clipped words cause my lips to tip up in amusement. Although we both hang out in the same crowd, it's no secret that both Devereux twins hate everything about me and the surname I wield as though it is a nuclear weapon.

Jealousy will do that to people. They can't stand that they're a step below me on the food chain, and if I have my way, they'll stay that way indefinitely.

Unfazed by his dominating demeanour, I peer past him, earning myself a growl.

"Easy there, tiger. No need to show teeth," I taunt, raising one brow in challenge.

I anchor my gaze to Saoirse's. "Hello, love." The words slide off my tongue. "Seems we meet again."

Seconds pass before she's brave enough to seek my stare. Then, finally, she turns those unique amber orbs my way, capturing every ounce of my attention. Something foreign pricks my skin, and for a split moment in time, Saoirse's widened eyes power the blood in my veins.

Is that fear I see dancing in her depths? Yes, the pulsing vein in my cock confirms.

Feeding off her fear, I propel forward, taking slow, unfazed steps until I come face to face with her falsely trusted protector.

He won't protect you, love. No one can. Not from me.

I don't miss the forceful swallow or the breath she catches behind her pouty lips.

Her whole body stiffens, her backbone stretching as she forces herself to stand tall. Whether or not she recognises me from that night remains a mystery. But, one thing's for sure: her body recalls how I made her feel — violently paralysed by crippling trepidation.

I can see it written plain as day across her tight shoulders. Fear dominates her wide eyes, a fear directed towards me and me alone.

I step forward, and her breath hitches. One audible intake of air, and she somehow sucks all the oxygen from the room. Then, with a back-step scramble, she places herself behind Liam, using his solid frame as a barrier. Little does she know, I could take him down with one small manoeuvre, but I won't. Not yet, anyway.

Liam jolts into motion, expelling himself forward and closing the minimal space between us. Then, nose to nose, he tries, but fails, to intimidate me.

"What did you just say?"

"Liam," I tease. "I am not a parrot. Therefore, I will not repeat myself." I peek past him, ignoring his death glare, and shoot a cheeky wink towards Saoirse. Her shoulders hunch forward, and folding her frame inwards, she shrinks in size.

Nope, that won't do. A queen should never bow, no matter how frightened she may be.

"Don't look at her," Liam growls like a cave dweller, dragging my focus back towards him. The landscape of his face tightens, seemingly unimpressed with my lack of shits to give. My presence unnerves him, as it should.

It's clear he has a soft spot for the returning Ryan heir, and as much as I hate to admit it, Liam is not as stupid as he looks. He's well aware of her importance, and he's threatened by my presence, so he's determined to keep her from me.

"It's a little too early in the game to be showing your cards, wouldn't you think?"

The twitch in his jaw showcases my theory, and it's not a good look for him. If I'm being honest, that is. Clearly, Daddy never taught him to hide his true feelings from the enemy. Showing weakness is a sure way to get yourself killed. That's Killybegs syndicate 101.

"Fuck off, Rí."

Feeling somewhat smug, I lean closer and trail my tongue over my teeth. "Or what, you'll hurt me?" I bark out a gruff laugh. We both know he can't touch me. Not only would the syndicate punish him for disrespecting a fellow member, but as big as he is, he's not as fast as I am. He'd never land a punch.

Suddenly, his fingers curl into a fist, knuckles fading to white with his tightened clench. Rolling his shoulders, his chest expands as his muscles pop with strain. He's itching to swing forward and clock me, making me bite out a huffed laugh.

Tiny hands reach out, curling around Liam's bicep. "Come on, Liam. Let's get out of here." Saoirse's concern titillates my every nerve, but the sight of her hands on him washes those feelings away just as quick.

With one last crescent squint aimed in my direction, Liam then reaches for Saoirse's hand. "Okay, free bird. It smells like last week's rubbish here, anyway."

In the next breath, he places his palm at the base of her spine and then propels her towards the exit.

Owning every last word, I shout after her, "See you real soon, love."

Really fucking soon.

Saoirse

ICE CRUSTS OVER MY BACKBONE AS FEAR-DRIVEN TREMORS quiver beneath my skin. My breath snags in my throat, held prisoner by my clenched lungs. The weight of Liam's open palm rests heavily on my lower back as he prompts me forward, towards Fiadh's office and away from...*him*.

Liam referred to him as Rí, and even though my Irish isn't as good as it should be, I know the term translates to King. Which, unsurprisingly, matches his demanding air.

The moment he stalked into the octagon, with confidence that screamed arrogance, all the air from the gym dispersed as though the energy he expels controlled everything and everyone around him.

Maybe it was how a dare marred his darkened brow, similar to that of a fearless predator. Or perhaps it was how he moistened his dry teeth with a swipe of his tongue. Whatever it was, he held everyone's attention as they, myself included, waited with bated breath for his next move.

He stood nonchalantly, shoulder muscles locked, ramrod straight, with his head held high. An air of importance swirled around him like a hurricane as he, the eye of the storm, held the centre, calm but equally dangerous. My heart stopped mid-beat as I anticipated what was to come.

Then suddenly, those eyes honed on me, and they transported me to a night I would kill to forget — the night they ripped my mother from me. Even if he never opened his mouth, piercing me with the parting words he used on me that night in the forest, I would have known it was him — the man behind the mask.

The same man who has haunted my restless sleep for the past few nights. Those unmistakable moss-green eyes seared into my skin, instantly revealing his true identity.

Then I stepped back, hiding myself and my vulnerabilities behind Liam's powerful frame. I couldn't stand the burning shackle of Rí's gaze as it roamed over every inch of my body, accessing every emotion on my face or the way my body stiffened at his presence. He saw it all, and I hated it.

What is it about him that crawls beneath my skin?

Every move he made, every word he spoke, every glance he stole, was perfectly executed to draw a response from whoever he directed his boldness towards. Unfortunately, that someone was me.

His presence brought a lot of questions to the forefront of my mind. Does he know what happened to my mom? How did he know where to find me? How does he know Liam? All questions I plan to find the answers to; not now, though. Not with Liam guarding me like I'm some lost lamb ready to be slaughtered.

I blink back our encounter, and next to me, Liam keeps our pace, ushering me further and further away. With each step, the pull in my stomach intensifies. Finally, the urge to turn around takes over, an unsettling need to seek him out and draw the answers I seek from him.

Realisation dawns. He knew.

That night in the thickness of the evergreen trees, he knew I'd come here. That's why he let me go, giving me false hope for freedom. He fucking knew I'd end up here, subsequently, right dab in the middle of the lion's den.

Rage filters through my bloodstream, and I narrow my eyes. The invisible thread tying me to this Rí guy forces me to halt my movements. Liam stumbles into me as my feet cement to the floor, unmoving. His smug smile flashes behind my eyes, and my teeth rattle with fury.

He thinks he's won.

In the next breath, my neck cranes as my eyes steal another glance at the unfazed guy leaning against the octagon, stalking every step I take.

As if sensing my appraisal, those same eyes trail over me, head to toe. A slow, serene smile tugs against his lips, matching the arch of his knowing brow. A thought enters my head, and my lips purse as I realise it's not my own but a silent conversation I'm reading on his taunting face.

The next move is yours, love. Use it wisely.

Suddenly, he slopes his head to the left as his brows jog behind the hair falling onto his forehead. I step towards him, but my movements halt when Liam's tattooed hand grips my wrist.

"Come on." The disdain in his voice makes him seem irritated. "He's not worth your time."

I hesitate for a second. My eyes jump between the two males who seem to be partaking in some kind of silent pissing contest. Then finally, my shoulders collapse and I turn my back on Rí, allowing Liam to lead the way. He doesn't waste a second, splaying his hand across my back as he guides me across the gym floor and away from the moss-green eyes boring a hole in my skull.

Dropping my voice, the words stumble from my lips. "Who is he?"

An array of emotions crosses his face as he diverts his

glare my way. His hardened stare cuts, eyes narrowing into slits and his lips drawn tight. "Who is he to you?" He cocks his brow as he waits for my response, calling me out before the words leave my mouth.

Uncertainty coils in my gut. Do I tell him about that night, about how the guy he called Rí, chased me through the woods before pinning me to a tree with only a look and a devious smile? Do I lay all my cards on the table, or do I keep it to myself?

Once again, before I can answer Liam's request, my eyes betray me. Peering over my shoulder, I seek him out. He's still there, leaning against the wall, arms crossed over his broad chest, amusement dancing across his lopsided smile.

Sweat licks his forehead, forcing the falling strands of his onyx hair to stick to his damp skin. His chest is bare, showcasing his lithe, muscular frame dotted with a scattering of patchwork tattoos. Finally, my attention drifts south, following the simmering glint of sweat that lingers in the crevices of his carved abdominal muscles. He oozes power, danger, and everything I should run from, but just like that night, I can't look away, and even worse, I don't want to.

How can a person look so dangerous yet so alluring at the same time?

Powerless to his chokehold gaze, I swallow back the lump swelling in my throat, then fight to free myself from his stare. Once successful, I allow my answer to filter through the thick air. "Nobody important."

Saoirse

With a crane of his tattooed neck, Liam's eyes align with mine, burning like hot embers as his curiosity carves tormented lines along his forehead. He doesn't buy a word of my omission. That much is evident by the clench of disappointment tightening his jaw. Finally, we reach the doorway of Fiadh's office, and he turns to face me, gripping my biceps to keep me from avoiding his stripping stare. "What was that?"

"It was nothing. I don't know who that guy is, let alone how he knew me."

"I'm calling horseshit."

Suddenly, the weight of my lie drops a stone block through my core, rippling waves of regret in its wake. I know Liam wants answers, but what am I meant to say?

How am I supposed to externalise my thoughts about the mysterious Rí when I can barely grasp them myself.

His stormy eyes soften as his shoulders collapse into a bowed heap. "I can't help you if you don't tell me everything you know, free bird. How do you know Rí?"

At his statement, my eyes narrow into anger-filled slits. How dare he demand my knowledge? Especially when all he does is feed me riddles, leaving me more confused and even further away from unravelling the web of lies my mother tangled me in.

"How about you tell me why I'm here first?"

His eyes close as he huffs out an impatient breath. Frustration twinges across his face as a deep frown worms its way onto his pursed lips. "I can't do that, Saoirse. You're not ready."

"Well, it seems we're at a crossroads, Devereux."

Unwilling to make any further concessions, his teeth slide over his bottom lip, drawing it into his mouth. His pierced nostrils widen as he tips his head. "Guess I better take you back to the house, then."

Turning his gaze away from me, his fingertips grip the door handle of Fiadh's office. "Wait here."

His tone scolds me as if I am a misbehaved child who needs reprimanding. Then, pleating my arms under my breasts, I level him with an unimpressed eye roll. "Whatever you say, Your Highness."

Liam's legs jolt forward, leaving me glaring at him from the open doorway. Bracing myself on the doorjamb, I take the weight of my tired legs as I follow every one of Liam's movements with my eyes. Finally, he stops in front of Fiadh's desk, drawing her attention. Too far away to decipher their hushed tones, I strain my gaze to their lips, eyes narrowing as I try to work out what they're talking about. Fiadh's lips bunch into a dubious pucker as Liam's hands move with great animation.

Suddenly, Fiadh's head swivels towards me, showcasing the deep worry lines surrounding her forehead and eyes. Her shoulders drop as she places her hands against her desk and pushes herself from her seat. A shadow of something unreadable glides across her defined features. Then, with a heavy release of breath, her nostrils widen.

Circling her desk, her legging-clad legs carry her towards the coat rack and closer to me. Her hands disappear into her handbag, and then she retracts her keys and holds them out for Liam to take. Thankfully, their new position grants me a better chance of hearing their conversation. Leaning forward slightly, my ears strain as I eavesdrop.

"Take her home, and for the love of God, don't push her into talking when she's not ready." She drops the keys into his palm while raising her brow in warning.

"She knows him, Mam. He said as much." Liam's

fingers tighten around the keys, his knuckles turning white as his hand silently begs to be let loose. "Why is she hiding it?"

"What she shares or withholds is her business. Understand, she doesn't remember the little boy who was once her best friend. Éanna removed all traces of us from her life a long, long time ago. She was never part of this world, Liam. Give her a minute to catch her breath and figure out who she can trust. Go easy on her. She'll come around."

At that, my brows deepen, shading my eyes with confusion. What does she mean, remember? Racking my brain, I scan through my childhood, searching for my earliest memories, but I can't seem to locate anything younger than the age of seven or eight.

More precisely, on the day of my holy communion, when a girl called Avril stood on my dress and tore it. After a colossal meltdown, my class teacher stapled it back together in time for me to walk down the aisle to receive the Holy bread.

Sure, there are a few other faded moments, but nothing of significance, not a single substantial memory. Did I know about the Devereuxs before this week? Were they a part of my life that somehow faded from my view?

"Is there any more information on Éanna?" At the mention of my mother's name, my ears prick, and my wide eyes train on Fiadh's scrunched face, desperately wanting and silently begging for her reply.

"No, nothing. The Gardaí are withholding any information they have on the fire. Your father has been relentless, calling them on the hour, every hour, and they won't budge."

"Not surprising. What about Reilly?" Liam's jaw clenches, sharpening his chiselled cheekbones. "Have you spoken with him?"

Fiadh's head twists, a sharp turn left, then right. "He won't answer my calls. Which can mean one of two things."

Unease rolls through me like a chilled, dark wave. *Who the fuck is Reilly, and what has he got to do with my mam?*

Liam tilts his head, giving a clipped nod. "He knows something and doesn't want to share it."

"Or, he knows something and he can't make a move, not yet," Fiadh finishes.

"Either way, he's withholding, and that's never a good sign."

Suddenly, my skin pricks as a shadowy figure steps behind me. "You know…" Rí's unmistakable confidence bleeds through those few syllables. "It's rude to eavesdrop on private conversations."

My gaze swings over my shoulder, locking on to his taunting face. "It's also rude to sneak up on people, yet you've done just that on several occasions. So much so, it seems to be your signature MO."

Rí's perusing glare roams over me as I hold myself against the doorway. He takes his time, slowly tracing my form with challenging eyes. The tip of his tongue peeks out from behind his twisted smirk, dampening his bottom lips as his fuelled-by-fire eyes linger on my breasts.

"What do you want from me?" The question rushes from my mouth like a runaway train veering off track. My tone is louder than I intended, clouded by my annoyance and coated with my need for answers. But unfortunately, my outburst has Liam and Fiadh's eyes shooting towards my space intruder and me.

Rí peers over my shoulder. When he takes in the annoyed expressions on Fiadh and Liam's faces, the twisted smile on his face widens with victory. Once again, he slowly draws his haunted irises back to me. "I want a lot of things from you, *mo bhanríon.*"

Stepping backwards, he expands the distance between us. "Prepare yourself, love. Soon, I will take what it is I want, and your little guard dog won't be able to stop me."

My throat seizes with a lump so thick it cuts off my breath. I force it down with an audible swallow.

"Which is?" There's no hiding the quivering mess his words reduced me to. But it's not fear lacing my words. It's something else, something I refuse to acknowledge.

Prowling forward, his precise movements eat up the distance he created, leaving nothing but a sliver of space between his mouth and my neck. His right hand cups my cheek, featherlight, and nothing like I would expect from his dominant bravado.

A rush of heat races over my skin when his hot breath licks my skin. "Do you really want to know?"

Without warning, Liam steps in behind me "Take your hands off her, Rí." His tone is low, throaty with a gravel of demand.

Anybody else would cower at Liam's dangerous growl, but I'm beginning to realise Rí isn't like anyone I've ever met. He plays by his own rules, preceding consequences.

When he glances at Liam's way out of the corner of his eye, I spy the unvexed look on his otherwise emotionless expression before he draws his focus back to me with a sly, devious smirk.

Suddenly, Liam makes his move, reaching out and grabbing hold of my elbow in an attempt to pry me from Rí's touch. "Come on, Saoirse. Lying with dogs will get you fleas."

"I…uh." Conflict knots my stomach as my brain twists and turns, undecided on what to do. On one hand, my mind roars at me to listen to Liam, to walk away from the haunted stare burning my skin. Then, on the other hand, my body begs me to stay, to hear what Rí has to say.

Before I can fully commit to any option, Rí steals my choice by dropping his hand from my face, and wrapping his arm around my waist. In a split second, he drags me closer, moulding me to his bare tattooed chest.

Liam reacts, stepping forward, shoulders squared and ready for a fight. Only, he doesn't get too far because, in a heartbeat, Rí's free hand extends, and his fingers clasp Liam's neck in a deathly clutch. Liam gasps for air when Rí adds more pressure, squeezing with so much force. In his struggle, Liam's hands circle Rí's wrist as he desperately tries to tear it away from his grasp, but it's useless.

My heart pounds against my rib cage as a sick, twisted grin lights up Rí's face. "Amazing what a pressure point can do, love. Big scary Liam could be the strongest cunt in this place, and yet, with the right hold, he's trapped. Isn't that right, Devereux?"

Liam responds with a murderous stare, a fire so ferocious it would intimidate most men.

Finally, my traitorous eyes swing back toward Rí, whose eyes are still locked on my face, paying no attention to the brute of a man he's immobilised with one well-executed grip.

This man before me is deadly, a lethal force that's impenetrable. Fear crawls through my veins, but it's mixed with a deranged sense of lust. *What the fuck is wrong with me? How can this sociopathic lunatic pull such contradictory responses from me?*

In the distance, I hear Fiadh's audible gasp, but it's quickly drowned out when Rí lowers his head once more, erasing everything around me but him and his toxic taunts.

His words tease my skin, burning me from the inside out. "Tell your lap dog to keep his hands to himself. You belong to me."

An unwanted rush crashes through my core, filling me with...no, it can't be desire. There is no way this psychotic arsehole is turning me on.

I realise how wrong I am when the next words slither from his lips, dancing like the devil over my skin.

"You are mine — to play with, to fuck, to shatter. I will destroy you, Saoirse, and you'll love every second of it."

With those parting words, he releases his unwavering hold from Liam's throat and stalks away as if he owns the place and everyone in it, leaving me transfixed as I watch him saunter away as if the last few minutes never happened.

His departure covers my skin with a chill while my heart thunders in my chest, fighting to find its rhythm.

"You'll fucking pay for that, King," Liam roars from behind me as Rí stalks towards the exit without a care in his arrogant step.

Once he reaches the door, he pulls it open, and then tosses a parting glance over his shoulder. "Send me the bill, Devereux. We both know I'm good for it."

Then, as if he was never here, he disappears, leaving me shaking from the core outward.

I have no idea what the fuck just happened, but one thing is for sure, the devil just claimed me as his new toy, and I've got a sinking feeling in the pit of my stomach he won't let me go — no matter how hard I fight him.

Saoirse

THE AIR IN THE CAR IS THICK WITH THE LOOMING TENSION that follows us from the gym.

From the corner of my eye, I steal a glance at Liam. His tattooed hands clutch the steering wheel in a death grip, showcasing his white knuckles as his fingernails dent his palms.

He keeps his sharp stare on the winding road ahead, refusing to meet my watchful eyes. His silence is so intense it's palpable, forcing me to hold my breath hostage in my lungs.

Finally, when I can't take another second of him blatantly ignoring me, my cheeks puff out, expelling an audible breath that cuts through the tension like a razor-sharp blade.

His eyes flick towards me as I shift in my seat, turning

my body in the chair to face him. Then, honing in on him, my gaze tightens at the corners as I wait for him to acknowledge my presence.

His eyes flick between me and the road, then back again. One eyebrow edges towards my hairline, deepening the wrinkle at the bridge of my nose as I silently call him out for his ignorant behaviour with just a look. Sure, he has every right to be pissed at what went down with Rí at the gym, but his silence is different from his usual cocky facade, and I don't know what to do with that.

"Stop looking at me like that," he spits the words out through gritted teeth, frustration and disdain wrapped in this demand.

"No." I shake my head and twist my lips into a pursed scowl. "If I want to look at you, I will." Childish? Maybe so, but I won't take the brunt of his bruised masculinity.

"Fine." Irritation laces his tone, forcing me to swallow the bitter taste that one word leaves in my mouth.

Flicking on his turn signal, he indicates into the Devereux Estate, slowing to a stop while the enormous gates open for us to enter. His beady eyes turn towards me as we wait, trapping mine with his burning glare.

"What's your problem?" I exhale a groan, rivalling a rusty hinge.

"Are you really that clueless?" His words sting more than they should. Maybe it's the hurt behind his eyes, or maybe it's his damaged ego talking. Either way, his arse-hole attitude is pissing me off. "How else do you expect me to be after that little show you put on with King?"

"Fuck you, Liam. I did nothing wrong, and you know it."

He holds my gaze for a moment before looking away without a word. Sloping his head to the right, an infinitesimal twitch curls on his upper lip, telling me I hit the nail on the head. His foul humour has more to do with Rí than me, not that he'll admit it. But unfortunately, I'm the one he's directing his rage towards.

Finally, the gates open wide enough for us to drive through, and Liam wastes no time pressing his foot down on the accelerator, excelling us forward. The short drive to the gate lodge is almost unbearable, but I focus my eyes out the passenger window, choosing to ignore the lump of a man in the seat next to me.

Once we pull up in front of the gate lodge, Liam cranks the handbrake and then shifts in his seat until he's facing me with his unrelenting stare.

"What you did in the gym was reckless, Saoirse."

My head bows. I hate the sound of my first name on his lips. He hasn't called me that since he dubbed me his free bird, a name that solely belongs to him and only him.

When I look back up, his hollow eyes slice my skin.

"It's my job to protect you, but I can't do that when you're lying to me."

"I'm not…I'm not lying to you."

Liam's shoulders drop with a sigh as he pins me to my seat with a raised brow. "How do you know Rohan?"

My mouth hangs open, but the words refuse to roll off my tongue.

With one last shake of his head, he stifles the engine's growl and flings his door open. "That's what I thought."

My stomach pits, flipping at his swift departure. Pushing my door open, I exit the car and speed after him. "Liam, please. Wait."

His feet come to an immediate halt, cementing him to the ground, and he freezes in place. Then with a heavy inhale, his firm, broad shoulders rise before concaving with a release of air from his lungs. Suddenly, he pivots on the balls of his feet, and then his stormy night eyes anchor on mine, impaling me with a dismissive look.

"Save it, Saoirse."

Over his shoulder, the front door opens and Beibhinn steps into view. Using her forearm as a crutch, she leans against the doorframe, watching our exchange with furrowed eyes.

Liam's hands fly into his messy hair, gripping onto the roots in frustration. His glassy eyes seem unfocused when he looks towards me again, void of all emotion. "Look, I'm not in the mood to fight with you. You want to crawl into the arms of the devil incarnate, be my fucking guest. But don't expect me to pick you up when you crash land from the height he drops you from."

With that, he storms into the house, pushing past Beibhinn without so much as a grunt.

"What's his problem?" she questions, her eyes darting between me and the space her brother just bulldozed through.

Pushing aside the regret sinking to the depths of my stomach, I shake my head and slump towards her. "I do not know."

Her footsteps match mine, her anticipation for a response propelling her forward. "Some shady shit must have gone down because Liam never loses his cool like he just did, ever."

As I make a straight line for the fridge, I shoot a glare over my shoulder. "It was nothing." My fingers wrap around the door handle, and I tug it open, peering inside for something to settle the fairies dancing in my stomach.

Opting for a sandwich, I pull out a pack of ham and the half-pound of Kerrygold butter, then close the fridge. Finally, I grab the sliced pan of Brennan's bread and a side plate from the press, all the while avoiding Beibhinn's knowing stare.

When I can't avoid her any longer, I glance back to

find her perched at the breakfast bar with her capped eyes on mine, complete with a raised *I'm-not-buying-the-bull-shit-you're-selling* brow.

Closing the distance between us, I slide onto the high stool opposite hers and begin making my snack. "You're not gonna let this go, are you?"

"Do I look like Elsa?"

Raising my hand to my mouth, I stifle the burst of laughter stirring in my gut because yes, with colourless hair that creeps down her spine, paired with stormy grey eyes, that's precisely what she looks like.

"Oh, shut up. You know what I meant." She reaches across the table and pulls an apple from the fruit basket, then tosses it at my head. "Stop avoiding my question, and tell me what happened between you and Liam."

"Fine," I punctuate with an eye roll before diving into everything from the moment Rí stepped into the octagon to when Liam and I pulled up at the house. Beibhinn remains silent, eagerly hanging on to every word. Once I finish, she breaks through the silence with her hysterical laughter.

Confusion mars my brow, and I pull my lips tight, deepening my smile lines. "What's so funny?"

Hoisting herself to her feet, she motions with the tip of her chin for me to follow her into the living room. "Come on, we'll put a movie on, and I'll tell you all about the life-

long rivalry between Liam Devereux and Rohan King."
She wiggles her brows as if she holds all the juicy secrets.
"But first, we need a drink."

Her feet carry her towards the glass cabinet next to the
tv. In the next breath, she has a full bottle of tequila
dangling from her fingers. We settle in, and Beibhinn
spends the next half hour running through Rohan and
Liam's never-ending competition to be crowned Killybegs' next King.

Rohan

I LOVE NOTHING MORE IN THIS LIFE THAN STEALING THE fight from my enemy's eyes. Especially when that enemy is none other than Liam Devereux.

For years, the slimy bastard has tried to one-up me, at school, in sports, even in boxing, but he never succeeds. Which…is all kinds of pathetic — if you were to ask me — considering his parents own the most reputable MMA gym on this side of the Isle and have even trained some of the best athletes this country has ever seen. Still, poor Liam always falls a fraction behind, and today was no different.

Let's face it; there wasn't a goddamn thing he could have done to stop me from drawing Saoirse into my chest, nor could he have controlled the way her cheeks turned a pretty shade of pink at my dirty words. Call me narcissistic, but the look of defeat in his eyes made my pursuit of Saoirse more satisfying. The way the fight drained from his face as my hand stole the breath from his lungs — pure crazed perfection.

Sure, to most of the public eyes, Liam and I are friends, standing together, portraying a united front for the sake of the syndicate, but behind the scenes, the MVPs know there is no love lost between the King and Devereux sons. There has always been a drive, a healthy rivalry that pushes us to be better, stronger, faster, and everything else in between. Now, it seems Killybegs' long-lost princess is no exception, which will only make my victory that much sweeter.

Liam may think I don't see through his pathetic protector act, but he's sorely mistaken. He might have naïve little Saoirse eating out of the palm of his hand, but I know better, and he's fucked in the head if he thinks he'll slither in and romance his way into a position that's rightfully mine because I will never allow it to happen.

See, the thing about me is, I'm a purebred arsehole, but at least I'm honest about it. I only have one face, and if you don't like it, I don't care enough to give a shit.

If Liam wants to take me on in a war of hearts for the Killybegs Queen, he better hitch up his jockstrap because this is another battle I refuse to fucking lose.

Finally, I come to a halt outside of my guest house,

raise my hand to the keypad and type in the code. The tell-tale click of the door opening resounds, and I push through to find Aodhán spread out across my couch, eating my fucking Pringles.

"Well, well, well." His eyes narrow on mine as amusement hooks his mouth to one side. "Are you done with today's episode of *Rohan becoming a Joe Goldberg level stalker?*"

Ignoring him and his smart remark, my feet carry me forward, past his slumped frame and into the open-plan kitchen. My throat swells with thirst, so I open the fridge and pull out a bottle of Evian, then bring it to my lips, allowing the freezing cold water to rush down my oesophagus, chilling my insides.

Once I've consumed the entire bottle of water, I crunch it in my fist, then toss it like a basketball into the recycle bin across the room.

Acknowledging the rattle in my stomach, I tear open the press above the sink, grab a share bag of original Hula Hoops, and head over to my favourite armchair before slumping down in the seat.

I pull the bag open and pour a mouthful of hoops into my mouth, savouring each chew.

Finally, I lock eyes with Aodhán's watchful glare. "FYI, today's stalking turned into talking." *Teasing, maybe a little touching.*

"Oh." He snickers behind closed lips. "Did you give Saoirse your virginity? How about hand-holding? Is that still a thing?"

Reaching beneath my arm, I grab one of the black throw pillows my mam insisted I needed and toss it straight at him, hitting him square between the eyes.

"Don't you remember?" I taunt. "Your mam already took my V-card. Apparently, Daddy Brady wasn't hitting that tight arse right."

"You're an animal."

"That's what she said." I hike a brow as I push myself from my seat. "Now, if you could politely fuck off to your own house, that would be great. I've got shit to do."

Pulling himself up, he shoots me a knowing grin. Then, as he skitters backwards, he raises his clenched hand in the air and pumps up and down. "Don't choke the chicken too hard, my friend. God forbid, he'll fall off."

I point to the door, but there's nothing I can do to wipe the slithery smug smirk off my grinning face. "Get the fuck out!"

THE SCALDING HOT WATER SPRAYS FROM THE OVERHEAD RAIN shower and rushes over my face. Lifting my hands to my face, I scrub up and down before running my hands through my wet hair, allowing all the excess water to flow down the back of my neck and over my shoulder muscles. Then with a deep exhale, I release today's tension woven beneath my skin.

Fuck, there is nothing like a steamy hot shower after a good workout.

My hands, still positioned at the base of my neck, needle the taut muscles as I stand rigid beneath the pounding water pressure for a few minutes.

Fuck, I love the way the blistering heat licks over my aching shoulders. Once I'm semi-relaxed, I grab my bar of Creed Aventus soap from the built-in shelf and lather up every inch of my skin. Before long, the shower fills with the tantalising top notes of Italian bergamot, blended with a subtle hint of pineapple, oakmoss and musk.

Suddenly, visions of Saoirse backed up against a moss-covered tree trunk flood my scenes. Followed by images of my knife trailing between her small pert breasts as her razor-sharp nipples teased me as they fought against the barely-there cloth of her pyjama top, begging me to slice through the material and draw each one into my mouth. At that moment, I wanted nothing more than to lower my head and graze my teeth over her hardened buds. It took every ounce of strength I had not to shed her from the confines of her sleepwear and fuck her into oblivion.

Imagining her and her olive skin glistening beneath

the bright white moonlight and how her soft pouty pink lips parted as she sucked in a breath when my words infiltrated her ears has my cock pulsing.

Without thought, my soapy hand glides over my taut abdominal muscles, travelling lower, until my fingers curl around my now thickening cock with a lung-compressing clutch. My eyelids slam shut, and Saoirse's face comes into view once more.

I start off slowly, dragging my hand from the tip to the base — once, twice, three times over. A low hum warms my body as snippets of her flash behind my eyes. It's not enough though; I need more.

Conjuring up the memory of that night and the way her hollow breaths rose and fell as I crept closer, caging her in so she couldn't run from me. Only this time, I allow my mind to roleplay, create a new vision, one I so desperately wished I had played out.

"Who are you?"

I prowl forward with slow, taunting steps, trapping her against the tree trunk, watching as every muscle in her body goes rigid.

Closing in, I mould my chest to hers. My head slopes to the left, levelling her with a devilish smile. Finally, I announce, "I think I'm the hero."

A crooked smile hooks at the corner of my lips. "And you

think I'm the villain." Then trailing my tongue across my teeth, I allow my words to settle in her throbbing chest.

Are you scared, darling? The thought spurs me on, feeding my desire to take every piece of her. Then, her words slice through my lust-induced fog.

"Which one is it?" Her shaky voice trembles with a tattered breath.

Slowly, I tease the edge of my knife along the curve of her neck, loving how the tip leaves a faint pink shadow in its wake. "I suppose it's a matter of perspective."

She sucks in a heavy inhale and judging by our proximity, I know my scent fills her nose.

"Creed Aventus."

"Huh?"

"The name of my aftershave. You seemed to take a good whiff, so I'd thought I'd tell you why I smell utterly un-fucking-touchable."

Frustration mars her brow, then raising her tiny hand, she pushes against my solid chest.

"Now, now," I taunt. "No need to be so aggressive."

"Says the guy holding me hostage with a knife," she mumbles.

"Listen, love. This"— I gesture between us with the tip of my blade —"doesn't need to be difficult."

Trailing the edge of my knife down her exposed throat, I cut through the flimsy material of her tank top. My mouth moistens *at the sight of her pert, pale pink nipples, the exact shade of her pouty lips.*

Greed ripples through me, a want so fucking strong it threatens to bring me to my knees. Bowing my head, I bring my mouth to her exposed flesh. My tongue slips past my lips, yearning for a taste. Finally, I give in to temptation, circling her hardened nub before scraping it through my teeth and biting down hard.

Her groaned moan fills the air as her back arches, drawing her closer to me. "Oh, God."

My free hand circles her waist, steadying her as I roam the tip of my knife over her stomach, travelling south until I meet the resistance of her pyjama bottoms.

Wasting no time, I drop to my knees and tear the fabric out of my way. In the next breath, my mouth is travelling over her soft, fleshy thighs, taunting her with tiny hate bites.

I peer up, savouring how her head bows back as I tempt her skin. Then, using the butt of my knife, I tease her slit through the fabric as I continue assaulting her thighs, leaving a trail of purple and red bruises in my wake.

"Please," she begs, needy and breathless.

The higher my lips travel, the more prominent her sweet yet musky scent becomes, and the more my need to feast on her strengthens. "Fuck, you smell so fucking tempting, love."

"Stop. I need you to stop."

My eyes find hers in the dark. "Stop touching you, or stop teasing you?" Not that it matters. Either way, I will have her legs perched over my shoulder as my mouth devours her sweet cunt.

A flush the colour of a winter morning's sunrise flashes on her cheeks. "Te...teasing."

"Right answer, baby."

Dragging my teeth across my bottom lip, I flip my knife around and press the blade against the tiny strings holding together her black thong. With a wrist flick, I slide beneath the flimsy material and pull, freeing her dripping-with-need pussy.

My tongue trails along my bottom lips as I lift the lace towards my nose, drawing in her scent before slipping the torn fabric into my back pocket. "You smell like fucking heaven, love." But I know better.

Saoirse Ryan is no fucking angel. Wrapped in temptation and dripping with sin, a woman like her was crafted behind the gates of hell.

Unable to hold back, I hitch her right leg over my shoulder, leaving her pussy exposed to me. My parched tongue glides over the roof of my mouth as I lean forward and finally slide my greed through her slit. My cock hardens as her exotic taste explodes in my mouth.

Then, like a starved man, I devour her, spearing my tongue in and out, until her hot, needy mess drips down my chin. "That's it, love. Keep riding shotgun on my lips."

Her body shakes beneath my palms, and I pull back, blowing a breath against her throbbing clit. Finally, when she's begging for me to let her cum, I suck her pink bud into my mouth and nibble until the force of her release ricochets through her body, and she becomes a boneless mess, clutching onto me for balance.

The vision ends as hot ropes of cum explode from my cock, coating the shower wall.

Fuck! My head falls back, and I ride out my orgasm as it rips up my spine, momentarily paralysing me.

No more waiting. Tomorrow, Saoirse Ryan will know precisely who her moans belong to, and it sure as shit won't be Liam Devereux.

Saoirse

EXHAUSTED FROM TODAY'S EVENTS, I INDULGE IN AN EXTRA-long shower before pulling on the fresh pair of pyjamas shorts and a matching cami top I borrowed from Beibhinn.

Then, finally, when I am scrubbed and shaved to within an inch of my life, I climb into bed, ready to succumb to the weeks' worth of sleep my mind has deprived me. Flopping backwards, my body bounces against the expensive mattress, forcing an appreciative moan to push past my lips.

I should never have left you this morning. I'm sorry, forgive me, please.

Every cell in my body screams at me to close my eyes, but my mind won't shut up for whatever reason. Restless, I twist and turn against the soft cotton, stretching out my aching limbs. I'm shattered from this morning's run and the long hours I worked out with Liam. Not to mention all the emotional shit that followed. Somehow, I thought I had tired myself enough to fight away the nightmares and get a decent night's sleep before I start school tomorrow.

The first day at a new school is always challenging. Trust me, I have had enough of them to last me a lifetime. If I have learnt anything with each fresh start, it's that they all begin and end the same. Let's just say I'm a pro when it comes to navigating the set of challenges being the new girl brings. Once I walk through those doors, things will go one of a few ways.

The weaker will cower, leaving me to fend for myself. Then the elite popular kids, the top tier, as I call them, will divide into two groups: boys versus girls.

The boys will view me as fresh meat, a game in which they'll try to win. The prize: which one will get dibs on the new girl? They'll spend the day wooing me with fake smiles and shitty one-liners, all while deciding if I am an easy lay or a waste of their time. I can tell you now, it's the latter, but that won't stop them from trying.

Then, there are the girls. This one is a little trickier because girls are unpredictable. They'll watch first, strike later. Then, either they'll circle, treating me as though I am their prey, before settling out to make my life miserable. Or they will invite me in, deeming me worthy enough to sit with them. Speaking from experience, it's almost always the former.

Yay-fecking-me!

My heavy lids fight to stay open, so I reach over to the side dresser, and just as I'm about to flick off the bedside light, a continuous rap softly pounds against my bedroom door, stilling my movements.

You have got to be kidding me.

Not in the mood for any more socialising and clutching onto the sliver of sleep I'm fading into, I ignore the banging and flick the switch before lying back and pulling the covers over my head.

There isn't a chance in Batman's cave I'm opening that door.

"Maybe if I ignore it, whoever it is will go away," I murmur. Only, I am not so lucky. The fourth round of taps ensues, then, with a frustrated groan — accompanied by several scissor kicks — I flip the covers off and pad towards the door, lips pursed, and my lousy attitude builds with each step.

My fingers curl around the doorknob as I twist, unlatching the door. Finally, I rip it open, ready to tear my intruder a new arsehole. "Go away. I'm slee—" The argument dies on my lips.

My brows furrow into a frown when my sleepy gaze lands on a shirtless Liam. His tousled hair stands up in a chaotic mess — as if he's spent the past few hours tugging it with his hands. His eyes are heavy, squinted into half-moons, and a glimmer of sadness lingers in the small smile tugging at his upper lip.

Like the little traitors they are, my sleepy eyes veer south, lapping up every inch of Liam's tattooed torso and God-must-have-carved-him muscles. For a long beat, I linger on the intricate canvas adorning his chest and abdomen. At first glance, it seems like a depiction of *The Last Supper*, but upon further inspection, instead of Jesus and his Twelve Disciples seated at the table, it's the Greek Gods of Olympus.

Christ, that's hot!

"Hey," he greets, drawing my attention away from his bare chest and back to his chiselled face. "Sorry, did I wake you?" His chin tilts down as he peers at me over the rim of his inky lashes.

"Erm, no, I, um…" I toss my thumb over my shoulder. "I was just, erm…"

Hello, ability to form a coherent sentence? Are you there?

"My mam wanted me to give you this." His sorrowful eyes are downcast to the floor as he holds out a black garment bag, gesturing for me to take it with the tip of his chin. "It's your uniform for school tomorrow."

"Oh." My fingertips brush against his as my grasp closes around the hanger, and quickly I pull back, taking the bag with me. "Thanks."

"I'll let you get back to…" He motions towards the bed and then turns on his heel.

For a second longer than I should, I lean against the door, allowing it to hold me up as I watch him retreat towards his bedroom. Two steps, and suddenly, as though he thought better of his exit, he halts. His shoulders droop with a stout exhale.

Finally, he turns around, latching his icy gaze on mine. His head shakes left and right as if he's debating with whatever conversation is going on inside his head.

"About earlier…" He lifts his hand to the back of his head, rubbing away his uncertainty and giving me a delicious view of his bulging biceps.

Stop it, Saoirse.

"I'm…I'm sorry." Those two words float between us, soaking up all the surrounding air. "Rohan…he gets under my skin, and when I saw you with him, it..."

"It what?" Crossing my arms across my chest, I wait for him to respond.

His gaze flickers over his shoulder, searching the empty hallway. When he looks my way again, the frown lines marrying his brow line deepens. "Do you mind if we talk inside?" He tosses his hand towards the open doorway behind me, into my bedroom.

My lips purse, and even though I'm still slightly pissed at how he behaved earlier, I want to know the reasoning behind his anger. From what I've seen of Liam since coming here, he's not someone who loses his cool quickly, not without good reason.

"Sure." I open the door wide and motion with my hand for him to step inside.

His slow, precise footfalls are hesitant as his eyes bounce around my room, taking in the small touches I've added in the few days I've been here. My clothes, or lack thereof, lie hastily across the chair by the bay window, and my minimal toiletries and make-up rest haphazardly on the vanity, next to the wooden box and the few mementoes I've studied so far. Sidestepping him, I quickly fix the blanket I tossed everywhere before answering the door. "Sorry about the mess. I wasn't exactly expecting to have anyone in here tonight."

Or any night, for that matter.

"Have you met my twin sister?" He chuckles lightly. "Her room looks like a tornado blew through it, and that's on a good day."

Sure, I've been in Beibhinn's room, and he's not wrong. Her floordrobe is almost as impressive as her walk-in closet. That girl could clothe half the country and still have enough left to clothe the rest.

"So, where were we?" I let the question linger as I climb onto the bed and settle myself into the centre in a Buddha style pose.

Liam drops onto the edge of my bed, turning his torso to face me. "I guess I was apologising for being a classic arsehole earlier. Not that it makes it any better, but it wasn't about you. Not really."

"What was it about, then?" My words come out clipped and laced with annoyance.

"There are things you don't know, free bird. Things that could unintentionally put you in danger. And Rohan King falls into that category. Fuck, he's right at the top of people you need to stay away from."

Logically, after everything that's happened, I should trust Liam when he tells me Rohan is dangerous, but there is still that tiny part of me that's unreasonably drawn to the darkness surrounding Rí. Besides, if anyone knows what really happened to my mam that night, it's him. I need answers, and fuck knows, the Devereuxs aren't very forthcoming.

Deciding I can use Liam's hatred to my advantage, I pry, "Why?" I punctuate with a raised brow. "Give me one good reason, Liam."

Once again, he averts his gaze to the floor, and his shoulders sag with a defeated sigh. "I can't. Trust me, I'd lay it all out if I could, but it's not time yet." Then suddenly, his hurricane eyes latch on to mine. His hand reaches forward, brushing the falling strands of hair from my face. "Soon, free bird. I promise."

Pulling back from his touch, unwilling to let myself become clouded by the way his fingertips scorch my skin, I level with him. "Give me something, Liam. Anything. I'm tired of all these secrets. Since I arrived at Killybegs, I have got more questions than answers, and that's the opposite of what I need right now."

His eyes close, and the tip of his tongue travels over the seam of his bottom lip. Finally, he tilts his chin towards me, and our gazes lock once more. "One question," he mutters. "But nothing pertaining to Rohan."

Before I can even think about what I want to ask, the question that's been tossing around my mind since I overheard Liam and Fiadh talking this afternoon freefalls from my lips. "What did your mam mean when she said, I don't remember the little boy who was once my best friend?"

A slow smirk slides onto Liam's face, accompanied by a twinkle in his eyes. "You caught that, huh?"

"Amongst other things."

"What other things?"

"Stop trying to deflect, Liam."

His chest vibrates as he holds back his chuckle, but his eyes flash towards the door as he mutters, "I can't answer that question either."

"Are you shitting me?" I cut him off. "You said…"

"Relax, free bird. Just because I can't outright tell you

doesn't mean I can't give you something to help you remember."

Confusion laces my brow, marring my forehead with tiny shallow lines. "What do you mean?"

Suddenly, he's on his feet and striding to the door. Peering over his shoulder, he stills me with a glance. "Do not move. I'll be right back."

Saoirse

My eyes stay trained on the open doorway as I fidget with my hands, waiting for Liam to return from wherever he ran off to. Finally, unable to remain still, I lay my palms flat on the duvet and hoist myself backwards until my spine greets the soft, grey, crushed velvet headboard.

Seconds turn into minutes, and before long, I toss my head back and stare at the ceiling. Straightening my legs out, I wiggle my toes, expelling some of the nervous energy building underneath my skin.

I wonder what he could have that would remind me of a time I know nothing about. I have no recollection of the Devereux twins or their parents. And unless there is a sizable chunk of my life missing, there's nothing Liam can show me that will convince me otherwise.

"Are you sleeping?" Liam's amusement pierces my

eardrum, forcing my head to drop to the side. Finally, I peel my heavy eyelids open to find a still shirtless Liam, blocking the entire doorway with his well-defined frame.

My brows crinkle when I spy the small object dangling from his right hand. "What's that?" I ask, tipping my chin towards the leather-bound book.

His feet carry him towards the edge of the bed. "Scoot over, and I'll show you."

Using my hands to steady myself, I bum-shuffle across the bed and then pat the space next to me. "Well, are you going to stand there all night, or will you show me what you're hiding there?"

A smile creeps onto his face, and he slides into the open space beside me. Then, mirroring my position, Liam stretches out his long, lean legs until they are straight out in front of him. Finally, he lays the 4×6 book on his lap.

Once he's settled against the headboard, he slopes his head to his left, catching my gaze. "You ready?"

Scooting closer, I mould myself to his side, our legs brushing as he raises his arm for me to duck beneath, allowing me to snuggle closer to his bare chest. My head nestles into the crook of his arm, finally resting against his taut, broad shoulders.

My left hand rests against his bare torso as I tuck my right beneath my cheek.

Suddenly, it strikes me how intimate the manoeuvre is,

but with the way Liam's fingertips twist the tip of my ponytail, I don't think he minds having me pressed against him like a band-aid. So, instead of pulling back, I bask in the warmth emulating from his chiselled body.

"Okay, ready when you are." I settle in, waiting for him to crack the book open.

Finally, he peels back the cover, revealing a photo album stuffed to the brim with old photographs. My curious gaze connects with the first image — two log cabins, side by side, standing tall amongst the shade of countless evergreen trees — and I gasp.

"The cabins." My words are nothing more than a breathless statement.

"Do you remember this place?" Liam dips his chin, peering down at me over the rim of his dark lashes.

My fingertips trail over the polypropylene covering, tracing the lines of the Belgian style log cabins. A sad smile curls on my mouth as a mirage of childhood memories flood my mind. "Of course. My mother took me to these cabins every summer for most of my childhood. It was the only place I ever truly felt at home.

"No matter how many towns we ran from or how many houses we upped and left with no return, this place" — I point to the cabin on the right — "was the one place she never took from me. Every year, without fail, we'd spend our entire summer vacation in these cabins. I looked forward to it every year. It was the only constant I had growing up."

"When did you stop going there?" He breathes against the top of my head.

"Erm." My eyes flicker shut, acknowledging the sadness that washes through me. "We were supposed to go back the summer after my thirteenth birthday, but right before we left to go there, my mam got a call from the owners. Apparently, they sold them, and the new owners weren't interested in renting them out."

I don't mention how disappointed I was that day or how I had spent the entire year building up to that vacation, hopelessly daydreaming about all the promises the boy in the sister cabin had made to me the summer before.

After all, I never saw him again, not after he stole my first kiss on my last night the summer previous. So telling Liam about him would be pointless, and I doubt he'd want to hear about the first boy I thought I loved as a pathetic preteen.

Beneath my cheek, the steady thump of Liam's heart pounds against his rib cage, slowly picking up pace with every word I speak. Finally, he flips to the next photograph, and I bolt upright, breaking free of Liam's hold, and tearing the album from his grip. Finally, I bring it closer to my face.

"Where did you…" The question dies on my tongue as I stare down at a face I haven't seen in almost five years.

"How do you have this picture?"

"Your mam sent them to mine every year."

"Why?"

"You are my mam's goddaughter. She wanted to stay updated on your life, even if she couldn't be part of it in the way she wanted to be."

Suddenly, Liam's front moulds against my back, and then his chin is resting on my shoulder. Cranking my neck, I peer at his smiling face out of the corner of my eye. "Who's the dork?" Laughter dances in his tone.

"Devin was not a dork. He was the coolest person I knew. He spent every year at the lake with his godfather in the cabin next to ours." My gaze falls back to the boy who stole my twelve-year-old heart. His lanky frame towers over me as his arm lies lazily over my shoulder. His braced smile is wide matching mine, and his mousey brown strands fall in dishevelled waves, concealing his bright, grey-blue eyes.

"Oh, did little Saoirse have a crush on the dork?" His tone is teasing, but it doesn't stop me from raising my hand and slapping his bare chest. "You're an arsehole, you know that."

"Stop avoiding the question." His wink sends a shiver down my spine.

My eyes roll at his ridiculousness. "If you must know, Devin was the first boy I kissed."

"Let's hope he grew into himself. Otherwise, you'd be the only girl who'd ever want to kiss him."

"Liam! Don't be so mean." I slap at him again, only this time he jumps back, trying to stop my hand from connecting to his bare skin.

The move knocks both of us off balance, and suddenly Liam's arms wrap around my waist as we flail back onto the mattress in a fit of laughter. Before I know what's happening, Liam rolls out from under me and then cages me beneath him. His eyes are wild, glistening with laughter and lust. "What was the last thing Devin ever said to you?"

It's a strange question, considering Liam's lips are mere millimetres from mine, taunting me as his tongue slowly travels along the seam of his mouth.

"Uh, eh…I don't remember."

"Try."

I hadn't thought of that day for a long time, and the words Devin and I exchanged are a distant, faded memory. But, doing as Liam asks, I think back to that last holiday and the bitter goodbye Devin and I shared before I had to leave to start my new school.

Closing my eyes, I recall standing next to my mam's

car and Devin sweeping the hair from my face as a foolish tear fell from my eyes.

"I don't want to leave."

"I know." His boyish grin swings free, lighting up his face and showcasing the tiny dimple on his left cheek. "But I'll see you again next year, and every year after that."

"Promise?"

"Always, free bird."

My lids swing open to find Liam's stormy eyes hovering above mine. I survey every inch of his face, searching for the awkward boy I once knew. Gone are the train track braces, replaced by a pearly white smile that lights up his face. Although they're familiar, his eyes are not as bright and innocent. There's a darkness to them now, something that wasn't there when he was a young boy. Although it's still the same shade, his hair is much shorter, showcasing the new tattoos along the back and sides of his skull. It's not shocking that I didn't recognise him. He's come a long way from the lanky boy he once was, but the longer I stare into those familiar grey eyes, the more foolish I feel.

"Devin?" The question reduces my words to a pathetic wheeze as a series of sputtering heartbeats pitter-patter against my rib cage.

"Finally, free bird. I was beginning to think that kiss meant nothing to you."

"But…where did Liam come from?" My confusion twists my face into a tight knot, making Liam — or Devin — snicker.

"Liam's my middle name. Being a twin is hard enough without having names that rhyme. I swear my parents were asking for me to be bullied. So, when I turned fourteen, I insisted everyone use my middle name instead. Besides, Liam suits me better, don't you think?"

I open my mouth to ask more questions, like where was Beibhinn all those summers we spent by the lake, and why didn't she spend the summers with their godfather, just like he did. But Liam's finger presses against my lips, silencing my thoughts.

"I know you've lots of questions, and I promise you, I'll answer them all, but right now, I need to…"

His roving eyes hone in on mine, expelling a flurry of goosebumps along my skin. I swallow the lump forming in the back of my throat.

"Need what?" I ask, airy and breathless, feeling the effects of our proximity.

He answers my question by sealing his lips on mine. He starts off slow, teasing my mouth open with a swipe of his tongue. I open for him, meeting each of his tender brushes with one of my own. Suddenly, my body ignites, and I'm diving into all things Liam Devereux.

My arms circle his neck, drawing him closer, and he

picks up his pace, devouring my mouth with greedy laps of his tongue.

This kiss is nothing like the one we shared all those years ago. Instead, it's doused in hunger, a need to claim something we lost as kids. His roaming hands slide over my rib cage, sending a shiver up my spine, forcing my back to arch into his chest, greedy for more. It's dangerous, and even though I know we probably shouldn't be doing this with everything else that's going on, I never want to stop.

I'm lost in him and the sensation he draws from my body. It's been too long since a man kissed me into oblivion, the way Liam is now. My skin is on fire, scorched by his touch. I need more…Fuck, I crave it. My hands trace over his back, sculpting the hard muscles defining his solid frame. My nails dig into his skin, and a deep groan rumbles against my lips. I'm seconds away from saying *fuck it* and taking everything he's willing to offer me. But before I can beg him to relieve the throbbing need building between my thighs, he rears back, stealing the air from my lungs.

His eyes find mine as he cups my cheek. "I've wanted to do that since the second I saw you lounging in the garden."

"Then why did you stop?"

"Trust me, free bird. Stopping is the last thing I want to

do, but we both know I have to. At least until I can give you the answers you need."

As much as I hate to admit it, he's right. That doesn't mean I have to like it, though.

He leans forward, stealing one more quick kiss. "Goodnight, free bird."

"Night, Liam."

Saoirse

My fingertips tug at the purple necktie as I glance at my reflection in the full-length mirror, checking out my new school uniform.

Honestly, I'm not mad at how the fitted black shirt slims my high bustline. Or how the purple and black pleated skirt elongates my short legs, making me appear taller than my five-foot-two self.

Finally, I swipe the fitted black blazer with the delicate purple trim from the edge of the bed and tug it on, completing the required Killybegs Secondary School dress code.

My hands brush against the double-breasted collar as I give myself one last once-over. I notice the school's crest stitched onto the left breast with purple and white stitching, a collective of four coats of arms, each one identical to the detailed lid of the box my mother entrusted me to take.

Beibhinn wasn't lying when she said the Kings of Killybegs and their families run this entire town. No wonder Mr Devereux could get me into my final year without a minute's notice. This town was built on his family name, along with mine and two others.

Once I deem myself decent, I take a reassuring breath before blowing out the nervous energy coiling in my shoulders.

You'd think by now, starting at a new school would be a walk in the park, but it gets no easier. The only plus is that with every fresh beginning comes the chance to put my best foot forward and showcase the best version of myself.

Today is judgement day. How I portray myself, is how my new peers will perceive me the rest of my time at KS.

There is no room for weakness. Instead, I must hold my head high and demand respect. Otherwise, this pretentious town and its royal status quo will shred me apart.

Sure, the Devereuxs hinted that I have a place amongst the elite and future generation of Kings. However, I'm sure there will be many who will make me work for whatever title I *supposedly* hold.

Besides, I'm not even sure I want the legacy attached to my name. My mother's past is foreign to me, and even though Beibhinn and Liam say I belong here, I don't know the first thing about what being a Ryan entails.

Whatever it means, I know my mother wanted nothing to do with it.

One thing is for sure; I need to survive today. Secondary school is a cesspit, one I am determined to get out of alive.

"No need to be nervous," I psych myself up. "It's just one more first day in an already long list of first days."

I hate the uncertainty in my tone, but the events that led me to Killybegs have muted my usual, sassy self. Instead, I've retreated inward with everything going on, and I hate it. Sure, there have been moments when snippets of *the real Saoirse* peeped out with a sarcastic comment or a bitchy comeback. But for the most part, I've hidden beneath the weight of the past few days.

But, no more! Starting today, I will not feel sorry for myself. This is my new reality until I figure out what happened to my mam and why she kept me from this life. I need to accept that where I am right now is where I need to be.

Time to get on with the hand life has dealt me. My new beginning starts today. Let's hope I am strong enough to handle whatever it throws my way.

Never feed your fears, Saoirse. Because if you do, they'll eat you alive.

My mother's final words to me ring through, filling me with the ache of her absence but also providing the confidence I need to take on whatever shitshow I'm about to walk into.

Placing my current life problems to the side, I plaster on a smile. "I am Saoirse Ryan, and I'm going to make Killybegs Secondary my bitch."

A bark of laughter sounds from behind me, and my neck cranes towards the amused chuckle.

"As much as I love the little pep talk you've got going on." Beibhinn's hand circles the air as she saunters into my room and plops down on my mattress. "My brother is making breakfast. And, unless you have a thing for burnt bacon, we should probably head down there before he sets our lodge on fire."

Heated cheeks aside, I turn to face her. "You heard that." My brows deepen as I scrunch up my nose.

"Oh, yes! I *particularly* loved the part when you said you would make Killybegs Secondary your bitch. That's the kinda energy I need from this friendship."

Her wide smile and the glimmer in her bright eyes ease my embarrassment. So, with a shake of my head, I shoot her a humour-filled eye roll and head towards the door. "Let's go then."

Beibhinn bounds off the bed and throws her fists in the air. "Killybegs Secondary School, you're about to suck our massive *metaphorical* dicks."

My head falls back as laughter barrels from my mouth. "You're crazy. You know that, right?"

Her arm circles my shoulder, putting me into a side hug. "All the best people are, my friend."

———

"Can I help with anything?" I slide in next to Liam as he flips the French toast on the pan with ease most eighteen-year-olds don't possess when it comes to culinary skills, especially those reared on a fully established estate with live-in staff.

With a side glance, he tosses me a wink. "Nah, I'm good. Take a seat, Bev and I have it covered."

Our eyes connect, and flashes of his lips devouring mine rush to the forefront of my mind. We've yet to speak about the events of last night or what our shared past means for us going forward. Was it two people lost in the nostalgia of what once was, or was it a new beginning for all that could be?

All I know is that kiss kept me awake, daydreaming about when life was easy and carefree. Then, when my eyes finally closed and sleep pulled me under, those innocent touches we shared on the lake and the boy with whom I gave my first kiss…faded. In place was the man before me, covered in tattoos and piercings, his touch anything but innocent as his calloused hands caressed my skin.

His luscious kisses were accompanied by a wicked smile as he devoured every inch of my wanting body until his name fell breathlessly from my lips under the pressure of my release.

I woke with a pounding heart, gasping for the breath my lifelike dream stole and an ache between my thighs that only Liam could satisfy.

With Beibhinn's presence, now isn't the time to broach the subject of what it all means, and honestly, I am not ready to dive into anything other than easy right now.

So, instead of dragging up the past, I mirror his smile and playfully hold my palms up. "You don't have to tell me twice." My body rounds the large island, and I hike my arse into the high stool directly facing Liam.

For a moment, I watch in silence as Liam and Beibhinn hustle around the kitchen, their movements complementing each other to perfection.

Since I arrived in Killybegs, I have not witnessed their twin bond in action until now. First, without looking her way, Liam holds out his hand, and then Beibhinn wordlessly places a plate into his palm.

A smile slides onto my face as I watch them effortlessly serve breakfast, reading each other's next move like a pair of synchronised swimmers.

Finally, Liam peers up over his lash line and raises his brow at my amusement. "What's so funny, free bird?"

"Nothing."

A glass of orange juice appears in front of me as Beibhinn scoots onto the vacant stool to my left. "You seem impressed."

"Well, I just didn't expect you both to be so…*domesticated*."

Liam lays a plate of French toast and bacon in front of me with a smirk. "It was one of the conditions of us moving out here after we turned eighteen."

"We had to learn how to cook and clean up after ourselves. Mam threatened to take away the staff, but we were determined to break free. We wanted our space more," Beibhinn adds before lifting her fork to her mouth.

"We still have dinner at the main house every night, per mam's request, but the rest, we had to learn." Liam holds up the crispy strip of bacon. "One burnt dish at a time."

"Well." I lean across the counter and snatch the piece of bacon from his grasp before popping it in my mouth. "Luckily for you both, I make a mean stack of pancakes. So, tomorrow, breakfast is on me."

"We won't say no to that." They both mirror each other, making my smile tilt to the side.

Rohan

M<small>Y FINGERS CURL IN ON THEMSELVES, AND MY NAILS BITE</small>
into my fleshy palm. Then, eyes blazing, they cross the
courtyard and laser in on the electric blue Ford Mustang
parked directly in my line of sight.

Firmly aligning my backbone, I cross my arms over my
chest and lean back, resting my arse against the picnic
table's edge as I zone in on the girl sitting pretty in Liam's
passenger seat.

Her warm, chocolate tresses freefall past her shoulders,
draping over the slight swell of her breasts, framing her
high cheekbones and shielding her alluring amber eyes
from my view. Her full attention settles on Liam as a wide
grin lights up her face, then suddenly, her head tips back
at whatever he said. Although I can't hear it, her laughter

rushes through me, and jealousy powers the blood in my veins as sudden malaise clenches my stomach.

No! That won't do, love. Those smiles — the ones that light your soul on fire — belong to me.

My thirsty eyes stay trained on her as she reaches for the door handle and gently eases the car door open. Then, her all-black converse-clad feet greet the tarmac before she pulls herself from the passenger seat to stand. My gluttonous gaze sweeps over the bare skin between the top of her knee-high stockings and the hem of her too-short school skirt.

Fuck me.

My tongue trails along my bottom lip, and I visualise what it would be like to mark those olive thighs with my teeth.

Finally, I draw my penetrating stare upwards over the fitted blazer until my eyes latch on to her temptress-like features. Pouty pink lips, a button nose dotted with barely-there freckles, and wide round orbs men like me crumble beneath.

My father warned me about the seductive allure that comes hand-in-hand with the Ryan women, but unfortunately for him, and maybe even my future self, I never listened to him or his shitty life lessons.

Within seconds, Liam and Beibhinn climb from Liam's

car, flanking Saoirse as though they are her bodyguards, and I suppose, in a way, they are. *Not that their protection will do her much good as far I am concerned. However, I have one motive in mind, and I sure as shit won't allow a Devereux to upheave any of my grand plans.*

Excitement flurries in my gut as she tilts her chin and squares her shoulders before she strides forward with a confidence I had yet to see from her.

Sin é, mo bhanríon. Ná léirigh laige nó beidh na vultures ciorcal. *That's it, my queen. Don't show weakness, or the vultures will circle.*

My insides itch, begging to push towards her. But when Liam's arm wraps around her shoulder — drawing her closer to his body as he glares at me with a victorious grin — I remain rooted by the possessive greed strangling my lungs.

I have two options, go in guns blazing by metaphorically pissing all over her or play the long game and lure her in slowly.

Both are good ideas, but only one of them will have her eating out of the palm of my hand. Which is why I stay rooted in place.

Reaching into the inside pocket of my school blazer, I pull out my silver cigarette case and flip it open. Then, I extract a blunt and guide it to my lips before sparking it.

The first drag coats my tongue and, with a heavy inhale, fills my lungs with its toxicants as I school my features to remain unfazed by the sight before me.

With a tip of my chin, I blow out the plume of smoke, polluting the fresh morning air.

"Here comes trouble." Aodhán slips in beside me, ignoring the curious looks from the rest of the table. "Seems like we'll be seeing more of your new plaything, or, should I say, Liam's new plaything?"

His low chuckle grates on my every nerve, but luckily for Aodhán, I'm far too preoccupied with the girl striding towards me to do anything about it.

I remain stoic, savouring every pull of my joint as I watch Liam lead Saoirse towards the picnic table exclusively reserved for the Killybegs Kings. It takes everything in me to hold back the urge to knock the cat-who-got-the-cream smirk off his smug-as-fuck mouth.

What a gobshite! He may think he's claimed her as his prize, but once again, he's sorely mistaken.

Take your fill, have your fun, cause when I finally claim her, all your sly touches will be a distant memory, paling in comparison, Devereux.

Dropping the blunt roach to the grass, I stub it out under the toe of my boot as manicured fingernails curl around my bicep. The rush of Hannah's overly sweet perfume invades my nostrils. "Who is with Liam and Beibhinn?" she asks, a tinge of disdain licking every syllable.

As the daughter of a syndicate member — a bishop to be exact — Hannah Crowe made it her mission to bed as many Kings as possible, all in hopes of bagging one of us and cementing her future. Her life mission is to climb further up the hierarchy ladder by locking any of us down. So far, she has not succeeded. She's merely a warm hole we pass around — or share — whenever an itch needs to be scratched.

I'm not one to slut shame anybody for their sexual preferences, but this girl has taken more dicks than a Pornhub Gloryhole, and although there have been plenty of nights I have indulged in what she so eagerly offered, I haven't touched her in weeks. Not since I first lay eyes on my newest obsession.

I'm seconds away from peeling Hannah from my side when Saoirse's gaze pricks my skin. Our eyes connect, and a slow, menacing smile forms at the corner of my lips. Her wide orbs bounce between me and the striking blonde plastered to my side before narrowing into curious slits.

Is that jealousy I see, love?

Deciding to test my theory, I draw Hannah closer, palming her arse. It's slight, but I don't miss the fleeting eye roll Saoirse gives me, or the tight set of her clenched jaw.

Suddenly, the last words I spoke to Saoirse repeat in my head as she closes the distance between us. *"You are mine — to play with, to fuck, to shatter. I will destroy you, Saoirse, and you'll love every second of it."*

A promise. One I have every intention to keep.

"Well, well, well…if it isn't the bus stop beauty," Aodhán chimes in, pulling me from my thoughts just in time to spy the cheeky wink he directs at Saoirse, drawing her fixation away from me.

"Oh, hey." She smiles back at him, probably seeking comfort in the familiarity of his boyish face. "It's Aodhán, right?"

"The one and only," he teases her with a flirty smile, forcing teeth to sink into my bottom lip.

"Seems my stellar direction telling worked out for you." He motions between Beibhinn and Liam, and a smile widens on Saoirse's face.

"They did. Thanks again."

"It's not a problem, doll." He briefly flicks his eyes towards me, his bright blues shimmering with mischief as he wiggles his brow at me. That little manoeuvre has my insides bubbling with molten rage, but I don't feed into his subtle taunt and instead remain stoic.

He's trying to rile me, and the fucker knows me well enough to understand his baiting is working, even if I'm not outwardly showing it.

"So, Beibhinn…" Hannah pipes up. "Are you going to introduce us to your *little friend?*"

Beibhinn's eyes rage at the condescension dripping from Hannah's words. Unfazed by the murderous glare, Hannah roams her hand over my chest before settling her head on my shoulder, undoubtedly trying to stake her claim. Any other day, I'd swat her away like the annoying little fly she is, but the glimmer of disdain shining back at me from Saoirse's annoyed features has me unmoving.

A part of me loves that she's so affected by the attention Hannah is giving me, and like the sociopathic fucker I am, I feed off it.

Tipping my chin, I bring my lips closer to Hannah's neck, speaking loud enough for mo bhanríon to hear. "Let's go, babe. Kings don't waste their time entertaining useless pawns."

Nor do they allow anyone to disrespect their queen.

Without hesitation, I turn on my heel, Hannah mindlessly following my lead, as I knew she would. Then, guiding us both towards the entrance of KS, I force myself further away from the watchful eyes scorching into my back. Then, right before I push through the stone-arched doorway, I throw one last look over my shoulder, challenging her with a burning glance of my own.

Feicim thú ag breathnú, mo bhanríon. Gach uair a bheidh tú réidh, beidh mé ag fanacht. *I see you watching, my queen. Whenever you're ready, I'll be waiting.*

Saoirse

"Hello! Earth to Saoirse." Beibhinn bumps her shoulder against mine, drawing my gaze away from the murderous glare of the devastatingly handsome arsehole who, mere seconds ago, dismissed me as if I were last week's trash.

Logically, I know I shouldn't give a shit what Rohan King thinks of me, but there was something about his distasteful appraisal and penetrating glower that left my skin crawling. As much as I hate to admit it, a hostile fire coursed through my veins when he tugged the nameless blonde closer to his chest, leaving me with unmentionable emotions I have no right to feel.

I couldn't be jealous. No, it's not possible.

My stomach knots as the weight of my realisation sinks in, knocking me for six. Yet, I refuse to give in to those thoughts and what they may mean, especially when all Rohan deserves is my hate, *not* my affection.

Shaking those thoughts from my head, I focus on Liam, Beibhinn, and Aodhán. "Sorry. I zoned out for second, first-day nerves and all that." The lie tastes bitter on my tongue, and judging by the three sets of eyes silently calling me out on my bullshit, they know better than to believe it.

Thankfully, Aodhán steps in beside me, breaking the heavy silence by wrapping his arm around my shoulder and pulling me into a side hug. "Don't stress, princess. I was just telling my cousins"— he tilts his chin towards Liam and Beibhinn — "to bring you to the party on Friday."

My eyes dart towards Liam, and I ignore the rage in his stormy eyes and do my best to keep things light. "You're related?"

"Our mam is his dad's sister," Beibhinn punctuates with an eye roll while Liam grumbles behind clenched teeth with clutched palms. "Unfortunately!"

"Now, now, Devereux." Aodhán whips his arm from my shoulder and prowls forward. His carefree smile is replaced by something far more devious. Nose to nose, Liam and Aodhán stand-off. "You're just sore because I'm Grandad's favourite." His taunting lilt is doused with condescension, but it's the way his eyes narrow with a threatening glare that has my skin prickling.

My heart pounds against my rib cage as my eyes widen at the sight before me. There's no denying the fight for dominance shining from both of their eyes.

Liam tilts his head to the side, lowering his mouth to Aodhán's ear before whispering something inaudible.

Aodhán cocks his head back, a laugh fleeing past his lips into the morning breeze. His feet fall back, creating space between them as he walks backwards. Once I'm within reaching distance, he halts, eyes trained on me. "You're *his,* Saoirse." His eyes slowly trail towards the entrance, where Rohan's eyes are still trained on me. "The sooner you realise that, the better off we'll all be."

With those parting words, he departs.

My confusion settles heavily on my brow as I whip my gaze back to Liam and Beibhinn. "What the fuck did he mean, I'm *Rohan's?*" I wave towards the dark figure filling the doorway with his stifling presence.

Behind rage-filled eyes, Liam remains mute before he strides off without a word. Finally, Beibhinn loops her arm through mine, guiding me towards the school. "It's just Aodhán being Aodhán. His charm will draw you in and gain your trust. But don't let his boyish dimples fool you. After all, a wolf dressed in sheep's clothing is still a wolf."

Her cryptic words stumble around my head, but now is not the time to question the meaning behind them.

"Enough boy drama for a Monday." Beibhinn steers our conversation in a new direction. "Let's get you to the office and get your schedule."

Slipping my confidence mask in place, I follow her lead, not missing the wink Rohan gifts me as I stride by him with my head held high.

You're his, Saoirse. Aodhán's words echo in my mind.

Think again, arsehole. The only person I belong to is myself.

AFTER BEIBHINN DROPS ME OFF AT THE PRINCIPAL'S OFFICE for my induction, Ms Kavanagh, Killybegs Secondary School's headmistress, gives me a rundown of my class schedule and how to navigate the black and purple colour coding on my timetable.

"As you can see from your map" — she points to the piece of paper in my hand —"we've divided the school into four floors, all colour coded for easier navigation. Your classes will all be held in the senior section stationed on the third and fourth floor." My eyes flick towards her, noting the sweet smile on her fresh face.

"The ones marked black are on the third floor, all the elective and common areas, the gym, library, computer and science labs, art and music rooms, etc, and of course, the cafeteria. All of your core classes are on the fourth floor, marked in purple."

I nod, hoping I understand the gibberish leaving her mouth. "My electives are on the third floor, marked in black, and my core subjects are on the fourth floor, marked in purple. Got it."

"Perfect. I've tried my best to place you in as many classes with the Devereuxs as possible, considering they're the only people you know here, but with your grades being as high as they are, it wasn't possible to have them in every class."

"That's okay. I'm sure I'll manage without the hand-holding."

A small smile tugs on her lips, but she lowers her gaze as she pushes out of her chair, hiding it from me. "Well then, let me show you where your locker is and give you a quick tour and then we'll get you to your first class — double period of Honors English with Mr Lynch."

Rising from my chair, I hike my bag over my shoulder and head towards the door she's holding open.

About twenty minutes later, our tour concludes, and she guides me towards room P14 before gently tapping her knuckles at the door. While we wait for the teacher to grant us access, she gives me one more piece of ominous advice. "Try not to get too tangled in the politics of this palace, Saoirse. From your transcripts, I can tell you are a smart girl, just like your mam was when we were younger."

Before I can question her or what she meant by that statement, the door swings open, revealing a well-dressed man in his mid-to-late thirties. "Ms Kavanagh," he greets before his bright eyes land on mine. "And you must be Ms Ryan."

I nod and swallow the nerves building in the base of my throat. "Come on in, and I'll introduce you to everyone and then you can take a seat."

I step forward, but Ms Kavanagh speaks once more, halting me in place.

"Saoirse, if you need anything, you know where my office is."

"Thank you."

She tips her head before spinning on her heel, leaving me standing in the doorway with over thirty eyes trained on me. It's then the whispers start.

Thrown to the wolves...here goes nothing.

"Everybody, settle down," Mr Lynch announces. "This is Saoirse, our newest student. So be on your best behaviour, and for the love of God, make her feel welcome."

"Oh, I'll make her feel more than welcome, sir." Some arsehole in the front row jeers, making the rest of the class burst with laughter, including the girl next to him, which just so happens to be the blonde wrapped around Rohan this morning.

Just my fucking luck!

"I apologise for the animals I seem to be teaching. Some of them really need to work on their manners." Mr Lynch holds his palm out, pointing between the two rows. "There's a free seat in the back row. Hopefully, Donnacha's poor attempt at flattery won't reach you back there."

The class laughs again, and I realise English won't be so bad, especially with Mr Lynch's easy-going rapport.

Following his guide, my feet carry me forward as my eyes roam over all the nameless faces. In the middle row, I spy Aodhán, who gives me a reassuring smile followed by a cheeky wink. Then, finally, the guy in the seat behind him, next to the empty chair, comes into view. When he lifts his head from his open textbook, my breath lodges in my throat as he peers up at me over his thick black lashes. His familiar forest terrain eyes connect with mine as a slow but smug smile forms on his lips.

You have got to be kidding me!

"We really need to stop meeting like this, love. I'm starting to think you're following me."

Ignoring him and the underlying taunt in his words, I take my seat before pulling my textbooks from my bag.

For a few minutes, he remains silent, piercing me with his unnerving glare, until finally, I can't take it anymore, and twist in my seat to stare back. "Stop staring at me!" I whisper with aggression, which only feeds his ego.

Leaning back, he balances his chair on the rear two legs as the dimple in his right cheek deepens. "No."

"Rohan!"

"Love," he counters as his chair falls forward, drawing him further into my personal space.

"Quit calling me that."

"Also no."

Irritation explodes, instantly souring my mood. Shifting in my seat, I slide the chair to the left, as far away from him as I can get without drawing any attention our way. Only, my slight reprieve doesn't last long because Rohan decides to follow my movement, closing every millimetre of the distance between us until our legs are brushing against each other.

Without warning, he drags the butt of his pen along my thigh. Gliding it over my skin until it's roaming dangerously close to the hem of my skirt. "How many times do I have to tell you? You can run, but I'll always find you."

I should ward him off and fight against his invasion, but the darker part of me craves the danger that clouds him. Curiosity killed that cat, and Rohan King may be the death of me.

His pen slips beneath my skirt, trailing higher, closer to the edge of my thong. My entire body becomes ramrod straight as shivers nip my spine and spasms cinch my core.

Frozen to my seat, the sound of my erratic breaths pound in my eardrums as the blood in my veins pumps towards the wanting destination between my thighs.

"What are you doing?" I manage to force the words out past my clenched teeth.

His eyes are on mine, searing past the exterior and exposing my soul. "Do you want me to stop?"

Goosed flesh pebbles at the base of my neck as my vocabulary lodges in my throat, cutting off my reply.

Then, with a slight flick of his wrist, his pen slides beneath my underwear, tracing my slit, once, twice. Shuffling in my seat, I draw my thighs together, hoping he'll remove his hand before anyone notices it has disappeared underneath my skirt. Unfortunately, my poor attempt backfires when my thighs push against his wrist, and the tip of his pen slips between my slick folds. The intrusion makes me gasp, but it doesn't stop him, and suddenly, every head in the room turns and all eyes land on me.

"Is everything okay, Saoirse?" Mr Lynch's brows crease with concern as my cheeks burn red.

From the corner of my eye, I spy the devious tilt of Rohan's lips. I open my mouth, and just as I acknowledge Mr Lynch's question with a breathless *yes,* Rohan pushes in further, and my hips thrust from the chair.

"Are you sure?" Mr Lynch presses as Rohan rips his hand away before sliding the pen between his lips.

A low hum rumbles from Rohan's chest as my taste touches his tongue, but I manage a quick nod, reassuring my English teacher. Once he turns back to face the whiteboard, I settle my glare back on Rohan.

His eyes glisten with mischief as he slowly slides the pen from his mouth before licking his lips. "Delicious."

"You're a fucking arsehole."

His eyes crinkle with humour as he lowers his lips to my ear. "Mo chorp. Mo phusa. Mo bhanríon. Mine." *My body. My pussy. My queen. Mine.*

"Says who?"

"Our last names."

Saoirse

IGNORING ROHAN'S PRESENCE IS PROVING TO BE RATHER tricky, especially when I can't steady the rapid thumping of my heart as it assaults my rib cage, nor can I ease the way my skin tingles under his watchful gaze.

My shoulders rise with short, shallow breaths as I keep my eyes trained on Mr Lynch as he rambles on about our Shakespearean set work for our final exams.

"Othello is a tale of sweet vengeance, led by deceit, jealousy, and lies. Othello is an eloquent, powerful figure, respected by all those around him. But, despite his elevated status, he is easy prey. He is a victim of his insecurities, which leaves him vulnerable, especially regarding the love he had for his wife. For homework this week, I would like you all to choose your favourite quote from the text and write a fifteen-hundred-word essay on why you chose it."

A collective grumble breaks out amongst my peers, but Rohan's low drawl breaks through the noise.

"She loved me for the dangers I had passed, And I loved her that she did pity them. Act 1, scene 3."

His words are not for anyone but me, but what meaning is he placing on them?

My head turns with a snap of my neck, eyes landing on his, my unspoken question shining from their depths. Suddenly, the bell rings, shattering the silence controlling our impenetrable stare-off. Then, without tearing his eyes from mine, he rises from his chair, swipes his books from the desk and flees the room, leaving me motionless and confused.

Finally, I pack up my books, reach into my pocket and pluck out my phone.

GROUP CHAT: Liam and Beibhinn.

Me: *Hey, I'm just leaving room P14. Are we still meeting in the common room for our small break?*
L: *I'll be there in 10.*

B: *Yup! I'm already here. Move that arse.*

Me: *Give me 5! If I don't show up, I got lost trying to navigate this stupid colour coding. Lol!*

B: *Walk straight until you get to the stairwell, down one flight, and I'll meet you at the bottom.*

Me: *Sounds good. OMW!*

Placing my phone back in my pocket, I start moving.

I'm halfway down the corridor when a side door opens and someone grabs my elbow and rips me inside. Another hand covers my mouth, silencing my scream. I blink, my eyes narrowing as they try to adjust to the dim lighting of what seems to be a janitor's closet. Suddenly, Rohan's unique scent fills my nose, and my breath hitches once more.

"If I remove my hand, promise me you won't scream."

I remain still, but I can feel the thumping of his heart against my back. Finally, when I realise he won't release me until I comply, I nod.

Once his hand drops from my mouth, I whisper-yell, "What the fuck are you doing?" then pull my elbow from his grip, turning to face him. "Are you insane?"

"Perspective."

"You say that a lot, but I'm yet to understand what you mean by it."

He creeps forward, forcing me to ease back until my

spine greets the metal shelving behind me. My chest rises then falls, over and over as I fight to fill my lungs. His presence unnerves me, and I unravel at the seams. I hold his gaze, mesmerised by the countless shades in his eyes. They remind me of a forest on a rainy day, a blend of greens, golden browns, and rustic oranges, intensified with the coating of heavy rainfall. Suddenly, as though thunderclouds roll in, the kaleidoscope of colours darkens, and I become consumed by the shadows that steal the light from his eyes.

He glides closer, moulding his chest against mine. "You want to know what it means?"

My throat clogs, then trailing my tongue along the roof of my mouth, I swallow my reply with a nod.

His head bows, lowering to my ear. His warm breath caresses my neck, sending a flurry of desire through my body until finally, it explodes, dampening the sweet spot between my thighs.

I shouldn't feel like this, dazed by desire and rattled by anticipation.

"Perception is a gift most people lack, Saoirse," he whispers. "But when we change the way we look at things" — his hand reaches up, brushing the hair off my shoulders, exposing my neck — "the things we look at change."

His lips trail over my pulse, leaving just a whisper of a kiss. "I told you before *all is never as it seems,* only those who choose to look—" His left hand crosses my chest, gripping my shoulder and spinning me in place. Suddenly, I'm facing the shelving, and my arms rush out in front of me, stopping my body from colliding with the steel frame. His head is hovering over my shoulder. Then, in the next breath, he whispers the rest of his response in my ear. "—will find the truth behind the lies."

"And you know the truth?" My voice drips with condescension.

"Yes!" His reply is firm, instant.

"Enlighten me then."

Suddenly, his hands fall to the bare skin above my knee before slowly trailing up my thighs. The higher his hands roam, the further up my skirt hitches.

My fingertips tighten on the shelf, biting into the metal.

I know this is wrong. I shouldn't want Rohan anywhere near me. But the lust, anticipation, and want pulsing between my thighs all sing a different tune. Danger and desire, longing and greed, my body bows beneath his hands, begging to be freed.

"We shouldn't." My mind kicks in, contradicting the submission of my body.

His breath lingers on my neck as he breathes out his reply. "Oh, but we should. After all, when all is said and done, you will be, and have always been, *mine*."

At the bluntness of his words, I squirm, and my back arches. But, in hindsight, it wasn't the best form of protest because now my barely-covered arse is resting against his harder-than-steel cock.

"Hmm." His groan pebbles against my skin, sending another dart of desire down my spine.

Skirt hiked around my waist, his fingertips dance across the small triangle of my thong before slipping beneath the lace and curling around the material.

In one swift motion, he tugs, ripping it from my body before guiding the flimsy material to my nose. "Smell," he demands. "That's what I do to *my* greedy cunt."

My mind rages against my lust, begging for me to push back, stop this foolishness, push him off me, and run as far and as fast as possible. But my skin is on fire under his touch, and my need for release far outweighs my urge to run.

"Deep breath, love." I follow his demand, submitting to the ache only he can ease.

Then, without warning, he stuffs the lace into my mouth, gagging me and muffling my cries.

Suddenly he dips to his knees, crumpling my skirt around my waist. "I can still taste you on my tongue," he mutters against my thigh as he laves along my flesh. "It's not enough, though. I need more, love."

His teeth nibble as he brings himself closer to my

pussy. Gripping my thighs, he spreads my legs, then lifts my left foot onto the first shelf, giving himself better access. "Good little Saoirse. You're glistening for me."

His praise washes through me, tightening my core. The pads of his fingers explore my thighs, and if I could, I would beg him to relieve me from the hell he's inflicting. Suddenly, his fingers slip between my folds, but the lace filling my mouth muffles the sigh trapped behind my lips.

Raising one hand to the small of my back, he presses down, and my arms buckle, forcing me to face plant the shelf before me. My back arches, and his mouth settles on my centre, his tongue lapping at my clit with merciless strokes.

He draws back slightly. "I want your cum coating my lips and dripping down my chin. Don't play shy, mo bhan-ríon. Ride my face with your pretty pink cunt."

His tongue spears into me, fucking my entrance like a man possessed. My thighs lock, and my arse clenches as my hips lose control, bucking beneath his relentless licks.

His strokes are ruthless, spearing in and out until I can't take the brunt of the pressure any longer.

I spit out the thong he used to gag me, and my words escape with a breathy beg. "Rohan. Oh, God. Please. Uhhh, Rohan."

His fingertips grip my arse as he slides his tongue from my pussy towards my aching clit. His teeth graze my pulsing nub, sucking so hard I see stars erupt behind my lids. "Oh, fuck! Yes, fuck! Oh, God, Rohan."

He doesn't relent, and my body sags above him, spasming with the pressure of my release. "Stop," I beg, desperately trying to catch the breath he stole.

The sensation builds, and my lungs scream at me, heavily sucking in air as the blood rushes from my head to my pussy. Suddenly a rush of want explodes from me, more forcefully than anything I've ever experienced before. "Ahhhh!" I shatter for him, not caring about anything else.

"That's it, my love. Break for me."

Rohan

Watching Saoirse crumble is my new favourite pastime — the way her body bows at my mercy or how her desire flitters from her pouty lips with breathless moans.

But the most satisfying of all is seeing her back curve as the pressure of her release ricochets through her, leaving her nothing more than a boneless mess held up by my palms — *Perfection.*

I could spend a lifetime drawing these reactions from her and still come up starving, an addict craving more.

I know I said I'd wait for her to make the first move, all the while luring her in, piece by piece, but all that flew out the window the second I licked her want from my pen and her sweet fucking nectar coated my tongue.

It took every ounce of my self-restraint to hold back

and make it through our double English class without bending her perfect arse over our desk and fucking her into next Sunday.

Hard as stone, I sat there enduring her unintentional torture, savouring every pathetic second.

After class, I should have walked away, but every particle of my continence shattered with that small taste, leaving me with no other choice but to claim her.

At that moment, my only desire was to make her mind bend and her body break.

I couldn't wait for a second longer, I had to have her, and it's a decision I don't regret. Not one fucking bit.

My cock pulses, begging to be freed from the confines of my school trousers, aching for release, anyway he can get it.

As I rise from my knees, I trail my tongue along my lips, gathering any reminisce of her release.

Fuck, she tastes how she looks — sweet and fucking dangerous.

Her breathing stills as I glide my palms up her thighs. Then, when I rest my chin at the crook of her neck, the air trapped in her lungs falls from her pouty lips.

Using my left hand, I gather her hair in my fist, then tug her head backwards, elongating her neck. My right arm circles her waist, and I needle her left breast through her blazer.

"Tell me, love." My teeth graze the column of her throat as my fingers bite into her shirt, squeezing her perfect mound until her back bows into me. "Do you want me to stop?"

Freeing her breast from my punishing hold, I slowly glide my palm over her buttoned blazer and the bunched skirt around her waist. Finally, I cup her dripping cunt. My fingertips slide through her slick folds, and I make slow, teasing circles over her still sensitive clit.

Her body shudders at my touch, still reeling from her intense orgasm, but it doesn't stop me from slipping my digit inside her. The warmth of her pussy wraps around my finger, squeezing so fucking tight. My head is spinning at the sheer thought of how my dick will feel nestled between her silky thighs.

Adding a second finger, I curl them, rubbing her G-spot before pressing down and pulling an appraising moan from her.

"That's a good girl. Let yourself crumble for me."

My wrist flicks, and I spear my fingers in and out in slow but hard pumps. "So fucking tight, love."

"Rohan," she cries out, back bowing as she chases the high only I can give her. "I hate you."

"We both know that's bollocks, Saoirse. You love how I make you feel. Admit it."

"Fuck you, Rohan." Her words filter through the small

narrow closet in a breathless whisper, wrapped in venom but soaked in need.

"Is that a request?" I push in again, hitting the spot that makes her eyes cross. "Because I'm sure fucking you is what I'm already doing."

Her eyes roll back as I tighten my grip around her hair. Finally, when my cock has had enough waiting, I rip my fingers from her tight cunt, and spin her around to face me. "Is it my cock you want, love?"

She bites down on her lip as her wild want-filled orbs capture my gaze.

Fuck me. She's gorgeous. The evidence of her release is painted across her blush-covered cheeks, free-flowing down the valley of her neck.

My dick twitches. Splaying my hand over her thigh, the pads of my fingers bite into her flesh. I raise her leg in one swift movement and place her foot on the shelf behind me, exposing her cunt. Tightening my grasp on her thigh, I hold her steady as I use my free hand to undo my belt and free my throbbing cock.

Her eyes follow my movement, but I see the apprehension building in her darkened gaze — it's a battle between what she feels is right and what her cunt wants. Of course, she'd never admit it, but the way her tongue slowly dampens her lips has me believing she wants this as much as I do.

"Have you dreamt about my dick splitting your cunt in two?" I wrap my fist around my cock, slowly pumping from my swollen head to the base and back again.

She swallows, eyes trained on my every stroke. "No."

Releasing her thigh, I bring my hand to her throat, curling my fingers around her neck until I can feel her pulse bobbing against my palm. "Oh, Saoirse. One day you will choke on all the lies you tell."

"I dream of you," I continue. "And all the things I want to do to your body. It always starts with me ramming my cock down your throat until you can't breathe, then I'd claim your cunt before flipping you onto your stomach and pounding into your tight arse, making every fucking inch of your body mine, just how it's supposed to be."

Her eyes widen, stunned by my words and my choke-hold clutch, but I don't stop announcing all the filthy scenarios I've played out in my head since that night I trapped her in the forest. I accompany each fantasy with a rigorous pump of my cock.

Before long, precum beads at the tip of my engorged head, begging me to ease the growing ache climbing at the base of my spine.

I need to have her. Now!

"Soon, Saoirse. Soon I will own every inch of you. But for now, I'll take this."

Drawing our bodies closer, I step between her thighs

and slide the head of my cock between her cum-stained lips. Her hips thrust forward at the contact, silently begging me to claim her pretty cunt as my own.

"Jesus, Rohan." Her words are muffled by my hold on her throat. "If you're going to fuck me," she sucks in as much air as she can, "do it already."

My brows hitch at her greedy command. "As you wish, mo bhanríon."

I grip her hip and lunge forward, impaling her cunt with my cock. Her head falls back at my intrusion, propelling her breast forward.

God, I wish I could rip her uniform off and expose everything underneath, take her nipples between my teeth, taste the sweat beading on her skin, all of it…but for now, this will have to do.

Pulling out slowly, I thrust forward, hard and aggressive, over and over, pulling a sweet appraisal from her lips. "Oh…my…God!"

Beneath the hand I have placed on her hip, I feel the faint buzz of her phone vibrating in her pocket.

Continuing with my punishing motions, I reach in and pull it out, spying Beibhinn's name lighting up the screen. A devious thought crosses my mind.

"Rohan," Saoirse breathes out as I grind my cock into her pussy, hitting the spot I've quickly learned drives her wild. "Don't you…ah, God, fuck."

A smile creeps onto my face, and I raise my brow in warning. Finally, I slide my finger across the screen, accepting the call, before placing Beibhinn on speaker. "Saoirse can't come to the phone right now." *Thrust.* "Would you like to leave a message?" *Thrust.*

Saoirse clamps her lips tight, keeping her pleasure contained with everything she has.

Beibhinn's silence draws a gruff laugh from my throat before I end the call, earning *another* glare from Saoirse.

"Lighten up, love." *Thrust.*

Dropping the hand around her neck, I lower it, gripping her leg before pushing it towards her chest, giving myself a better view of her soaked cunt. I pick up my pace, hitting her with deeper, more brutal propulsion. Her moans fill the small space, cheering me on. Then, right on cue, just as I knew he would, Liam's name flashes across Saoirse's phone screen, still clutched in my left hand.

Coincidence, I think not! Everyone knows Beibhinn always runs to big brother, and it seems today is no different.

"Oh, look," I taunt. "Seems your little guard dog is looking for you. Should we answer it?" I grind my hips, making her eyes roll back. "Doh…" I cut her off by placing the vibrating phone against her clit. The pulsation lasts for three rings before stopping. Then it picks up again. Once she overcomes the sensation, it starts again, stealing her ability to form a sentence.

Her head falls back, elongating her neck. Her inner walls tighten, gripping my cock so fucking tight, I'm seconds away from filling her with my cum. "Does it turn you on? To know he's one swipe away from hearing you scream my fucking name."

"Rohan!" It's a warning, but one I'll gladly indulge. "Do not answer that goddamned phone."

My tongue trails along my bottom lip as I pound into her, rattling the shelf behind her. Her hips buck as she chases the high my cock is delivering. "That's it, love. Squeeze my cock with your pretty pussy."

"Oh, God, I'm gonna…"

I swipe to answer just as her filthy moans reverberate around us. "Oh, yes, Rohan. There, right there. Don't you dare stop!"

I follow her over the edge, filling her with my cum. Then I raise the phone to my ear. "Hope you enjoyed that little audio, big man. Tell me, does she scream like that for you?"

Saoirse

After Rohan releases me from his hold, my boneless body sags as my feet greet the floor. My legs are jelly, and it takes me a second to overcome the orgasm-induced haze fogging my brain. Finally, after a few seconds, I compose myself and gather my bearings. But then reality bulldozes in, and the weight of what *we* just did kicks me in the face, dragging me under all over again.

I just had sex in a supply closet with the same sociopath that broke into my house and flipped my entire life on its axis. *Fucking hell, Saoirse. What were you thinking?*

You were thinking with your pussy, the whore on my shoulder chimes in. *Why does she sound eerily similar to my new friend Beibhinn?*

It's official. I've lost the run of myself. It's the only explanation I have for my brief moment of insanity.

"I cannot believe we did that," I mutter — more to myself than Rohan — as I swipe my hands over my crumpled uniform, righting everything in place.

Sure, I can't deny the sexual chemistry between Rohan and me, but fucking hell, what he just did to poor Liam… fuck me, I've no words. It's grade A narcissistic behaviour, but what else did I expect from someone like Rohan King.

How am I supposed to walk out of his closet and look Liam in the eye? He will hate me, and to be honest, I deserve it.

I know Liam and I haven't talked about whatever's brewing between us — if there is anything to it at all. But, regardless of our situation, he deserves better than an audio play-by-play of me coming all over another man's dick.

Panic settles in as my eyes flutter around the small space. I need to get out of this room before the walls enclose on me. Wide-eyed, I peer around the small area, looking for my belongings, not to mention the part of my mind I have misplaced.

When my gaze connects to humourous hues of taunting greens, my internal freak out turns into soul-destroying regret. Rohan shoots me a lopsided grin, seemingly pleased as fuck with his unwanted 'Big Dick Energy', which only annoys me further.

"Was your little pissing contest fuckin' necessary?"

"Eh." He shrugs his broad shoulders. "Necessary? No. Satisfying? Fuck yeah!"

"You're a pig. You know that?"

"So you've mentioned, and yet—" He steps forward, then lifts his hand to the lapels of my blazer before straightening them out with a brush of his fingers. Once more, he sets his malevolent eyes on mine as the tip of his tongue traces the seam of his lips. "—you still let me feast on your pussy, and then fuck you into next week."

Anger burns molten beneath my skin, and as much as I'd like to blame the sociopathic narcissist before me, some of it, or maybe most of it, is directed at myself and my own lust-crazed stupidity.

"Just give me back my phone so that I can get out of here, Rohan." My shoulders slump, my mental state of mind entirely done with this situation. I need to leave this poxy closet and forget this ever happened.

Ignoring my request, Rohan reaches behind me and plucks my balled-up thong off the shelf before attempting to stuff it into his pocket.

"And I'll take those, too." I reach forward and tug my now tattered lace undies from his grasp. "You owe me a new pair of knickers."

His eyes roll to the side in that sexy, unfazed, bad-boy way. "I prefer you without any."

My nostrils flare, irritation whirling beneath my skin,

but before I can react, Rohan holds my phone up to my face, unlocking my phone screen with my face ID. *Fucking Apple and their technology.*

Reaching out, my hand snaps at him, trying to retrieve it, but the fuckface raises it above his head, out of my reach, and then turns his back on me.

My fingertips tug at his elbow, but he remains unmoving, tapping the screen with ease.

"What are you doing? For fuck's sake, Rí, give me the damn phone."

He taps my screen a few more times before finally, he spins to face me, holding out my phone with his devilish grin. "If you insist."

Pulling it from his grasp, I spin on my heel and walk the three steps towards the door. My fingers curl around the doorknob, but right as I twist and pull, Rohan's palm shoots over my shoulder, slamming it shut again.

He's so close. His chest moulds to my back as his warm breath brushes along my neck.

A heavy breath rushes from my nostrils as my neck cranes to peer over my shoulder. "What do you want?" My eyes close briefly, and I shake my head slightly, done with the little game he insists I play.

"I'm not the bad guy, Saoirse." His voice drops to a roughened whisper, brushing across my skin, and sending a shiver down my spine.

"Really? You could have fooled me," I bite back with a sardonic snide.

"Believe what you want, love." His palm curls around the doorknob, covering my hand. "But when the truth you seek knocks you on that gorgeous arse, just remember I tried to warn you."

"Warning me," I bark out a sarcastic laugh as I twist to face him. "Is that what you're calling it? First, you show up out of nowhere and take the only person I had in this world away from me. Then, just when I thought I'd found my place here, with the people who can help me figure out whatever the fuck you and your masked accomplice did to my mam, you show back up again, and what…try fucking me to silence?"

"That's not—"

I hold up my hand, cutting him off. "I don't know what game you're playing, Rohan King," I spit his name with a venomous slur. "But count me the fuck out."

My finger pokes his chest, but he remains still, unfazed by my outburst. Hot angry tears freefall from my eyes, burning with hate, sadness, and regret. "There's only one thing I want from you, Rí. So, unless you're willing to tell me what happened to my mam, then go fuck yourself. Then, once you get off on your sick, twisted fantasies, do it all over again. Cause one thing is for sure. This" — I motion between us — "was a one-time thing."

His hand reaches for my face, then suddenly, he swipes my fury from my cheek with a gesture so sweet and un-Rohan-like it makes the breath in my lungs dissipate. Unwilling to lean into his gesture, I continue to release all my pent-up emotions on him, only this time, there's less fight behind my words. Instead, they're littered with defeat. "Just let me leave, Rohan. Please."

He acknowledges my plea with a dip of his chin before wordlessly twisting the doorknob and pulling the door open.

Relief floods my lungs, and I turn on my heel, but right as I'm crossing the threshold, Rohan calls my name, halting my escape.

My shoulders sag as I toss a glance over my shoulder.

"I know you don't owe me anything," Rohan starts. "But you can't tell the Devereuxs about that night at your house."

"Why not?"

He bites down on his tongue, eyes downcast to the floor. Finally, he tilts his chin, peering at me over his thick black lashes. "Time to open your eyes, love. A hero disguised as a villain is still a hero."

"You expect me to believe you're the hero here?"

"No. Not exactly."

"Then what is it you want?"

"Trust is earned, Saoirse. You shouldn't give it freely."

My heart freezes mid-beat. Those words are so similar to the ones my mother wrote on the back of the photo that led me here. But how?

I blink through my confusion, eyebrows furrowed as I work through how he knew what to say to gain my attention.

Finally, he steps forward, brushing past me with these parting words. "The truth is more powerful than the lie, but only if you have the full story. Be careful who you confide in, Saoirse. Sometimes the devil you think you know is far worse than the devil you don't."

Saoirse

RETURNING TO THE REST OF MY CLASSES IS THE LAST THING
I feel like doing. My mind is still reeling from Rohan's
ominous words, and my need to run from this school and
go home and take a shower is high on my list of priorities.
I feel dirty, thanks to Rohan's disregard for protection and
the evidence of my colossal fuck-up that's now sticking to
my thighs, not to mention my lack of underwear situation.
God, stupid fucking, Saoirse.

Shuddering off the ick crawling beneath my skin, I
send a silent thank you to the birth control Gods. Logically, I know that won't protect me from a potential STD,
but I'm hoping for my sake that Rohan doesn't normally
wield his sword without using a shield. But, judging by the
fact he just had unprotected sex with a stranger, I should
probably schedule a check-up soon to be safe.

Pushing through the crowd of students gathered in the hallway, my feet carry me towards the exit, but then the realisation that I'm running from Beibhinn and Liam and their reactions has me halting in place. My gaze falls to the phone clutched in my palm, and I debate with myself before finally pulling up our group chat.

GROUP CHAT: Liam and Beibhinn.

The cursor blinks back at me from the text bar as I mull over what it is I should say, but every time I try to formulate a coherent apology, it seems to fall flat.

Me: *I know you guys must hate me right now, and honestly, I deserve it. But I just thought I'd let you know I'm heading home. I'm really sorry.*

Three dots dance across the screen before disappearing, then suddenly, Beibhinn's name flashes across my screen as my phone vibrates in my palm. I suck in a breath, preparing myself for her wrath. Finally, I swipe to accept, then draw the phone to my ear. "Hello."

"Hey." Uncertainty lingers in her pause. "Are you okay?"

Her question startles me because honestly, I don't deserve her concern.

"Em, I don't know how to answer that honestly."

"Then don't." I can almost see her pity tugging at the corner of her mouth. "How about I meet you at the picnic table we were at this morning, and I can take you home?"

"You…you don't have to do that," I stutter as I shuffle through the crowd towards the entrance. "I can walk into town and get a taxicab back to the house."

"What are friends for? I'll see you in five, no arguments, okay?"

My eyes prick at her kindness, and I blink back the emotion brewing in them. I feel like such a bitch for the way Rohan behaved when he answered both of their calls, but I know he's not solely to blame either. I knew about the animosity between Liam and Rohan, Beibhinn mentioned the rivalry between them during our movie night, and yet, it didn't stop me. Sure, I wasn't expecting Rohan to be such a devious bastard, but I still made the choice. He asked me if I wanted him to stop, and I said no. So, I'm as much to blame as he is, regardless.

"Okay." I nod, even though I know she can't see me. "See you then."

A FEW HOURS LATER, AFTER I WASHED MY MISTAKES FROM my skin with a steaming hot shower and a change of clothes, Beibhinn and I watched a few episodes of *The Reacher* on Amazon Prime before she insisted we go and get some ice cream.

She's yet to broach the giant hippopotamus in the room, for which I'm thankful, but as we sit across from each other at Maeve's Melt's, munching on two glassfuls of Kinder Bueno ice cream, I can feel the question brewing in her eyes before it finally tumbles past her lips. "So, Rohan King?"

My eyes close briefly as my face contorts with shame-filled regret.

Her barked laugh pulls my focus back to her and the raised brow dancing dangerously close to her hairline. "Oh, don't give me that look. I was next to my brother when Rohan answered your phone, and those moans were nothing to regret."

Planting my elbows on the table between us, I drop my face into my palms. "You heard that?" My question comes out muffled by my hands.

"Oh, yes! God, yes!" she mocks, trying her best to control the laugh dancing behind her eyes.

Pulling my hands away from my face, I swat at her, making her giggles erupt. "Stop that. I'm mortified. I can't believe he did that."

"Oh, I can." She nods, lips curled outward in a know-all pout. "Rohan King is a law unto himself. Always has been.

And when it comes to one-upping my brother, especially with tonight's fight brewing, there's no telling how far either of them will go to win."

"What do you mean by *tonight's fight*?"

"Did Liam not tell you?"

Drawing a spoon full of ice cream towards my lips, I shake my head.

She rolls her eyes, shaking her head in disbelief. "How do you expect her to survive her trials if she doesn't know a thing about it?" Her words are muttered as if she's directing the question more towards herself and not me.

"Trials?"

Beibhinn drops her spoon into her empty glass and then leans back in the booth before folding her arms across her chest. Her eyes divert upwards as though she's mentally analysing how much she can tell me. Finally, her gaze settles on mine. "Fuck it!" She leans forward, folding her body over the tabletop before lowering her voice so the other customers can't hear our discussion. "I shouldn't be telling you any of this, so if it crops up, play stupid, okay?"

I tilt my chin, acknowledging her with a nod.

"Do you remember when I told you that the Kings of Killybegs were made up of families?"

"Yeah."

"Family names don't guarantee a spot at the syndicate

table. In order to claim a rightful place, each heir has to go through a set of trials, and they begin right after the person turns eighteen. Tonight is one of Rohan and Aodhán's trials. They both turned eighteen in the past few weeks."

Lost for words, my brows narrow, listening intently to every word she spews. *What kind of culty shit is this?*

"Most of our generation has completed the trials, well, everyone who is of age, except for Rohan, Aodhán, and…" She trails off, eyes searching my face until finally, her unspoken words dawn on me.

"And me." *Is this what Fiadh meant when she said I need to learn how to become a Ryan? Was she trying to prepare me for what is to come when I turn eighteen in a few weeks' time?*

"You said tonight is one of Rohan's trials? What's that got to do with Liam?"

"Rohan and Aodhán have to fight — and beat — a syndicate member to pass this part of his initiation. That's where Liam and Donnacha come in; they've both completed their trials."

"That's…barbaric?"

"You're telling me. I was the first of our generation of girls to reach eighteen. I had to fight my mam and that woman trains the best fighters in the country. To this day, she swears she didn't go easy on me, but I know she's lying."

I sit wide-eyed, blinking back my disbelief. "Did my mam have to do all this, too?"

"Yes, and from what I heard, Éanna Ryan was a badass. She was the very first female to take the trials, and because she was the first, she had to take down a male member. Apparently, Rohan's dad got his arse handed to him that night, or so my mother told me."

Before I know it, the question that has been tumbling around my head since Beibhinn insinuated my role in all this stumbles off my tongue. "What if we don't want to initiate?"

"We don't get a choice, Saoirse. There has only been one person who refused to complete all of the trials."

It dawns on me. "My mam?"

Beibhinn nods, her eyes brimming with sadness and pity.

Is this why she ran, why she refused to never tell me about her life, why she spent years of her life running? Because of the syndicate?

"We were born into this life, Saoirse, and either you're in it or you're silenced. There's no other option."

Beibhinn looks down at the time displayed on her phone screen before she pushes from the booth and tips her chin towards the door. "We should get going. The fight will be starting soon."

Rohan

Couped at the top of the round tower, I stand with my arms folded across my chest, glaring out the small arched window cut from the centuries-old stone.

Light beams across the courtyard from the free-standing floodlights, blurring the faces of the rowdy crowd gathered below while also illuminating the walls of Kill Castle. In the centre of the old ruins, a large octagon consumes the courtyard, drawing the attention of every watchful eye. Most of the syndicate — or, as the locals know them, Kings of Killybegs — sit ringside, monitoring every jab and kick that is exchanged between the first two opponents.

Tonight is the night many of them have waited for, the night the last two male heirs fight for their place at the head table, leaving only one heir who is of age to claim their seat — Saoirse Ryan. Saoirse is a direct descendent of Caolain Ryan, the man who founded Killybegs and the empire it thrives off. It's no wonder she threatens my father with her presence because with the right knowledge, and with enough power, she could strip him of his title, and leave him with nothing but the hair on his head. Something her mother, Éanna, failed to do.

Suddenly, the locked iron gate behind me rattles before the ancient-old hinges cry out as it's pulled open. I don't turn around to see who is disturbing my quiet sanctuary, because I already know.

"What are you doing hiding up here?" My company questions as he stalks into the room with soundless footsteps.

"Hiding." I bark a laugh. "Kings don't hide, they observe. How is he doing?" I continue, keeping my eyes trained on a blurred Aodhán as he glides effortlessly around the octagon, dodging every one of Donnacha's advances. From this height vantage, the two figures dance around the canvas, ant-like, but that doesn't stop me from leaning forward, squinting my eyes for a better view.

Ignoring my question, his broad frame appears beside me, fresh as fuck in a black tailored suit, black shirt, and black Gucci shoes. The burning glow of the cigarette dangling from his lips lights up his hard features, but then my eyes meet his amber depths, the mirror image of his daughter's.

"Did you know my daughter was coming tonight?" he questions, eyes trained on the fight happening below us as he fills his lungs with nicotine.

"Saoirse's here?" As far as I was aware, nobody told her about the trials. We were all instructed to keep our mouths shut. And although our generation doesn't always agree, the syndicate vote was unanimous. Well, except for… "Beibhinn."

"Seems so. They arrived together."

"Fuck." My hands raise to my head and I bury my fingers into my hair, tugging on the longer stands.

"Don't worry. I've eyes on her. Nobody will touch her, not here."

"If my dad gets to her…" I don't finish that thought.

"Leave your dad to me. I'll handle it. Nobody will touch my daughter, Rohan. I can assure you that."

Suddenly, our conversation gets cut short by the thunderous roar of the crowd below. My eyes trail towards the octagon to see Gabriel King holding up Aodhán's arm in victory while Donnacha lies unconscious against the canvas.

"Looks like you're up, kid. Are you ready?" He leads me through the open gate and begins our descent.

Rolling my shoulders, I release the tension knotting my muscles. "Born ready."

"Don't get too cocky, Rí. Devereux is a mean fighter. That's the reason they paired you with him. He is the only one who will give you a run for your money."

"I got this." My confidence echoes down the spiralled stone staircase. "Devereux may be good with his fists, but that's not what's gonna win this fight."

"Oh." His brow hikes up. "Enlighten me?"

I tap my temple. "Being a warrior is a state of mind, boss man. Brains outsmart brawn…every fucking time." His lips quip into a slight smile, seemingly pleased with my confidence. "Besides," I continue, "the best soldier the syndicate's got didn't train Liam. He trained me." I wink, earning myself a rare smile.

"Save the flattery for whatever girl you're fucking. That shit doesn't work on me, kid."

He wouldn't be saying that if he knew who I was fucking.

STANDING IN MY CORNER, I BOUNCE ON THE BALLS OF MY feet, trying to keep myself warmed up as the late evening dew settles on my bare torso. Music pumps through the open air around us, filling the crowd's growing anticipation with something other than mindless chit-chat.

My father flanks my front, gripping my face in between his palms, black eyes focused on mine. "Whatever you do, do not fuck this up, Rohan."

It takes everything in me to not spit in his fucking face. In the months leading up to my eighteenth birthday, he's done nothing to prepare me for any of the trials I'm due to face. But now, after Donnacha — his little pet project — lost the last round to Aodhán, he suddenly gives a shit.

Nah, there is only one reason. Daddy King is in the ring with me, and it's because all eyes are on me, and his surname is at stake. Fuck that, I *will* win this fight, but it won't be for Daddy Dearest's approval.

"Cause that's what I do, right? I fuck everything up." I raise a smarmy brow, egging him on.

His nostrils flare as he bites down, clenching his teeth. "Don't test me, boy."

My mouth curls to the side as my eyes narrow, a look I know he despises. He shakes his head, levelling me with one last look before exiting the ring. Finally, Luke Brady, Aodhán's dad, steps into the centre of the octagon. The music fades and then he raises his microphone to his lips. "Killybegs, are you ready?"

The crowd wails out a deafening cheer, and then Luke proceeds. "Almost twenty years ago, Oliver Devereux won his first trial when he defeated his opponent, Gabriel King. It was a legendary battle. One most of us here will remember for eternity. And now, almost two decades later, their sons repeat history, only this time, can the youngest Devereux hold his undefeated title or will Rí beag (*little king*) reign supreme." He pauses for effect before deepening his baritone into an echoed gravel. "It's the fight you've all been waiting for. DEVEREUX VERSUS KING!"

The floodlights dip as the opening intro of "Only One King" by Tommee Profitt and Jung Youth bleeds through the speakers. Liam and I walk forward, meeting in the centre of the octagon. Forearms stretched out, we raise our wrapped knuckles before tapping them together.

My eyes drift to the left, seeking *her* out. I scan the crowd until finally, my gaze settles on Saoirse Ryan. Hand clenched into a fist, she holds it over her mouth, biting into her knuckles. Her shoulders sink forward, barely holding her up. She's nervous, but for who? Finally, her eyes greet mine, and time stills.

How is it I can hear her heart pound in my head? Why can I feel her fear crawling under my skin? My lungs tighten, but it has nothing to do with the fight. It's her. Dominance courses through me, a need so fucking strong it rattles my bones. Before I walked into this octagon, I knew I couldn't lose. But now, with her wide amber orbs scanning my every move, I have a lot more to prove.

Forcing myself to look away, I bring my attention back

to Liam. His grey eyes flick between Saoirse and me. Rage flushes his skin as molten red anger trails up his neck and pinches his cheeks. Good, our brief phone call earlier had the effect I was hoping for, and you can bet your fucking granny I'll be using it to my advantage.

Poor little Liam always shows his hand too soon.

Finally, Luke shouts, "Fight!" and then everything else fades from view. I'm here to do one thing. Win!

EIGHT ROUNDS HAVE PASSED BY IN A BLUR OF PAIN, AND I won't lie, my legs are minutes away from buckling beneath me, my rib cage is on fucking fire, and I can barely see through the stream of blood that's dripping onto my lash line from the deep slit Liam busted into my eyebrow.

Icy rain falls from the sky, pleating my sweat glistened skin and burning through my aching muscles, but I hold myself strong, unwilling to break, and determined to win, no matter what the fucking cost. Liam lunges forward, jabbing his fist towards my ribcage. I sidestep, drawing my elbow up before launching it into his nose. His head whips to the left, blood spraying from his nostrils. He looks as rough as I feel, shoulders sagging as he drags his exhausted body around the canvas.

Swiping my forehead with my forearm, I wipe away the trail of blood trickling down my face. "Come on, big man." I taunt, egging Liam on as much as I can, hoping his reaction will grant me the one shot I need to end this, once and for all.

I stay on my toes, relying on my speed and agility. "Is that all you've got?"

"Go to hell," he spits, his blood blending into his saliva and spraying across the octagon floor.

"I've already been, and she tastes delicious." I bait before spearing forward and landing an uppercut to his stomach. "Tell me, D," I prompt as he catches his breath, "did you get to slide your cock between her pouty lips? How about her tight cunt?" I shake my arms out as I bounce on the balls of my feet.

Bent over with his hands on his knees, the slight narrowing of Liam's eyes signals his next move, and then, as predicted, he bounds forward with a gritted, "Fuck you!"

I dodge right, reserving my energy for my final blow. Suddenly, Liam comes at me again, this time swinging with his left, connecting it to my right cheek. My neck cranks with the force of the impact, and all the blood inside my body rushes to my ears. *Fuck me, that stung.*

Dazed for a moment, I shake it off before sliding my tongue along my bottom lip. The taste of copper assaults my senses, but I don't let it slow me down. My victory is within my grasp. I can feel it in the energy surrounding me. *Patience, Rohan. Watch for your opportunity.*

"Do you know how it feels to have her clenching down on your dick while your name falls from her lips?" My eyes dart towards the crowd, pointing at Saoirse with a tip of my chin. "Because I do. And it was fucking ecstasy."

Finally, he breaks, charging at me without thinking it through. Blinded by his rage, he misreads my stance and veers left, leaving his jaw vulnerable. My fist connects, and the sound of bone crunching bone silences the crowd. Liam's eyes roll back and his legs give out as he sways off his feet before greeting the floor.

"Light's out, motherfucker."

As Luke bounds into the cage, I drop to my knees, allowing my exhaustion to take over.

"Winner by K.O, ROHAN KING!"

Saoirse

MY STOMACH PITS INTO TIGHT COILS AS MY PULSE thunders. Acid bubbles in my gut, whirling beneath my chest as I watch the medic shine a small torch into Liam's eyes. He sits forward and wraps his hands around his shins, nodding once at the doctor.

Then finally, he swigs a gulp of water from a bottle the medic hands him and rinses his mouth before spitting the contents onto the floor. His back expands with each breath he draws, settling the unease gripping my stomach.

He's okay, I reassure myself. *He's okay.*

What feels like the first time since Liam collapsed on the canvas, I steal a breath and then divert my gaze to the other opponent.

Rohan sits in the centre of the ring, his body perched on his shins. His wrapped hands cover his face, showcasing the blood-stained once-white cotton. Mesmerised by the rawness eluding from him, I count the rise and fall of his shoulders as they accentuate his deep, laboured breaths.

I follow his hands with my eyes as he drags them over his forehead and buries his fingertip into the long, soaked strands of his fringe before pushing them off his face. His shoulders drop when he cranks his head and tilts his face to the night sky.

Rainfall dances from the blackened clouds above, puncturing the air and dampening his sweat and blood covered skin. Yet, he seems unfazed by the ice-cold droplets, and instead, bathes in them.

The light from the large floodlights reflects the beads of water clinging to his exposed torso, making him appear unnatural, like an actor in the latest action feature.

He's dangerously intoxicating, and I hate how my body reacts to him. No matter how hard I try, I can't seem to fight the invisible thread that ties us together. Whenever Rohan is in my presence, he becomes a thief, stealing every ounce of my attention, whether or not I want him to.

Blood flows from his busted brow like a narrow river's steam, trailing over the high contours of his cheekbones until, finally, it pools in the commissure of his open mouth.

My breath traps in my throat when the tip of his tongue peeks out, capturing the small pool with one careless swipe.

I know it shouldn't, but for some unbeknownst reason, that one slight movement fills my core with a pulsation only he could reach.

My attraction may seem crazy, but the danger — the deceit, the desire, all of it — is alluring. But isn't that how angels fall? The devil was the most strikingly beautiful man. A temptation we should never indulge in, a sin we must not commit. But even so, the stories say he was once God's favourite creation. Rohan King is my very own devil, a beautiful enigma wrapped in thunderclouds and coated in the most tempting of sins. Am I strong enough to defy the pull he has on me, or will he drag me under until I burn in his flames?

When his captivating eyes flick towards me, stealing the breath in my lungs, I get my answer. Rohan King will be the death of me.

AFTER WE LEFT THE KILL CASTLE GROUNDS, BEIBHINN drove us back to the gate lodge before she disappeared to her in-house library with a book tucked underneath her arm. Apparently, Liam got a gym, and she got a room with wall-to-wall smut books. Her words, not mine.

Anyway, she said she needed to clear her head after the fight. Not that I blame her because I'm still reeling from the sadist brutality of it all.

For almost an hour, I pace the floors, waiting for Liam to return. I haven't spoken to him since this morning, before that embarrassing phone call with Rohan, and as much as I'd love to avoid the topic of my sexual exploitations, I feel he needs some sort of explanation.

Finally, a little after ten, the front door clicks open and he hauls himself inside, his right arm clutching his left side, holding his rib cage.

Flicking the tv off, I place the remote control on the table and lift myself from the chair before walking towards him with hesitant footsteps.

"Here." I gesture to his gym bag. "Let me help you with that."

His eyes narrow, darkening when they settle on my face. A harsh gasp rushes past my lips when my eyes land on his battered appearance. There is an enormous bruise forming along his jawline, not to mention the deep cut sliced into his bottom lip. There's congealed dried blood beneath his nose and his left eye appears non-existent behind the swelling of his eyelid.

"I don't need your help," he grits through his teeth. I

know he's mad at me, and he has every right to be, but he's clearly in pain.

"Just piss off, Saoirse. I'm not in the fucking mood for your fake sincerity. If you wanna play nurse, I'm sure your dickhead of a fuckboy would be happy to have you." His words sting more than I'm willing to admit. Then he pushes past me and drags himself up the stairs, grunting with each step. My eyes stay trained on him, and when he sways halfway to the top, clutching the banister for support, I rush up the few steps and stand behind him. He may not want my help, but he's getting it.

Placing my palm in the dip of his back, I stop him from rocking back.

"I said I was fucking fine."

I ignore him, sticking to him like a shadow. Finally, once I successfully get him up the stairs, I trail him to his bedroom door and open it for him. He wordlessly brushes past me for a second time, dropping his gym bag right inside the door before he strides across the bedroom towards the en suite.

Flicking on the light, he kicks the door open and hauls himself inside, leaving the door open. I take it as an invitation and follow behind him. Finally, I come to a stop in the doorway and lean my shoulder against the jamb. My eyes track his every movement as he lowers himself to the cabinet beneath the sink and pulls out a first-aid kit. His left hand is still clutching his rib cage, so using his right, he flips the clasp holding the green plastic med-kit open before pulling out a bottle of antiseptic and some cotton balls.

Feeling helpless, I push from the doorway and close the distance between us. I grab the bottle from his grip and level his unamused look with one of my own. "I know you're mad at me, but that doesn't mean you don't need my help."

His nostrils flare as he huffs out a defeated breath. Once again, I ignore his stubbornness, and twist the cap off the Dettol bottle and dampen a few of the cotton balls with antiseptic. The distinct scent of antiseptic floods my nose, reminding me of freshly laid tarmacadam on a newly surfaced road.

Finally, I close the toilet seat and then gesture for him to sit. As he lowers himself onto the lid, he grunts, his eyes closing with the pain. "Motherfucker."

Once he's settled in, I place my fingertips beneath his chin and tilt his head, giving me a better angle. Suddenly, his eyes fly open, landing on mine. Behind his stormy grey depths, hurt and pain swirl, stealing the air from my lungs. I feel like a colossal bitch for everything that happened today, and now, after the fight, I realise, deep down, Rohan only used me as a pawn in his game against Liam. I feel stupid for letting it happen, but the hurt written all over Liam's face makes my careless inhibitions even more regrettable.

With a fake smile, I push through the guilt swarming through my core and raise the cotton ball to his lip. A hiss escapes him as I gently press down on the open wound, but he never takes his eyes off me. The weight of our unspoken words feels like a boulder on my shoulder, but I don't think now is the time to broach what happened with Rohan, so I remain silent, working quietly to clean up the traces of blood and clean any open cuts so they don't get infected.

Finally, once I've applied a generous amount of Savlon cream to any open wounds, I drop the supplies onto the bathroom countertop and then turn back to face him. A fire blazes in his eyes, then suddenly, he reaches out, gripping my hip before tugging me forward. My heart hitches as I halt between his legs, peering at him through my lashes. Even seated, his face is level with mine, his eyes searing through me, making a blush tinge my heated cheeks.

A sexy smirk widens across his face as his hands roam downwards, over the material of my sleep shorts, until they burn against the exposed skin of my thigh. My core clenches, overcome by the darkened lust swirling in his eyes.

He leans in, and just as I think he's going to claim me

with a kiss, he stops, leaving just a breath between us. Our gazes lock once more, as he utters his next words against my lips. "I really want to fuck you, free bird. But not while his cum is still dripping from your pussy."

His words slice through my chest with the sharpness of a thousand tiny razor blades, forcing me to step back. Trying my best to ignore the ache, I focus on helping him clean his wounds.

"Do you need me to check your ribs?" My words are barely audible with the dryness coating my throat. So I dampen the roof of my mouth with my tongue, then swallow the giant ball of regret lodged there.

With a nod of his head, he pushes off the toilet seat and slowly stands to his feet, tugging the bottom of his t-shirt but doesn't get very far. Deciding he needs my help more than I need his approval, I reach for the hem of his shirt. His eyes latch on to mine once more, peering into my soul as I raise his shirt up, only stopping when he yelps. "Fucking hell."

It's then I realise his left shoulder has locked up, suspended mid-point, and he's unable to raise it any further. It takes a little manoeuvring, but finally, I get his shirt off and assess his bruised ribs. "Should I wrap them?" I ask, unsure of what the protocol for bruised, and possibly broken ribs are.

"No. You shouldn't wrap broken ribs because they can

keep you from breathing deeply, which can increase the risk of pneumonia."

"Um, okay." I don't ask how he knows that, but judging from what I saw tonight, I doubt this is Liam's first rodeo.

"You can leave now." He motions to the doorway with the tip of his chin. "I can manage the rest."

"Are you sure?" I prompt, peering around the bathroom, looking for anything he may need help with.

"I said I was fine, didn't I?" His tone is aggressive, but I try my best to not judge. Even though we never discussed what the kiss we shared meant, I knew he had issues with Rohan, and seeing them fight like that tonight only opened my eyes further. Nobody could deny the hate between them; it was glaringly obvious with every strike. So, giving Liam what he needs, I turn on my heel and walk out of the bathroom. Maybe someday, we can talk about what this means for us and our friendship.

I'm two steps from leaving his room when he calls my name.

I spin around, and my eyes glide over him as he leans against the open bathroom doorway. "Yeah."

"I've one question, but you have to promise me you'll tell me the truth."

My eyes close briefly, but then I peer back at him over my lashes. "Okay."

"If you could start the day over, would you still let him fuck you?"

My throat closes, hesitating my response. It's then my conscience sweeps in, hitting me with a reality I don't want to face. Do I regret what I did with Rohan? I regret the hurt our actions caused. I regret his motive behind it. But if I was in that closet again, would I stop him? Deep down, I know the answer is no.

"Come on, Saoirse. It's a yes or no question. Would you still let him fuck you?"

Swallowing the lump encased in my throat, I ask, "The truth?"

Liam nods, his tongue lapping at the deep cut on his lip. "I need to hear it, please."

"Yes. I would." It's only a few words, but his face crumbles with the force of them, chipping off a piece of my heart.

"Close the door on your way out."

I nod, unable to ease the ache I caused us both. "Goodnight, Liam."

Saoirse

As I walk away from Liam's room, my body feels laden, worn down by the hate that flickered in his eyes. When he asked me that question, the last thing I wanted to do was lie to him. Not when I'm consumed by a lifetime's worth of those already.

He deserved my truth, no matter how detrimental that truth may be.

My temple tightens as the heaviness of the day settles behind my eyes. Rubbing my closed eyelids with my fingertips, I can feel the first signs of a migraine brewing. Bypassing my bedroom, I take a quick trip down to the kitchen for a glass of water and some migraine relief. I pop two pills onto my tongue before washing them down, then drag myself to my room, more than ready to sleep off this shit show.

Finally, exhausted from my rollercoaster of a day, I push through my bedroom door, but halt mid-step when I notice the stretched-out figure fast asleep in the middle of my bed. Once I'm in the room, I peer out into the hallway to see if anyone is watching. My eyes dart left and right, then I shut my door gently and twist the lock, making sure neither Liam nor Beibhinn barge in to find a half-naked, passed out Rohan in my bed.

Shit! What the actual fuck? How did he even get in here?

My feet carry me towards him, but the closer I get to the bed, the more prominent the distinct stench of alcohol becomes, so fucking potent it floods my nose until I can almost taste it on my tongue. A wrinkle appears above my nose as my stomach churns.

Fucking hell, Rohan, how much did you drink?

Lying flat on his stomach with his forearm tucked beneath his head, his neck cranes to the side as the moonlight shimmers through the window, highlighting his face. My hand reaches out to shake him awake, but just before I reach him, I stop in my tracks, noting the half-smile gracing his sleeping face. He looks so different from the usual cocksure arsehole I'm used to. Gone are the sarcastic taunts and the dark cloud that seems to hang over his head. In his sleep, he looks…almost peaceful. As though all his worries, responsibilities, and whatever haunts his soul doesn't reach him in his dreams. He looks young and vulnerable — a complete contrast to the walking devil with the sinful smile.

Somehow, that thought brings a smile to my lips. Finally, I reach forward, brushing the hair off his face.

A gasp escapes me when I see he hasn't bothered to wash the blood off his face or tend to any of his wounds. Appears he numbed whatever pain he was feeling at the bottom of a bottle instead. My fingers twitch, needing to erase the blood-stained evidence from his face. Instead, I kneel on the floor, resting my head on the mattress next to his head, and like some crazy creeper, I watch as his lashes flicker while he dreams. Inaudible murmurs vibrate against his lopsided grin, and for a brief second, I wonder who he is talking to, and is it them who has him smiling like a little boy who just met the real-life Batman.

Finally, I give in to the urge to touch him again and allow my fingertips to brush over his bruised cheek. "Who is the man behind the monster, Rohan?" It's a breathless question, barely a whisper in the breeze, but he stills. His chest goes rigid, with no evidence of his exhale, almost as though he heard every syllable. Suddenly, he shifts, rolling over on his back, and giving me a full view of his tattooed torso. This is the first time I've seen his naked chest up this close, and fucking hell, he belongs on one of those thirst-trap TikTok videos. You know, the ones with the *'This is a Work of Art'* sound.

My greedy eyes drink up the patchwork designs dotting his torso, mismatched pieces of art that all make up the man lying before me. Everything from skulls, roses, knives, and even a small grave with the words *'I Blame Society'* engraved on the headstone. Finally, my eyes land on the largest piece that covers most of his left side — three swords overlap in the shape of a six-pointed star and surrounding the blades, right where the three swords cross, is a crown. Upon closer inspection, I see the initials etched onto the sword's handles. B, K, and D. Then, right in the centre of the crown, is the letter R surrounded by jewels. The original Kings of Killybegs — Brady, King, Devereux, and finally, Ryan.

It's a beautiful piece, and it looks far fresher than the rest of the work. The ink is darker and more vivid. Finally, my gaze falls south, tracing the sharp edges of his hip bones down to the delicious V that disappears into his sweatpants. My mouth waters at the small scattering of black hair beneath his belly button, a landing strip that leads to his dick.

Jesus, what is it about this guy that stuns me stupid?

I draw my wandering eyes back towards his face and nearly swallow my tongue when I find his sleepy eyes glaring at me with amusement. "Well, hello, love." A wide smile steals the bottom half of his face, showcasing his perfectly white teeth. "I fell asleep." His tone is strange, lilted with humour and playfulness. "Come here. I need a snuggle." He barks out a laugh, and his chest rises as he chuckles. "Snuggle," he repeats. "What a funny word!"

My cheeks heat, and I'm sure if I were to look, they would be an obnoxious shade of pink. "Rohan, how much did you drink?"

He lifts his hand off the mattress, suspending it in the air. He holds his pointer finger above his thumb, leaving a tiny space. "Just a little, ma'am. I swear."

He's clearly wasted. "What are you doing here?" I prompt. "And how did you get in?"

Pushing up on his elbows, he lifts his head from the pillow and sways forward. I grip his biceps, holding him steady while he kicks his feet over the edge of the bed. Once I feel like he's stable enough to hold himself up, I release him.

"Window."

Peering over my shoulder, I notice the window pushed out further than normal. "You climbed up here drunk? Jesus, Rohan, you could have hurt yourself."

"I'm already hurting, mo bhanríon. Come, kiss my boo-boos better."

Rolling my eyes, I ignore his drunken advances. "Stay here. Do not move." He flops back, his head bouncing off the mattress as I head for the bathroom attached to my room.

Lowering myself to my hunkers, I root through the cabinet beneath the sink until I find a small packet of make-up remover pads. I stand, then run them beneath the hot water faucet, dampening them. It's not the best-case scenario, but at least I can remove the dried blood from his brow and cheeks.

When I inch back into the room, Rohan is lying horizontally across the bed. His arms criss-crossed over his face. "Love?" he questions.

"Rohan. How many times have I told you? Stop calling me that!"

He raises his arms higher, dropping them above his head before twisting his neck so his eyes are on me. "Never. You are love. I am hate. But who will win these wicked games we play? Oh, that rhymes. Ha!"

I shake my head, amused by this version of Rohan. He's almost…cute. Finally, when I make it back to the bed, I sit beside him and usher him to sit up so I can clean his face. "Up you get."

"Oh, I may be as pissed as an ole boot but have no fear, mo bhanríon. For you, I'll always get it up."

"Shut up, you eejit. I meant for you to sit up so I can clean your wound. You don't want to get an infection, especially so close to your eye."

"Why do you have to ruin my fun, love?"

Doing as I ask, he pulls himself up with a grunt. "It's only a cut, Saoirse. Trust me, I've had far worse."

The sadness in his eyes halts my breath, but now is not the time to dive into the meaning behind them. "Just sit still and let me clean it, please."

"If you insist." He sways forward, bringing his face closer to mine, leaving only mere inches between our lips. Suddenly, a thought strikes me out of nowhere.

My God, this man has had me in many vulnerable positions, and we've never even kissed. My eyes flick towards his mouth, and I wonder what it would be like to be consumed by his mouth. No! *Stop, no! We are not going there.*

Dragging my gaze back up, our eyes connect, but I fight past the pitter-patter of my heart and do what I set out to do. I raise my hand and slowly press the cotton pad against the congealed blood that has dried into his brow, taking extra care so I don't hurt him.

With his eyes burning into the side of my face, and the heat of his warm breaths brushing against my skin, I find it extremely hard to concentrate, but finally, I finish, and then pull back, needing to add some space between us.

"There, all done."

His gaze lingers for a beat, and then he shoots me a wink before he flops back again, nestling against my pillow. "You smell good too, you know. Like lavender and pomegranates."

"You're not sleeping here," I announce as he pulls the duvet over his body, ignoring me.

"I think I am, love. Now, be a doll and flick off that lamp. It's blinding my eyes."

"Rohan," I warn. *Nothing.* "Rohan!" I call again, this time shoving his shoulder. But again, nothing. Suddenly, his breathing thickens, and I know I'm fighting a losing battle.

"This is a bad idea," I announce to nobody in particular.

"Come to bed, love. Drunk Rohan loves snuggles."

"GO TO SLEEP OR GET OUT!" I whisper-shout as I begin making myself up a bed on the small reading nook beneath the window. There isn't a chance in hell I'm getting into that bed next to him.

"Fine, be a party pooper," he utters before bringing my duvet beneath his chin and snuggling in. Once I think he's finally dozed off, I pull the throw cover off the end of the bed, but right as I'm about to settle onto my makeshift one, he mutters my name, halting me on my feet. "Saoirse?"

"Yes, Rí?"

"Did you clean Liam's wounds too?"

The question comes out of left field, and my reply

lodges in my throat. What is it about these two? "Erm, I don't think you have the right to ask me that?"

He bolts up, knocking the blankets off him. "I don't share my toys, love."

His possessiveness irks me, and in the next breath, I do what I should have done as soon as I found him here.

"I'd like you to leave. Now!"

Rohan

THERE ARE SEVERAL REASONS WHY I CHOOSE NOT TO DRINK on the regular — the lack of control, the inability to survey my surroundings and keep my guard up, and finally because *apparently,* I turn into an incoherent mess who needs to be held.

Trust me, nobody wants to see that, least of all me.

Last night only solidified my feelings on the matter, because, in true Rohan fashion, I got shitfaced after the fight, mainly because of my cunt of a father and his constant dissatisfaction with everything I do. And then, to make matters worse, the little boy trapped inside me came out to play, seeking any form of fucking affection he could get. Which is possibly the worst thing a guy like me could do. Vulnerability is not in my vocabulary. A king never shows weakness, ever. Hence my swift fucking departure from Saoirse's room in the early hours of this morning.

I did not mean for her to see that side of me, ever. Unfortunately, I remember every word I uttered to her, and now I can't erase the pathetic visual from my mind.

Regretting last night's decisions, I tip my head back and balance it on the back of my couch. "Fuck me, I asked her to snuggle me," I mutter, my thoughts falling from my lips as I close my eyes.

"You did what?" Perched on the seat across from me, Aodhàn's ears perk up, his attention now pulled from whatever Netflix shit he's watching. "Fucking hell, that's gold. Liam must have gotten a few hard hits at that thick skull of yours, huh?" He howls with laughter.

Scrubbing my face with my palm, I try to erase the image of my body curled around Saoirse's tiny frame from my mind. "She's a quick fuck and a means to an end, nothing more." *A fact that I wish were true, but it's not.*

Across the living room, Aodhan wraps his arms around his waist, running his hands over his back like he's kissing someone. "Oh, Saoirse. Your snuggles are magic. They give my tiny penis life."

Plucking up a cushion from next to me, I chuck it at him. "Can you please shut the fuck up?"

My eyes squint tighter as I massage my temples with the pads of my fingers. "Monkeys are already banging cymbals in my head. I don't need you adding to it with your ridiculous hyena laugh and ridiculous kissing noises."

"I can't help it. You've painted this picture in my head, and fuck me, it's hilarious."

Lifting my head slightly, I level him with a murderous glare. "Final warning, A."

He side-eyes me, raising a brow before bringing his joint back to his lips and taking a drag. Behind a poof of white smoke, he pokes me once more. "I'm shaking in my boots. Big bad Rohan is angry and he might snuggle me to death." Another round of laughter barrels past his lips and he throws his head back as he clutches his rib cage. "I have to know — Were you the big spoon or the little spoon?"

In one swift motion, I reach forward and tear open the drawer beneath my coffee table, and then pull out my Agency Arms Urban Combat G19. After reloading the chamber, I straighten my arm and aim slightly above his head before pulling the trigger.

He ducks, covering his face as his arms cups his head, and the bullet smashes through the wall behind him.

His eyes widen as he ticks his neck back and forth between me and the fresh hole I put in the plaster. "What the fuck? Did you just try to shoot me? That was low, man, even for you."

"Don't be ridiculous. If I wanted to shoot you, I wouldn't have missed."

He nods, knowing full well I am right. Most of the King's kids have been shooting a gun since they were fourteen years old. Being a part of the syndicate brings its own set of troubles, ones we need to be prepared for at all times. Money, drugs, power, and guns, they're all part of this lifestyle. Besides, it's not the first time I've aimed my gun at him, and honestly, it probably won't be the last either. After all, Aodhán has a tendency to get on my nerves.

Finally, I push myself from my chair, grunting as every aching bone screams at me to sit the fuck back down. "I'm heading to bed for a few hours before tonight's meeting."

Walking past him, I clip him in the back of the head. "Feel free to make yourself at home, arsehole."

He throws his middle finger up in salute, before facing back towards the tv. "Always do, snuggle bunny. I always do."

THIS IS EXCRUCIATING.

Not only would I kill to be anywhere but sitting at this ridiculously long, pretentious, old mahogany table, but I'd also rather gouge my own eyeballs out with a rusty fork than have to spend the next hour perched across from my cunt of a sperm donor and his holier-than-thou attitude. My head is still pounding from last night's miserable attempt to dull the demons in my head. Not to mention the slight embarrassment lingering from my night at Saoirse's house, drunk off my fucking arse.

But rules are rules, and we must obey them. So here I am, fulfilling Daddy's request. Horse shite!

Everybody here knows the older generation loves a good power play, especially when it involves their heirs. Delegating us to the 'kiddie side' of the table while they sit high and mighty on their thrones is a prime example of that. Who are we to think we deserve a seat next to them? We've yet to prove our strength, our loyalty, and our devotion — all three trials we must complete before earning our title as one of them. I'm not a fan of some of the old traditions, but with my father running this sinking ship, I need to comply. For now, at least.

"Let's get down to business," My father looks back and forth at the line of men and women sitting to his right and left. "How are the operations going? We will start with the Bishops, Kevin, and Lorcan," he prods, peering at the two men sitting to his left.

"All the hospitality businesses are doing well. Bars, restaurants, and clubs are all back in business. We've secured the liquor company, too. Which will be a great way to clean the cash we get from the shipments." Kevin shifts in his seat, buckling beneath the weight of my father's stare. Honestly, I don't understand how he made it this far. Not only is he a ball-less bastard, but he's also about as useful as a chocolate teapot. Fucker can't stand the heat.

"And what about you?" He tips his chin at Lorcan. "Everything okay on your end?"

"Yeah, all good. We had some minor issues with the shipping company a few weeks back. There was some product missing. But I dealt with the issue personally, and he won't be a problem in the future."

My shoulders shuffle at Lorcan's unfazed response, earning me a beady look from my father. "What?" I poke the bear. "We all know that problem is now decomposing at the bottom of a septic tank, most likely in a few pieces."

"Rohan."

"What? Come on, Daddy. We know what goes on here. No point calling a spade a shovel, when it is, in fact, a spade."

The rest of the meeting goes much the same with my father working his way along the line of the wealthy business associates who pose as a front for the biggest crime organisation on the Isle, while I jab at him with sarcastic remarks and a blunt attitude.

Welcome to the Killybegs syndicate, where we build hopes and dreams at the price of your integrity.

Finally, once he's covered all the shady shit, my father congratulates Aodhán and me for completing our first trial. "Celebrations will begin this Saturday at Kill Castle at 8 PM sharp. As usual, it is a black-tie event, so please, leave those rags" — he points towards me and my current attire — "at home."

Rolling my eyes, I ignore his underhanded insult — only my father would think my short-sleeved, black Gucci button shirt, and my favourite black ripped AIRMI jeans are rags, even though my attire, as he so eloquently phrased it, cost more than most people's monthly mortgage payment — and rise to leave.

"Wait." He holds up his hand, stopping me mid-suspension. "We're not done here. We still have to address what we are doing about Ms Ryan's arrival."

My teeth clench at the mention of Saoirse's name, but I slowly ease myself back into the chair, curiosity taking over my limbs. Honestly, I knew he'd bring her up sooner rather than later, but I thought he'd wait a while so he could give himself enough time to suss her out first.

Gabriel King doesn't make rash decisions; he's a *sit it out and then pounce when the time is right* kind of guy. The fact he is so hellbent on removing Saoirse from the equation doesn't sit well with me. I'm missing something here, but what?

My eyes skirt across the table, scanning from end to end until finally, my eyes connect with Saoirse's father. To anyone else at the table, he seems unfazed by my father's words, but I can tell by the tight set of his shoulders and the slight crinkle surrounding his eyes that's not the case. Nobody knows about his secret daughter, except for yours truly, and it will stay that way for as long as possible. He's Killybegs' very own trojan horse. The only difference is he's been hiding his vendetta behind the castle walls a lot longer than I have, for over eighteen years, in fact.

"Do we know how much she knows?" Lorcan asks, the tip of his tongue probing the corner of his mouth.

"Not very much," Liam chimes in before Beibhinn adds, "Only what we've told her. She knows she's part of Killybegs' heritage, but I don't think she understands what that means, not fully."

"Has she mentioned her mother?" Darren, a syndicate knight, chimes in, cranking his neck as he peers down the length of the table towards Oliver Devereux.

Oliver slips his hand over his hair. "No. As far as I can tell, she doesn't know where Éanna is. Last time she saw her was when Lorcan and Rohan arrived at the house. She thinks they took her or killed her."

"So, Éanna hasn't reached out to her?" Lorcan sits

forward, resting his elbow on the table while cupping his hand over his mouth.

"I don't think so," Beibhinn offers. "She hasn't mentioned her mam much."

"Are our guys still looking?" My dad twists in his chair and directs his gaze towards Lorcan.

"They are. But she hasn't shown up anywhere yet. No activity on her bank cards, and her phone is off."

"Okay, keep looking and inform me if she reappears. She will not leave Saoirse here for long. It's not her style. She's planning something, I can guarantee you that."

Kevin nods in agreement. "This is why we need to get Saoirse initiated ASAP."

"Thanks to Beibhinn, she knows about the trials. But, is she aware she has to take them?" Oliver questions his daughter with a stern, clipped tone.

"No." Beibhinn's eyes briefly flick to the floor and back. She's lying, but why? "She's not ready. She's barely been here a week. Liam has only begun training her."

Liam nods his head in agreement. "She needs a few sessions, at the least. Otherwise, she'll fail the trial."

I clench my fists beneath the table. If she fails the trial, they'll kill her. But maybe that's what my father wants. Get her out of his hair once and for all. I hate that Liam had his hands all over her, but I also know she needs all the help she can get. She's out of her fucking depth. I look towards Aodhán and send him a silent plea to say something. Thankfully, he picks up on it. "Maybe we should wait a while, let her settle in before throwing her off the deep end without a life jacket."

My father contemplates it for a second, then asks, "When does she turn eighteen?"

"May 5th." Shit! The date flies from my lips without thinking, earning me more than a few curious glances from everyone at the table, including a pissed off Hannah. Fuck her. The only reason I showed her any interest yesterday was because of the gorgeous brunette with the sultry smile.

Doing my best to flog that thought from my head, I lean back in my seat and place my hands at the back of my head. "Why so surprised? You asked me to monitor the girl, and I did my homework."

My father's brow narrows as he scans my body language for the lie I am telling, but I remain stoic, except for the side smile curled on my smug lips. *Fuck you, you hairy bollox. You're getting nothing from me.*

Displeased, he releases an explosive sigh. "Three weeks is all I'll allow. After she turns eighteen, she initiates. We won't bend the rules for her. If she's not ready by then, tough shit." My teeth sink into the soft flesh at the side of my mouth, biting down at his dismissal. "For now, make sure she is at the party. Who better to introduce her to her life than the king himself?"

His eyes roam in Donnacha's direction as a sly smile lights his eyes. An eerie feeling courses through my veins as they exchange a silent conversation. They're up to something, and if I had to take a stab at it, I'd guess it involves getting Saoirse to the party, but why?

AFTER LEAVING THE MEETING, I FIND MYSELF PULLED UP outside the gates of Devereux manor, staring up at Saoirse's open window. Reaching over to my glove compartment, I flick the latch open and pull out the Celtic Knot USB I stole from her that night. Her mam asked me to keep it from her until she was ready, but we are running out of time. Twisting it around with my fingers, I contemplate my next move. Suddenly, my phone chimes with an incoming text.

TEXT MESSAGE: É

É: *Use that charm of yours to convince my daughter to be your date on Saturday. You need to keep her close, Rohan. The vultures are circling.*

Me: *What makes you think your daughter would go anywhere with me?*

É: *Because she's more like me than she realises, Rohan. Your danger excites her. You know that, and her father saw it the night of the fight.*

Me: *I'll see what I can do.*

É: *Ask her, Rohan. Her answer might surprise you.*

Throwing my phone onto the passenger side, my head flops back against the driver's seat. Still spinning the Celtic knot through my fingers, I think of ways to get Saoirse to agree to come as my date, but come up empty. I'm not the roses and chocolate kind of guy. And I'm pretty sure showing up with her over my shoulder kicking and screaming is not an option either. I need a plan, and I sure as shit won't find one sitting here stalking her from my car window.

Stuffing the USB back in the glove compartment, I then press down on the accelerator and take off towards my house.

I may not know much about wooing a woman, but I know who does, and more than likely, he's camped out on my couch, as always.

Saoirse

Art and Design class has always been my favourite elective. Not only am I fascinated by the historical aspect, the styles gracing each period or how each artist has a signature stamp, but I also love the practical side and the escape it gives.

Today, we're focusing on perception and viewpoint in life drawing, which is twenty-five per cent of our final exam. Usually, I'd be excited to dive right in, losing myself in the strokes of my pencil. But I can't focus on anything but the blank stare of our class's model as he tries to avoid eye contact by keeping his eyes trained on the wall behind me.

It's been four days since Liam kicked me from his bathroom, and he's barely uttered a word to me since. Not that I blame him, but living in close quarters and sharing most of my classes with him is hard, especially when he won't acknowledge my existence.

"He's still pissed at you, huh?" Beibhinn mutters from the seat next to me as my pencil glides across the page, my gaze darting between Liam and the coarse A3 sketch pad.

"Yeah. But, honestly, I deserve it."

Without lifting her pencil, she peeks at me from the corner of her eye. "Do you, though? It's not like you guys were dating. Sure, you two have a past, but that doesn't mean he can swoop back in and pick up where you left off. You were kids back then. He's changed, as I'm sure you have."

I glance her way with a sad smile tugging at my lips. "You're right, but so is Liam. He asked me to stay away from Rohan, and I did the opposite. If I were in his shoes, I'd hate me, too."

She huffs a humourous breath. "I know my twin, Saoirse. And I assure you he does not hate you as much as he'd like to." I follow her gaze until it lands on Liam, and my lungs freeze when I find his eyes focused on me. Lost in his appraisal, I'm captivated by the sorrow clouding his storm-grey eyes. The depth of his gaze burns through me as the quip of his lip pulls into a sad smile.

Foolishly, I can't look away.

I want to tell him I'm sorry for creating this tension between us, but I can't, not without denying the pull I feel towards Rohan. Stupid as it may seem, both of them make me feel something in totally different ways.

Liam is broad and bulked with muscles, his body a decorated canvas of art and piercings. Then there's Rohan, tall, toned, and dangerously dishevelled, a chaotic masterpiece from head to toe.

It's hard to compare them. When I'm with Liam, I feel protected, as though nothing in the world could hurt me. With Rohan, nothing is safe. He's a skydive, utterly reckless, but the fall is exhilarating.

Calm or chaos. It should be simple, right? Needing the mental space to gather my thoughts, I pull my eyes away. At some point, Liam and I need to clear a few things up, but right now, I don't see how it's possible.

Not when I refuse to lie.

Keeping my head down for the rest of the class, I draw him from my memory, only peeking up when I need to see how the light contours the sharp edges of his features. Finally, when the bell rings, I pack up my stuff before telling Beibhinn I'll meet her at the cafeteria for lunch. Then, slinging my backpack over my shoulder, I keep my head down, avoiding the grey eyes following me out the door.

As my feet carry me down the hallway, I am lost in my thoughts when a large tattooed hand clamps down on my shoulder. "Hold up, free bird."

Shooting around on the balls of my feet, I spin to face Liam and accidentally collide with his chest. His arms wrap around my waist, keeping me from falling on my arse. My chin tilts up, catching his bright eyes.

"Hey." It's unsure, almost awkward, but when he stares back at me with the same expression, my smile widens.

A stutter falls from my lips. "I, eh…" And at the same time, Liam prompts, "I wanted…"

Stepping back, I raise my hand to my face and brush my hair behind my ear. "You go first."

His hand tugs the strap of his bag as he looks around the bustling hallway. Then, finally, his gaze falls back to me before he grips my hand and pulls me to the side, out of the heavy foot traffic. With my back against the wall, Liam towers over me. His forearm rests against the wall above my head, shielding me from the students rushing past to get to their next class.

His eyes flicker around my face for what feels like forever. Then, finally, he reaches out and lifts my chin with the pad of his finger. "I'm sorry for how I spoke to you the other night. I don't have any excuse for it. Other than…I was jealous."

"Liam, I…I'm sorry, too. But, I-I couldn't lie to you. You deserve better than that."

"Look, I get it, okay. You've obviously got something going on with Rohan, but you're not his. So if there's even

a slight chance you'll pick me at the finish line, I want in."
His eyes are piercing, punctuating how much he means
the words he's saying. "If you need time to figure some
shit out, that's okay. But please, don't count me out.
Because although the fight between Rohan and me is over,
I'm not done fighting for you."

Those words seep through my chest, squeezing my
heart.

"Give me a chance to prove I'm the better option, and I
promise you, I won't fuck it up, free bird."

Lost for words, I nod my reply, and Liam wastes no
time leaning in and claiming my lips with his own.

Unlike the last time, this kiss doesn't start slow.
Instead, he's all in, making me a prisoner to each stroke of
his tongue, stealing the breath from my lungs before
breathing life back into me. His hands settle on my hip,
drawing me closer until I'm pressing against his chest
with his arm wrapped around me, holding me steady.

It's all-consuming, and for a moment, I forget we are
standing in a packed hallway with a hundred eyes
passing by.

Finally, he pulls back, and I gulp in a breath, dazed by
what just happened. The smile on his face makes my chest
clench. "Be my date at the syndicate party tonight."

I don't hesitate. "Okay."

His smile widens as he backs away, his eyes still locked on mine. "See you later, free bird."

Shaking my head at his silly, carefree grin, I toss him a wave before heading to my next class. My happy daze doesn't last long, though. Especially when I turn around and my gaze locks on the murderous expression on Rohan's face, glaring at me from across the hall.

It's only then I realise why Liam dragged me to this side of the hallway...he wanted Rohan to see us.

Shit!

"I'LL BE TWO MINUTES, MAX." I GLANCE AT BEIBHINN OVER my shoulder as we both run up the stairs to change out of our uniforms before we rush into town to go dress shopping for tonight's party.

"Okay, hurry though, cause we need to get back and get ready. It starts at seven, and we still have hair and make-up."

"Two minutes, I promise."

Leaving her at her bedroom door, I continue down the narrow hallway. Once I'm at my room, I push through the door with my hip and drop my school bag to the floor.

It isn't until I have my coat off that I notice the large black box lying in the centre of my bed.

With curious but cautious steps, I walk over to find a note on the top.

Mo bhanríon,

Ní bhíonn gach ríocht faoi rialú ag ríthe. Sábháil damhsa dom. (Not all kingdoms are ruled by kings. Save a dance for me.)

R x

Inside my chest, my heart pounds wildly as a flood of emotions takes hold. I haven't spoken to Rohan since the night I threw him out of my room. Today in the hallway — after my kiss with Liam — is the first time I've seen him since then, too.

Floored by his written words, I sit on the edge of the bed and slowly draw the box onto my lap.

It's huge, like the ones you see at a designer fashion boutique in Paris or Rome. With a deep breath, I gently glide the lid off until it pops open with a release of air. Placing the lid next to me, I unfold the layers of white packing paper, until my eyes land on the delicate lace bodice surrounded by tulle. The colour is beautiful, somewhere between orchid and lavender, and I know it will suit my olive skin tone perfectly.

My heart beats wildly as I gently lift the dress from the box, assessing every intricate detail. Lost in a daze, I don't hear Beibhinn enter until she's next to me. "Holy shit, is that a Ciara Keely dress?"

"A who?"

She lifts the dress from my hands and holds it out for inspection. "She's a new Irish designer. Highly sought-after and her dresses cost a kidney and a liver." She draws the dress closer to her chest, peering down at herself as though she's envisaging what it will look like on her. "Ah, it's gorgeous. Did Liam get you this?"

My face falls into my palms, and suddenly she's placing the gown over the back of my vanity chair before sitting down next to me and wrapping her arm around my shoulder. "Hey, what's wrong?"

Peeping at her through the cracks in my fingers, I sigh. "It's from Rohan."

"Well, shit." Her mouth pulls wide, understanding why I'm so flustered. "I won't ask how he got it in here." Her eyes flick back towards the dress.

"It's stunning, isn't it? I can't wear it, B."

Her head swivels back to me. "Why the hell not?"

"Well, for one, I'm going with your brother, and wearing another man's gift is not exactly appropriate."

"Let me tell you something you need to hear," she prompts, turning her body to face me fully. "You are not dating either of these guys. If they want to woo you with fancy shit, let them."

"I know, but it's too much."

"It's not, Saoirse. I vote, wear the dress. A little competition won't do either of those guys any harm."

"I can't. I'm already on a high cliff with Liam, and I think wearing something Rohan bought might just send him over the edge."

"Look, just try it on. And then, if you decide you're in love with it and all its beauty, wear it. What Liam doesn't know won't hurt him, right?"

I knew the second Beibhinn suggested it — wearing this dress was a terrible idea, but the second I see Liam's gleaming face as I descend the staircase, the reality of just how bad this situation could turn out, settles in, leaving my stomach in a twisted knot.

Is it too late to change?

Rohan

I FUCKING HATE WEARING A TUXEDO. NOT ONLY DO I LOOK like an entitled prick with more money than God, but it also makes my resemblance to my father more prominent, which, to be honest, is where most of the hatred stems from. Thankfully, his looks are the only thing I inherited. Although, many would probably attest to that fact.

Tugging at the collar of my shirt, my foot taps against the mosaic tiles surrounding the open bar as Aodhán drones on and on about banging Hannah in the bathroom.

Elbows resting on the bar top, I face the growing crowd and stay on guard. The Killybegs Kings are not the only syndicate attending tonight. Members from the other parts of the Isle are here, too. The families who run the remaining three provinces of Ireland — the Ulster, Munster and Connacht syndicates. For the most part, each syndicate remains in their territory, only crossing paths for events, such as tonight, or when one of the Kings lets his greed overpower his intelligence and declares a war on a quarter. And that never ends well.

"No dates tonight." Lorcan approaches the bar, gesturing to the barman with his empty whiskey glass for another before dropping the Waterford crystal on the vintage mahogany bar top, then mirroring my stance.

"Not tonight, Lorcan," Aodhán clears up. "Poor Rí here lost his date to a Devereux." The humour lacing his tone pisses me off, but there's no way I'll let Lorcan see how much I'm fazed by Aodhán's remark.

Lorcan's curious gaze hones in on my face. His eyebrow creeps over his forehead, dancing dangerously close to his hairline. A slight smile teases the tilt of his lips. "Is that so?"

"Oh, yeah," Aodhán punctuates with a nod of his head. "Want to know the best part?"

"Go on," Lorcan adds, clear amusement lingering on his features, thanks to my discomfort.

My eyes shoot a death glare at Aodhán, warning him to *shut the fuck up*, but his devious grin widens. *Arsehole.*

"His pussy-whipped arse still bought her a fancy gown, costing more than most high-end used cars. My bet is she won't even wear it."

"Five hundred says she will." Lorcan laughs, feeding Aodhán's incessant need to wind me up.

"You're on, boss man."

Trying my best to ignore my *former* best friend, my attention diverts around the ballroom, scanning all the faces in attendance. *You're late, love.*

Then, as if right on cue, the large oak medieval-style doors push open. Ashamed to admit it, I ignore the organ in my chest when it stops fucking beating, and focus on filling my lungs with a much-needed breath. I can't deny it. She looks stunning.

The dress is perfect, just as I knew it would be. The pale pinky-purplish colour makes her tanned skin glow. I don't know what all the material is called, but the way the tight, detailed bodice accentuates her waist, moulding her breasts before latching around her neck like a choke-hold…Fuck. It has my mouth watering.

Hair pulled back, fastened at her nape as loose strands frame her face, showcasing her wide amber eyes. Not to mention her pinked pouty lips, matching the shade of her dress, making me want to stride across the ballroom and mess it up with a searing kiss. My pulse quickens, thumping in my throat as I fight to keep my feelings buried beneath my stoic disguise. But the second she steps forward and her toned leg peeks out from the thigh-high slit, all bets are off. My eyes trail her, laser-focused on every step she takes.

"Holy shit." Aodhán follows my gaze. "You are completely and utterly fucked, mate."

"I do not know what you're talking about." I draw my glass to my lips, hoping to conceal my emotions.

"Bullshit. She's wearing the dress."

Lorcan's open palm appears extended across my chest, waiting for Aodhán to pay up.

Aodhán pulls his wallet from his suit jacket with a grumble, before slapping a wad of fifties into Lorcan's palm. "Pleasure doing business with you, boys."

He tips the rest of his whiskey down his throat before slapping his empty glass on the bar. Then his hand lands on my shoulder as he lowers his mouth to my ear so only I can hear. His voice deepens to a roughened brogue, his always concealed Belfast accent shining through his threat. "'Member what I told ye, kid. There's no place for a Ryan in a wee King's bed."

Pulling my gaze off Saoirse, I face him with a raised brow. "Don't know about you, boss man. But FYI, I don't need a bed."

Finally, I slam my glass down next to his and walk away with my head held high.

IT'S BEEN AN HOUR, AND I STILL CAN'T TAKE MY EYES OFF her. Every time she throws her head back, laughing at something Liam said, or when she keeps stepping on his toes as he teaches her how to waltz, I have to stop myself from beating the smug look off his face.

Every now and then, the smug prick glares over Saoirse's shoulder and catches my eye. He knew I was going to ask Saoirse tonight, and like the slimy cunt he is, he decided he'd beat me to it. He's not fooling me with his newfound gentleman façade, I am well aware what's beneath his cool calm demeanour, and it sure as shit isn't the gentle giant he's pretending to be.

One hand in my pocket, the other resting against my chin, I stand at the edge of the dancefloor, surviving off the tiny glances she keeps throwing my way.

"Wanna dance?"

The question pulls my lingering gaze off Saoirse, directing my attention toward Beibhinn. My eyes drag over her body from head to toe. She's nothing like the girl I crave. Tall, slender, white-blonde hair that freely flows down her back in thick waves. Finally, my aggravated glare focuses on her silvery eyes. "I don't dance."

"That may be so." She shrugs. "But she" — she tips her head towards my fixation — "does."

She holds her hand out, waiting for me to take it. Sliding my thumb along my bottom lip, I mull the decision over, before finally taking her hand in mine and leading her out onto the dancefloor. The band begins to play a cover of "Heart of Darkness" by Sam Tinnesz and Tommee Profitt as I draw Beibhinn closer to my chest. Placing one hand on her back, between her shoulder blades, while the other takes her hand, I step forward, forcing her back as we waltz around the dancefloor alongside the other members.

Tilting her head slightly, she hits me with a sly smile. "I thought Rohan King doesn't dance."

Effortlessly guiding her around the polished floor, I counter, "I said I don't dance. Not that I couldn't."

Her eyes roll at my reply, but she remains silent, scanning my face as I glare over her shoulder, keeping my eyes trained on Saoirse as Liam leads her around the floor with his hand settled on her bare back.

"It's not like you to let someone take something you want."

"Who said I wanted anybody?"

A small laugh bubbles past her lips. "A dress worth twenty grand screams everything, Rohan. Sure, money has never been an issue for any of us, but a man would never drop that kinda money for a taste of a *nobody's* pussy."

From the corner of my eye, I catch her gaze. "So eloquent, as always."

"Cut the crap, King. You want her, admit it."

"I'm just doing what my father asked us to, Beibhinn."

"Is that why your eyes haven't left her since she stepped foot into this place?" Trust Beibhinn to call me out on my bullshit. It's the type of girl she is. She and her cousin, Aodhán, are more alike than either of them would care to admit.

Taking my eyes off Saoirse, I glance down at Beibhinn, surprised by the teasing quip of her lips. "Believe what you will, B. The only thing I want is the keys to this kingdom."

"So, you do want her."

"That's not what I meant, and you know it."

"Semantics."

Not liking how close to my truth she's getting, I steer our conversation in a different direction. "One would think you wanted your brother to lose, Beibhinn."

"Has it ever occurred to you…maybe I want *her* to win?"

Feeling the heat of an onlooker's eyes boring a hole in the side of my face, I sidestep, spinning us both in place, and peer over Beibhinn's shoulder.

Suddenly, Saoirse's wide pools of honey hold every ounce of my attention. We're locked on each other. Not so much as a blink could interfere. With every step I take, her eyes follow. The intensity of our stare-off claws through my exterior, pumping the blood in my veins, making my palms itch to reach for her.

With Beibhinn still in my arms, I follow Liam's footsteps, never freeing Saoirse from my potent glare. Each step quickens the thumping thud in my chest. When I can't stand it any longer, I drop my hands from Beibhinn's grasp and stalk towards Saoirse with intent. "Fuck it."

I'm done watching from the sidelines.

Making my way over, I cut in. "How about that dance you owe me, love?"

Her chest rises as she draws in a breath, but once again, those eyes linger on mine as she nods. Liam clamps down on his jaw, unimpressed by my intrusion.

"Are you sure, free bird?" His little term of endearment pisses me off, but I am wise enough to know that picking a fight with him won't get me what I want.

With one last flick of her eyes, she tosses a concerned look at Liam. Then, placing her hand on his chest, she assures him. "One dance. Why don't you go get some drinks and I'll meet you at the bar in a few minutes."

I'd be lying if I said her words didn't sting, but I don't protest them either, unwilling to forfeit the dance she's granting me. So, instead, I graciously bow, holding my hand out to Saoirse, the picture of the perfect gentleman.

Finally, she places her palm in mine, and Liam bites down on his lip as I draw her into my chest, not leaving a sliver of space between us.

As I shoot him an *I win* look over Saoirse's shoulder Liam grinds down on his teeth before striding off.

Taking a moment, I glance down at her as she peers up at me over her thick lashes.

"Thank you for the dress. It's…em, it's beautiful."

Wrapping my arms around her waist, I settle my hand on the curve of her back. "Only on you."

Raising her hand to my eye, she traces over the cut Liam left on my brow. "This is healing well."

Emotion at her small, delicate touch forms in the back of my throat, but I gulp it back, and cover her hand with mine, intertwining our fingers. A new song begins, and I step forward, guiding her back. Our eyes never leave each other as the singer lilts out "Taibhsí no Laochra" by The Coronas.

We exchange no words, solely feeding off the magnitude of the moment. Some looks can kill, but in her eyes, she holds a far greater power, the power to bring this king to his knees.

She doesn't know it yet, but every move I've made has been to protect her. Sure, at first she was a job, a means to get everything I've ever wanted. But now, she's an obsession, an itch beneath my rib cage I can't reach.

As the song slows, my eyes veer over her shoulder, catching sight of Liam, Donnacha, and my dad. They're looking this way, focusing on every moment Saoirse and I share. Hardening my features, I loosen my hold on Saoirse. A king never shows weakness, and as much as I try to hide it, I know the girl in my arms is mine. Lowering my head, I bring my lips to her ear. "Only love a king when he deserves it. That's when he'll need it most."

With that, I step back and turn on my heel, leaving her standing in the middle of the ballroom floor.

Saoirse

I'm lost in a daze, frozen to the floor as I watch Rohan's retreating frame.

What the fuck just happened?

One moment I'm swept away by the tsunami of emotions he unapologetically makes me feel, and then the next, he turns to stone, leaving me longing for the warmth he took with him.

A small part of me wants to follow him and ask him what happened, why the sudden shift from sweet and attentive to dark and detached. But the larger, more sensible side of me knows better. Chasing a guy like Rohan only leads down one road — destruction.

One thing is for sure; there are far more sides to Rohan than he allows anyone to see, but boy, is he giving me whiplash.

Peering over my shoulder, I search for Liam, but can't seem to see him anywhere. My feet carry me off the dance floor towards the bar area. But as I crank my neck above the crowd, I suddenly collide with a solid frame. "Oh, I'm so, so sorry. I wasn't watching where I was…"

"Don't worry about it, sweetheart." His slow, toxic smile creeps across his face. I remember him from my English class, the guy who made the smart remark on my first day. "It's Donnacha, right?"

He tips his chin forward. "And you're Saoirse."

I hold my hands out wide. "In the flesh."

A slight laugh huffs past his closed lips. "Would you like to dance?" He tosses his thumb over his shoulder, pointing towards the dancefloor. "We can call it an apology for the shitty comment I made on your first day at school."

Unease rolls in the pit of my stomach, and my internal sat-nav blares at me to turn around. My eyes dart around the ballroom, looking for a reasonable excuse to tell him no.

Finally, my eyes land on Liam standing at the bar talking to a man I recognise from the photo in Fiadh's office, Mr Gabriel King, Rohan's father. "I should probably get back to my date." I step forward, but he shifts in front of me, blocking my path.

Donnacha's dark eyes follow my line of sight. "Are you sure? He seems a little busy with my dad."

My eyes whip around so fast they bulge out of my sockets. "You're Rohan's brother?"

At first glance, I'd never make the connection between the two, but as I look closer, I see it lingering in the finer details. His hair is slightly lighter, more brown than black, but the cut of his sharp jawline and the set of his eyes are identical. They are even the same forest shades but lack the mischievous sparkle. Donnacha's eyes appear lifeless, void of any emotion, and it unnerves me.

Stalking forward, Donnacha forces me to retreat, and then suddenly, the cool night breeze from the balcony behind me brushes against my skin.

He steps closer, closing any space between us. His mouth lowers to my ear before he whispers, "Technically, I'm his half-brother. But, shh…" He lifts his index finger to my lips, silencing me. "Because I'm Daddy's best-kept secret."

My heart clammers up my throat, lodging in my airways, but somehow I convince my feet to take a few steps back. Distancing myself from him, I place myself out onto the balcony. Which, in hindsight, was a dangerous move.

Stupid Saoirse. Stay where the people are.

My stomach lunges into my chest, knitting into a tense ball of anxiety. My chest rises and falls, reducing my breaths to an erratic wheeze as I fight to fill my clenched lungs with air.

Inside the ballroom, people dance to the band, but nobody seems to notice as Donnacha creeps forward, backing me further into the dark and enclosing me so I have no way to escape. I open my mouth to scream, but nothing comes out. The sound is trapped in my throat, muffled by the blood rushing to my ears.

Tears sting my eyes, burning my retinas and the inside of my nose, but I refuse to let them fall. Fear dances along my spine, vibrating every internal organ.

Suffocated by this prowl, my eyes dart left and right as I look for an escape, but the only way past him is through him.

Taking my chance, I rush to the left, hoping to take him off guard so I can push past him. Suddenly, he grabs me by the elbow and draws me closer to his chest. "Did I say you could leave, sweetheart?"

Using all the strength I have, I tug my arm, fighting to remove it from his grip, but it's useless. His fingertips dig into my flesh, holding me steady. "What's the matter, Saoirse? You've already thrown yourself at my baby brother and Liam."

"How did you…"

"Just because I'm silent doesn't mean I'm not paying attention. After all, the villain always hides in the shadows, sweetheart. That way, when he strikes, nobody will be watching."

With an aggressive tug, he spins me around, one hand coming up to cover my mouth as the other pushes me forward, shoving me against my back. My ribs greet the iron rail enclosing the balcony with a heavy thump, making me cry out into his palm.

He muffles my pleas as I beg him to stop, to let me go, but my attempts are futile. I grip the railing, squeezing so tight my knuckles turn white and my fingers go numb. Pushing against his hold, I scream into his palm.

"Stay still, you fucking bitch." He applies more force, moulding his chest to my back as he releases his hand, tugging the tulle skirt of my dress up and exposing me in all the wrong places.

Finally, the tears I tried so desperately to conceal seep from my eyes, burning their way down my cheeks, pooling in the seam where his palm covers my mouth.

The liquid fear coats my upper lip as he pulls my thong to the side. Closing my eyes, I block it all out, the feel of his hand sliding through my slit as he wets my entrance with his saliva, the intrusion of his fingers as they force their way inside me.

Holding my breath, I rob my lungs of air.

I pray…I pray I'll blackout, so I don't have to relive this moment every day for the rest of my life.

I thrash, wishing I was strong enough to force him off me.

When nothing works, I give in to the reality of what is happening and my body goes limp, numb to his fingers buried inside me as he forces me to stretch for him.

"I'm really going to enjoy tearing your cunt with my cock."

My blood pulses as my fear electrifies every cell in my body. "Stop," I cry out, but it hits his palm, dulling the sound into an intelligible muffle.

Behind me, he shuffles, undoing his pants. Closing my eyes, I brace myself for the intrusion, but it never comes.

Suddenly, the weight holding me down disappears, but with my body still shaking, I can't move. Someone tugs my dress down, covering my legs, then arms wrap around me, pulling me against a warm chest.

My vision is nothing but blurred shapes, distorted by the tears freefalling down my cheeks, but the crunch of bone reverberates through the air, followed by Rohan's gravelly threat. "You rotten son of a bitch. I'm going to bury you. Nobody touches her and lives. I'll kill you fucking all."

The pounding continues, hit after hit swooshes through the air, but I can't look.

"Rohan, stop, you're going to draw attention."

"Just get her the fuck out of here."

"But—"

"Now, Aodhán." The grip on me tightens, but he doesn't move. "Now!"

In moments, I am floating through the air, clinging to him like a lifeline. "Aodhán."

"You're okay, Saoirse. I've got you. I promise. You're safe now."

Before I know what's happening, my body greets cool leather as Aodhán places me onto a passenger seat before tugging off his suit jacket and covering me with it. He's still standing outside the car, but he hunkers down next to the open door, bringing himself to my level. "Can I get you anything?"

Wrapping my arms around myself, I avoid his eyes and shake my head.

"Are you okay?"

I don't answer. Instead, I focus on the windscreen, losing myself in the thick treeline. Finally, he stands, and from the corner of my eye, I watch him pace up and down, back and forth over the asphalt, muttering to himself. When the silence becomes too much to bear, I croak out, "Where has Rohan gone?"

His hands rush through his blond hair, tugging on the long strands on top of his head. He halts, spearing his concerned gaze towards me. "He's coming, sweetheart."

"Don't call me that, please." My voice cracks. "That's what he called me. Please don't call me that again."

"Shit. I'm so sorry, Saoirse." His usually carefree humour-laced face drops, but right now, I can't bring myself to comfort him.

Another few moments pass until finally Aodhán releases a relieved breath.

"Where is she?" Rohan roars. Peering in the rearview mirror, I spy him as he rushes towards the car. Within seconds, he is dropping to his knees next to the open passenger door. His blood-stained hands cup my chin before carefully bringing my eyes to his. The look on his face breaks me, and I squeeze my eyes shut, unwilling to accept the thoughts and emotions swirling in his eyes.

"Don't do that, love. Don't hide from me."

Tears leak from the corner of my eyes and trail down the slope of my nose, but I refuse to open them.

"Please, mo bhanríon. Look at me." The emotion behind those few words cracks my eyes open.

"I'm going to take you somewhere, okay? Somewhere you'll be safe."

I nod, the words I want to say lodging in my throat.

"Good girl." He leans forward, dropping a chaste kiss on my forehead. Rising to his feet, he turns to face Aodhán.

"What do you need, mate?"

Interlocking his fingers, Rohan raises his hands to the back of his head before his shoulders drop. "Find Lorcan and get that piece of shit off the balcony before anyone else finds his unconscious arse. But whatever you do, do not kill him. When he dies, my face will be the last face he ever sees."

Aodhán nods in understanding. "You got it."

After exchanging some sort of man-shake, Aodhán peers around Rohan. "Don't worry, Saoirse. You're in good hands." For the first time since arriving here, I believe those words. Rohan is not my villain.

Before I can muster up the strength to reply, Rohan shuts the door. My eyes stay trained on him as he talks to Aodhán, then he rounds the front of the car, and climbs into the driver's seat.

Reaching over, he tugs on my seatbelt, strapping me in.

"Where…where are you taking me?"

"Home."

"Rohan. I don't want to go back to the Devereuxs."

His eyes glance my way. "I am taking you home, Saoirse. Not to the Devereuxs, and not to my house. Your home, Saoirse. I'm bringing you home."

I lose his meaning to my wandering thoughts, but I'm trusting him to keep me safe as he promised. "Rohan?"

"Yes, love?"

Dampening my dry throat with a swallow, I rest my head against the headrest and close my eyes. "Thank you…for saving me."

"I'm not the only one doing the saving, mo bhanríon."

Rohan

Anger spirals from the pit of my stomach, boiling with a growing need to turn this car around and bury that motherfucker once and for all.

Slamming my palm against the steering wheel, I thrash my shoulders off the seat and release a curse. "Fuck!"

I should have been there, watching her and keeping her safe. I knew, I fucking knew Donnacha and my dad were up to something, but never in a million years did I believe they'd stoop as low as rape.

Jesus Christ, where was I when she needed me to protect her? Too busy trying to purge the emotions she awoke in me from beneath my skin, that's where.

I allowed our dance to creep into my chest, and instead of doing what I was supposed to do, I let her down.

Even though we got there before he…*Fuck, I can't even think it.* He violated her. Stole her right by forcing her down while he played out his sick game. Her reaction is valid, but I hate how he dimmed the gold glimmer in her eyes.

He's lucky getting back to her was my first and only priority, because I would have killed him, and honestly, a quick death is not something I'm willing to give. Donnacha's time is fleeting, and when I finally get to deliver his execution, the fear I'll instil in him will follow him into his shallow grave.

My eyes drift across the cab, settling on the girl passed out in my passenger seat. Even in her sleep, she clenches her eyes tight as she grinds down on her teeth. Tonight has followed her into her dreams, and I don't know how to fix that.

Reaching over, I trail my busted knuckles over her cheek. "You don't know it yet, mo bhanríon. But, tá mo chroí istigh ionat." *My heart is in you.*

Suddenly, my phone rings through my Bluetooth as Lorcan's name flashes from the screen. Connecting the call, I greet him. "Tell me you have him." *Silence.* "Lorcan?"

"He wasn't about."

"What do you mean, he wasn't about? I tied him to the railing myself."

"He'd disappeared. When Aodhán and I got there, he was away." Sometimes his northern slang can be hard to follow, but his message rings loud and clear. When he and Aodhán got back to the balcony, Donnacha was gone.

"Motherfucker. He was out cold, Lorcan. There's no fucking way he walked out of there by himself. Where the fuck did he go?"

The line goes quiet, and I know I will not like whatever he's going to say next. "Gabriel is away, too."

"Fuck. Fuck. Fuck," I mutter, not wanting to wake Saoirse while I am on this call.

"We'll find 'em. They'll not be gettin' away with touchin' my wee one."

My eyes trail back to Saoirse — who is still fast asleep — curled up in the seat next to me, her head resting against the passenger window. When I don't reply, Lorcan prompts, "How's about 'er?"

"She's sleeping. I'm taking her to the Ryan Estate. Tell Éanna to meet me there."

"No."

His stern tone cuts through the speaker like a knife through paper, leaving no room for argument, but it doesn't stop me from trying. "What do you mean, no? She needs her mam."

"Not yet. If Gabriel finds out Éanna is in Killybegs, it's game over."

"She. Needs. Her!" I repeat, punctuating each word and hammering my point home.

"It's too risky. This is bigger than t'night. One wrong move and the last twenty years go down the fuckin' shitter. I didn't miss out on my daughter growin' for nothin'. We have to see this thing through." His accent bleeds through his frustration, thickening with an angry bite.

"Fine. But I'm telling her everything. She deserves the truth."

His heavy breath courses through the speakers. "Grand. Do what you need to. I'll give ya a call tomorrow. Oh, and Rohan?"

"What?"

"You know I love you, kid. But if you break my baby's heart, I'll put an ounce of lead behind your ear."

Normally, I would blast back at him with a cheeky comment, but I'm wise enough to know Lorcan Reilly doesn't make idle threats, and right now, I know he means every fucking word. "Understood, boss man."

After I disconnect the call, we pull up to the entrance of Ryan Estate within minutes. Unlike any of the other syndicate members, the Ryan Estate is a restored 18th-century castle that sits at the peak of Killybegs. With a 185-acre panoramic view of the Dublin/Wicklow mountains, it's the most sought-after piece of property on this side of the border.

For years, it sat idle, gathering dust as the ghosts of lifetimes past roamed the halls. Recently, Lorcan had the place cleaned and prepared, knowing one day soon all of this would belong to his daughter. The second Saoirse turns eighteen, all of this becomes hers. The only Ryan Heir who is eligible to run the Killybegs Syndicate. But first, she has to pass her trials. If she even makes it that far. My father is clearly desperate to keep his false throne, and tonight only solidifies how far he's willing to go to keep the title he stole all those years ago.

Punching the entry code, the Ryan family crest splits in two as the two enormous wrought-iron gates separate, giving way to a sweeping avenue lined with hundreds of mature cherry blossom trees. Foot to the floor, the car accelerates forward, guiding us up the mountainside until finally, the Ryan Castle Estate comes into view. Gliding my car to the entrance, I press the handbrake button and climb out before rounding the car to the passenger side.

Finally, once I have the door open, I unbuckle Saoirse's seatbelt and then slide my arms beneath Saoirse and lift her out. She stirs in my arms, her eyelashes flicking as she fights to stay asleep.

"Rohan?" Her voice is hoarse, strained from everything that has gone down tonight.

"I got you, love." I comfort her, drawing her closer to

my chest. "Can you wrap your arms around my neck so I can carry you inside?"

Without hesitation, she circles her arms around me, holding on as I climb the steep stone steps to the front door.

Finally, we get to the top and I set her on the deep-set concrete window ledge, and grip her face with my palms. "Hang tight. I need to open the door, okay?"

Her eyes soften, and it sets off a whole load of shit I don't have the words to describe. "As much as I like this side of you, you can stop fussing so much. I'm a little battered, Rohan. But I'm not broken."

I nod, wondering if I'm overcompensating because I feel guilty, or because I genuinely want to take care of her. Affection is foreign to me. For as long as I can recall, there has only been one person who has ever cared about me and what I need, and let's just say Lorcan Reilly is not the hugs type. For all intents and purposes, he's the only father figure I have.

Every year, he'd take off for a few weeks during the summer. Then, I found out he was spending those weeks with Liam on stupid fishing trips... And well, if I were to be transparent, that's how mine and Liam's rivalry began. I hated Liam for stealing the only person in the world who saw me as more than an heir. It was then I did everything in my power to be superior to him in every way. After a while, it grew into a competition, a game we've continued to play.

When I turned sixteen, Lorcan finally told me the real reason behind those trips — he was going to see his daughter, and because he couldn't risk Gabriel finding out that he was Saoirse's father, he concealed those trips under the disguise of a bonding trip with his only godson, Liam.

Eventually, when my hate for my father was undeniable, Lorcan trusted me with his biggest secret, and in return, he told me story after story about his little princess who would one day return to Killybegs and claim her title as Queen. For two years, I helped him watch her from afar, until one day, my father announced he'd finally found them.

After that meeting, Lorcan and I put a plan together, one that led us to this very moment.

Pulling my keys from my pocket, I retrieve the one for the electronic keypad and open it before punching in the code. The door unlatches, and I push it open. My neck cranes as I peer over my shoulder, and hold out my hand for Saoirse. She places her hand in mine and I pull her to her feet. "Are you ready?"

Her brow raises. "Ready for what?"

"Your return to home."

With one hand circling her waist and the other in my

hand, her mouth drops open. "What? I thought…Is this not your house?"

A small laugh bubbles past my lips at her wide eyes as she glances at the stone-faced castle. Turning on my heel, I face her fully, then raise her hand. "Hold out your hand." Finally, I drop the keys into her open palm. "What's a queen without a throne? Welcome home, love."

Rohan

"ARE YOU OKAY?" IT'S BEEN ALMOST AN HOUR SINCE WE arrived at the estate, and after a very brief tour of the hallway, Saoirse veered into the living quarters and has barely moved an inch since. Not to mention she's hardly strung a sentence together, only acknowledging me with one-word responses and the odd head nod. I'm out of my depth and sinking rapidly. "Still cold? Do you want a blanket?"

Her face remains stoic, void of any emotion as she peers around the expansive room, her gaze lingering on various pieces of artwork decorating the walls. Finally, she settles her wandering eyes on me. "I'm fine, Rohan. Stop hovering. Your nice guy act is weirding me out."

Stalking forward, I then hunch down in front of her, meeting her at eye level. "For one, you don't look fine. And two, it's not an act. A lot has happened to you tonight,

Saoirse. Is it so fucking wrong that I'm concerned about your well-being?"

Her amber eyes glimmer with unshed tears. "What do you want me to say, Rohan?"

"I want you to be honest with me."

"Ha! That's a little rich. Especially when everything and everyone in this fucking town thrives on deceit and lies." She pauses, sucking in a deep inhale through her nose. "Fine…You want my truth, have it. I feel as though I'm stuck in this constant freefall, spiralling further and further into a bottomless black hole, and I don't know how to make it stop." An angry tear seeps from the corner of her eye, carelessly sliding down her cheek.

"You're overwhelmed by your emotions. Frustrated by your need for answers. Upset at the lack of control you have over your life. Angry at every person who has kept you in the dark. I get it, Saoirse. But sitting here, staring blankly at the walls, will not help you sieve through any of that."

Raising my hand, I catch her fallen tear with my thumb and then swipe it from my fingertip with my tongue before giving her some truth of my own. "I have never lied to you."

"Haven't you?" Her eyes narrow, effortlessly holding me accountable for a sin I haven't committed.

"No. Sure, sometimes I've withheld the truth, but not once have I lied."

"You're playing the omission card. *Really,* Rohan. How big of you."

"Look, I get that you're hurting, love. But I promise you, anything I've withheld was for a reason. I was trying to protect you."

"That didn't work out so well for you, did it?" she barks, but her statement punctures my skin like a ferocious bite.

My eyes drop to the floor, her words affecting me far more than I care to admit.

"I'm sorry," she whispers, placing her fingers beneath my chin and tilting my face until our gazes intertwine. "That was a shitty thing for me to say. I shouldn't blame you for someone else's wrongdoings. I'm just tired of it all, Rohan. Over a week ago, I was just an average teenage girl. And now, here I am, thrust into a lifestyle I know nothing about. Every time I think I get close to figuring out the answers, a new tidal wave of questions appears and then I'm drowning all over again."

Reaching out, I push the fallen strands of hair from her face.

Her eyes dance around the room, bouncing from wall to wall. "I spent my childhood hopping from matchbox house to matchbox house, and then suddenly, you're handing me the keys to an entire estate and telling me it's mine. I'm confused, Rohan. When did this" — she holds her hand out, gesturing around us — "become my life?"

Placing her palms on the couch, she pushes herself to her feet and moves past me. She crosses the room until she's standing in front of the enormous fireplace, her back to me. Following her lead, I stand up and place my hands in my pockets, allowing my feet to carry me towards her.

I watch as she draws her palms together, sliding her hands up and down, creating heat with the friction. Then she holds them above the open flame. Finally, she peers up at me. "I don't know who I can trust."

Reaching for her, I wrap my arms around her and draw her into my chest. Her arms circle around my waist, and she rests her head against my shoulder.

"You can trust me," I whisper into her hair.

Pulling back an inch, she peeps over her thick lashes. "I want to believe that, really, I do. But all of this started with you."

As I glide my hands over her arms, I step back to look at her. "There's where you're wrong, mo bhanríon. Me and you — we are not the beginning of this story. We're the end."

"Jesus, Rohan." She pulls out of my hold completely

and then turns her back to me. Her hands cover her face as her shoulders rise and fall with her large intake of breath. Finally, she turns around. "Can you stop being so fucking cryptic? You are driving me insane. I can't take it anymore. Everything out of your mouth has an underlying message, a hidden snippet of information for me to decipher. My life is not Hansel and Gretel. I don't want to follow your breadcrumbs. For fuck's sake, just spit it out." Her hands fly through the surrounding air, accentuating every word while everything from the last week and a half finally boils over. She spews every ounce of her frustration at me until finally, a defeated breath rushes from her lungs. "I need answers."

"Sit down."

Her brow hitches, making her doe eyes crinkle.

"Sit. The. Fuck. Down. You want answers, Saoirse, fine. You can have answers, but you better make sure you ask the right questions."

Shaking her head, she stalks towards the couch, muttering something under her breath about me and my fucking whiplash.

Once she's sitting, I take a seat directly across from her and then rest my elbows on my knees. Her eyes laser in on mine, and we sit there, staring for a moment. Finally, her first question breaks out of the gate. "Do you know where my mam is and is she okay?"

"Yes, and yes."

Her chest expands with her intake of breath, finally falling when relief collapses her shoulders. Her teeth graze over her bottom lip. "Where is she?"

I keep it simple, not wanting her to know everything, not yet. "Killybegs."

Her full moon eyes glaze over as anger and hurt rear their ugly heads. "She's been here the whole time? Why didn't she call me and let me know she was okay?"

"She's fine. Missing you, but in order to put an end to all this, she had to stay away from you."

Her frustration pushes her to her feet, and her hands fly to her head. "An end to what? What is she running from? Stop avoiding it, Rohan. Tell me what the fuck is going on."

"There are some things I can't tell you, Saoirse. Purely because I don't have all the information." I rise from the couch and place my hands on her shoulders, eyes searing into the window of her soul. "But for you to understand the bigger picture, I have to go back to the beginning."

She nods before stepping out of my grasp and lowering herself back onto the couch, directing all her attention on me.

"The syndicate is a criminal organisation founded hundreds of years ago by the four High King families of the Emerald Isle — The Ryan, Reilly, Connelly, and

Murphy clans — one King for each province of Ireland. Caolain Ryan was the original High King of the Leinster syndicate but over the years, crime changed and expanded beyond the reach of one person. Everything became more accessible — drugs, money, power. The High Kings knew they needed to extend their reach. That's when they brought in more families, ones with enough connections to keep them at the top of the food chain."

"And that's when the Kings, Devereuxs, and Bradys became Leinster's Killybegs Kings, right?" My gaze flicks towards her, wondering how she knew that. She answers my unspoken question with one word. "Beibhinn."

I nod, lowering myself onto the couch, and taking a seat next to her. "I should have known she was feeding you snippets. Anyway, Caolain brought in our families to strengthen his reach. Then, with each new generation, the keys of the kingdom got passed down to the next heir in line. But first, they had to pass their trials and prove their loyalty. Your mam was the first female heir to step up and demand a seat. She was the oldest Ryan heir, but normally women didn't initiate." When she tips her chin with acknowledgement, I carry on.

"At first, the Kings didn't want a woman leading any province, but after putting it to a vote, they agreed that if women could pass the same trials as the men, then why not?" Your mam cleared the way for all women. But some men weren't happy about having a woman as their leader."

Her tongue peeps out from her parted lips, trailing along the seam. I follow the movement with my gaze until she finally asks, "Beibhinn said my mam never finished her trials. Did something happen? Is that what made her run?"

"Yes…but that's not my story to tell. It's hers."

Her eyes roll back, agitated by my response. "She's had almost eighteen years to tell me, Rohan, and she hasn't. What makes you think she will now?"

"She's no choice, love. You're in this now."

"Can you take me to her?"

"Not yet. Especially after what Donnacha did tonight. That attack wasn't a fluke, Saoirse. If I hadn't realised you'd disappeared from the dancefloor, God knows what he would have done to you."

She hesitates for a moment, dropping her gaze to the floor. It's clear by her facial expression that the events of tonight are flashing through her mind. Finally, she peers back at me. "What do you mean when you say it wasn't a fluke?"

Reaching over, I take her hand in mine and draw it on my lap. With my free hand, I draw lazy circles on her palm. "When your mam failed to complete her trials, the syndicate crowned my dad as King of Killybegs, but only until the next Ryan became of age and passed their trials. You're my father's biggest threat. Not your mam. You. You're the only eligible Ryan heir. And with that title comes enemies. Ones that would do anything to remain in power. As far as I can tell, my father knew he was running on borrowed time, so he got his pet project to take care of the problem. But, thankfully, Aodhán and I stopped him before Donnacha could finish whatever it was he was going to do to you."

She stiffens, and her eyes gloss over before she squeezes them tight and forces back the emotions she is feeling. Finally, after a few deep breaths, she continues, "So, what…your father told your half-brother to rape me?"

Deciding to brush past the fact she knows Donnacha is my brother — because that is a story for another day — I give her my thoughts on what happened tonight. "My guess is my dad sent Donnacha to get rid of you, but Donnacha got greedy and thought he'd have his way with you first."

Her lips clamp down as she gulps her emotions back. Bringing a hand to her face, I cup her cheek, and she leans into my palm.

"I don't have a good relationship with my dad, Saoirse. But I know he wants to remove you from the equation. No more Ryan heirs means he can continue his reign without interruption."

"He's the reason you came to my house that night?"

"Yes, and no. We knew he'd found out about you, and we had to act fast before he got to you."

"Who is…we?"

I knew this question was coming, and honestly, I don't think she's ready to hear it. But I promised her I never lied to her, and I will not start now. "Your dad."

Saoirse

EVERY MUSCLE IN MY BODY GOES RIGID AS MY BREATH HALTS in my chest. All I can hear is the rapid pulsation of my heart as it echoes in my eardrum. Closing my eyes, I force myself to summon a deep breath, drawing it through my parted lips until it burns my parched lungs. Slowly, my lashes lift, and Rohan's concern is the first thing I see.

His gaze holds mine, patiently waiting for my reaction. Finally, my mouth opens, but nothing comes out.

A thick fog settles behind my eyes.

It's too much. After everything I've been through, I never would have thought it would be those words that would split my chest wide open.

I've spent years wondering who my father was, hopelessly imagining if he thought of me as much as I did him. Sleepless nights speculating whether he knew of my existence. Birthdays, school dances, the first time I brought a boy home, all the times he should have been there but wasn't.

I've too many questions. Who is he? Where is he? What is he like? Do I look like him? Is he one of the Kings? So many fucking questions, and yet, I can't find the words to ask them.

Pushing from the couch, I stalk across the living quarters until I'm peering out the deep-set floor-to-ceiling window that overlooks a beautiful walled garden. Lost in my thoughts, I don't notice Rohan creeping in behind me until his arm snakes around my waist. My breath hitches at the contact as images of Donnacha's hand forcing me down against the balcony railing erupt behind my eyes.

"Breathe, love." Rohan's velvety rasp licks my skin as he settles his chin on my shoulder. The scent of his cologne wafts around me, instantly erasing all the tension I'm holding in my shoulders. "I'm the villain in many a man's stories, but never in yours."

My back sinks into his chest, wanting to believe every word. Time and time again, he told me he wasn't the bad guy. But how do I trust anyone when every ounce of my life is nothing but secrets and lies? Would it be stupid to allow myself to fall for a man raised on the devil's backbone? Am I naïve to believe the thunderstorm and chaos wrapped around him isn't exactly what I need to escape the flames of hell marring my skin after inflicting Donnacha's seedy touch?

I can't deny the pull he has on me, or how my body reacts every time he almost touches me. Rohan King is my escape, the person who rips all logic from my headspace, and I'll be a liar if I said he's not what I need right now. He is someone I run to, a corner of darkness where I can hide from all the noise blaring in my head.

With him, I know there is no safe place to land. No matter how I look at it, if I allowed myself to dive into the things he makes me feel, I'd be falling forever.

Constantly bewitched by his ever-changing sides, Rohan is an enigma wrapped in the devil's temptations. And silly me, I crave his every sin.

"I'm not ready to forgive, but make me forget," I whisper those words as his breath caresses my neck, leaving nothing but desire in its wake. "Replace his hands with yours, take away my pain."

His knuckles barely dance along my spine, a tender touch so delicate…I feel like the most precious thing he's ever held in his arms. The hand around my waist skirts along my rib cage, tracing the detailed lace along the bodice of my dress.

"Ar do shon, mo bhanríon, loiscfinn an domhan." *For you, my queen, I'd burn the world.*

My head falls back, and his tongue trails along the

curve of my neck. It's easy to lose myself in the touch of his roaming hands. Finally, his fingers tease my throat with a gentle, featherlight hold.

Breathing out a lustrous sigh, I cave to the sparks exploding beneath my skin.

His stance widens, feet on either side of my hips as he gently leans me forward. My hands greet the window, bracing for the fall that never comes.

"Tell me where he touched you, love. And I'll destroy myself to erase it from your mind."

I clench, needing his promise more than my next breath.

Pulling back slightly, he undoes the three pearl buttons at the nape of my neck, unclasping the halter neck of my dress. The front falls forward, pooling around my waist and exposing my breasts. Next, he dots kisses along my spine as he lowers himself onto his hunkers. "Was it here?" He licks along the base of my back, paying extra attention to the two small, intended dimples. His palm glides over my arsecheek, soft and teasing, making my back arch until my exposed chest presses against the windowpane.

The cool glass brushes against my nipples, darting shockwaves of desire over my skin. Finally, he finds the small, concealed zipper and slowly glides it down, freeing my hips from the weighty layers of tulle material.

Taunting me, he eases the dress over my hips until it pools around my feet.

"Who is touching you?" he demands in a gruff whisper.

"You."

"Who is touching you, love?" he repeats before lifting my right leg and pulling the material out of his way. He repeats the action with the other leg, tossing the dress to the side.

"Rohan." His name flitters past my lips.

"The second I saw you in the dress, I fucking knew I'd be the one to take it off you," he whispers against the inside of my parted thighs, his hot breath dampening my pussy. Finally, his lips grace my flesh as the tip of his tongue traces his name along my inner thigh. He moves higher and higher until he stops at the crevice, where my lace-up thong conceals his destination.

As his hands drift up my outer leg, his tongue slides over the lace. "So fucking wet for me, love." At last, his fingers curl around the edge of my underwear before slowly teasing them down. "Step out."

I do as I'm told and peer over my shoulder as he tosses them next to my dress. His gaze catches mine. "Good girl," he praises. Completely bare before him, his sweeping gaze roams over every inch of me as he curls two fingers through my aching slit.

"Who owns this pussy?"

He eases his digits past my entrance as he lowers his mouth to my arsecheek, grazing his teeth over my flesh before treating himself to tiny nibbles. "You."

Satisfied by my response, he curls his fingers, drawing them in and out in slow, torturous thrusts. "That's right, mo bhanríon. Mo chorp. Mo phusa. Mo chroí. Minach." *My body. My pussy. My heart. Mine.*

"Oh…my…God." I tighten around his fingers, feeling the familiar ache as it builds with every single curl of his fingers. "Rohan, I need…"

He tears his hand away and stands to his full height. His hand circles my neck, drawing my head back until I'm peering at him over the top of my head. "As much as I want to feast on *my* glistening cunt, I want inside you more."

Twisting in his arms, I turn toward him, needing to see his face. With two steps, he forces me back. My spine greets the window, and I bite down on my lower lip at the contact.

Raising his hand, Rohan swipes his thumb across my lip, freeing it from my bite. His eyes follow the movement, staring at my mouth like it will be his last meal.

I've dreamt of his first kiss, wondering which side of his personality would shine through. Would he be soft and gentle or would he steal a part of me with his dangerous greed?

Needing to touch him, I roam my hands over his black shirt. Finally, I tease the buttons with my fingertips, never taking my eyes off his. He reaches up, covering my wanting hand with his, hesitant about letting me take control by undressing his tattooed skin. Finally, he drops his hand. "Is leatsa mise an oiread agus is leatsa." *I am yours as much as you are mine.*

His intimate stare gives permission, and I don't waste any time, popping each button until my hands are gliding between the material, pushing his shirt off his shoulders, until it falls to the floor. Next, my hands reach for his belt, undoing the buckle and pulling it from the loops.

His shoulders rise and fall, his heavy breaths steadying his need to devour me whole. He releases his control, giving it to me freely. Once I have his suit pants undone, I sweep my hands beneath his boxers, pushing it all down in one slow motion. Lowering myself, I leave a trail of kisses along his deep, rigid torso until I am at eye level with his hard, thick cock.

My mouth waters as I kneel before him, peering up at him over my lashes. Finally, I clasp his cock in my fist, gliding my palm from tip to base and back again, until his need is seeping from his engorged head. My tongue darts out, sweeping across my lip before I take his tip past my lips. His taste explodes on my tongue as I lower myself further until he hits the back of my throat.

His approving hiss infiltrates my ears as he brings his hand to the back of my head, cradling me in as I hollow my cheeks, sucking, licking, devouring every single inch.

"Fuck." His curse stains the air. "Jesus." His fingers tangle in my hair as he applies just enough pressure to spur me on. My strokes become firmer when his hips thrust forward, fucking my mouth with his cock. "I've dreamt of choking you with my dick, love. But, fuck me, it didn't feel like this."

Cupping his balls, I apply a bit of pressure, and then he's bucking into my mouth, chasing the temptation until, finally, he falls over the edge. "Ah fuck."

His fingers still tangled in my hair, he carefully eases me to my feet before lifting me off the ground. I wrap my legs around his waist and he forces my back against the cold glass.

My arm circles his neck, and my fingernails dig into his skin as he traces my collarbone with his tongue. His mouth mashes against mine, stealing the breath from my lungs.

Not prepared for his savage intrusion, my nails bite into his skin as I hang on for dear life. With every swipe of his tongue, I fall a little further into all things Rohan.

Before long, his greedy strokes fade into a kiss so raw and intense that I forget my own name. Our eyes connect, and the longing in his eyes stirs something in my chest, something I am not ready to acknowledge.

"Fuck me, Rohan," I whisper against his lips.

Reaching between us, he lines up his cock with my pussy. His eyes find mine again, and the intensity behind them cuts through my chest, leaving my heart exposed, ready and waiting for him to steal it.

He holds my gaze as he spears his hip forward, bending my back with his forceful thrust. A needy cry escapes me as his fingers dig into my hips, holding me steady.

Our hips move together, perfectly in sync, matching the steady thumping of my heart.

I'm lost to his touch as his hands skate over my skin, fuelling the fire building in the pit of my stomach. His mouth is everywhere, my breasts, my collarbone, my neck. His hand grabs my breast, squeezing down as he thumbs my nipple. Shockwaves of lust rush through me, spiralling my need for release.

My nails run along his back and shoulders, pulling him closer. It's all too much and not enough at the same time. He feels it too, the incessant need to mark every part of each other.

His thrusts become frantic, harder and deeper until I'm a panting mess in his arms. "Oh, yes. Yes."

"Look at me," he demands, his fingers grasping my chin and drawing my gaze back to him.

He doesn't let up, pinning me to the window with his deep, steady thrust, all the while holding every ounce of my attention. Something passes between us at that moment and every cell in my body pulses beneath his touch. I'm a slave to my desire, and Rohan King is the only one who can set me free.

"Fall for me, mo bhanríon, because you already have me on my knees."

At those words, my body vibrates, and my pussy clamps down around him as the familiar build-up takes control of my limbs. My thighs start to shake, and I know I'm seconds away from coming all over his dick.

"That's it, mo bhanríon. Take all of me."

My body explodes with the vulnerability lacing his words, and before I know it, he's chasing me over the edge.

"Mo ríocht." *My kingdom.*

Rohan

My back rests against the couch as I sit — bollocks naked — on the carpeted floor with Saoirse perched between my legs.

Her back moulds against my chest as I draw lazy circles along her exposed thigh, both of us enjoying the after-effects of our orgasms as we share a joint and a bottle of whiskey we found in the liquor cabinet.

This moment holds more intimacy than I'm used to. I've never been the guy who hangs around after sex, but when Saoirse gently trails her nails up and down my arm, I know for certain there's no place else I'd rather be than right here in this moment with her. Nobody expels the demons of childhood past from my head the way she does.

As I trail my hand over her body, my fingertips caress

her skin with a barely-there touch while my other hand draws my blunt to my lips.

I inhale a drag, then drop my head back onto the couch before I blow it out, billowing a cloud of smoke into the air.

Between my legs, Saoirse rolls over and rests her folded arms on my lower stomach before laying her head on top of them, peeking up at me over her thick lashes.

Her mouth is so close to my dick that there is no stopping the twitch that follows her giggle.

"You're insatiable." She laughs as she picks up the crystal decanter of whiskey next to us and draws it to her lips.

Next, she tilts her chin back and takes a swig before swiping her tongue along her bottom lip, savouring every drop. My eyes follow the movement, completely entranced.

Finally, she rests the bottle back on the floor, dropping her head back onto my stomach as she traces the ink of my tattoos with her index fingertips.

"I love this one," she mutters, and I feel she wasn't supposed to say it aloud.

"It's my syndicate tattoo."

"I saw it when you came to my room that night after the fight."

My heart stops fucking beating. Saoirse hasn't mentioned that night, and neither have I. It was the first time I allowed myself to lower the walls I'd spent years building. Fuck, it was first time in my life I *allowed* anyone to see all of me, not just the cocky prick the years have hardened me into.

"The swords piercing through a crown represent loyalty, respect, and strength. Then the crown is who we do it all for. Remove the crown, and the swords will fall."

"Which one are you?"

"What do you mean?"

"Well, every sword is marked with an initial, so which sword are you? Loyalty, respect, or strength?"

"For you, I'm all of them." I brush off Saoirse's comment by teasing her sides with my fingers.

"Gah." She giggles, the effects of the whiskey and second-hand weed allowing her to let loose and be nothing more than a seventeen-year-old girl spending time with a boy. "That tickles."

"Oh, does it?" A smile breaks loose across my face before I shift my hips and roll us over.

Saoirse's back greets the carpet, and I hover above her with one arm. Lost in her laughter, I bring my joint back to my lips and take another hit, loving how her nose rumples as the smell floods her senses.

"You know smoking is bad for you, right?" Her brow

arches, but I see her humour as it dances around the corner of her eyes.

"Is that so?" I mirror her facial expression before taking another drag and lowering myself until my mouth is millimetres from hers. Then I exhale, blowing the smoke into her mouth.

Her back arches, pushing her bare pussy against my rock-hard cock.

Jesus, the glimmer in those eyes will be my undoing.

"You're treading a dangerous line, love." My voice drops to a growl as she wraps her legs around my waist.

Bringing my mouth to her ear, I nibble on her earlobe, twisting the delicate diamond stud earring with the tip of my tongue. Finally, I draw it into my mouth, sucking hard before releasing it with a pop.

Her moans spur me on as I kiss along her neck, over her collarbone, until finally, I circle her nipple with my tongue before drawing it into my mouth and biting down hard.

"Rohan!" she squeals as I lick the mark I left behind.

Suddenly, she rolls out from beneath me and jumps to her feet. The wicked smile on her face stirs something inside me. Her gaze flicks toward the door, and instantly, I know she's going to make me work for what I want. "Don't you dare, mo bhanríon."

She takes off running, and like a stupid love drunk, I

follow.

Her laughter echoes off the high ceilings as she rushes up the stairs. Taking two steps at a time, I finally catch her on the first small landing and wrap my arms around her waist, before spinning her around to face me, and kissing away her ridiculous giggle.

Her arms wrap around my neck as I lift her off her feet, and then I carry her up the rest of the stairway, kicking open the first door I come across, which, thankfully, is the master bedroom.

"I think you want me to punish you," I tease as I drop her onto the mattress. Her hair splays across the white bedding, and she looks like everything I never knew I wanted.

"Maybe I do." Her eyes blaze with desire as a sultry smile quips the corners of her mouth.

Gripping her ankles, I drag her to the edge of the bed and rest her legs against my shoulders. My teeth gaze the inside of her calf, leaving little bites and sucks along her soft skin. Finally, when the temptation of her wet cunt becomes too much, I scoot her up towards the headboard before crawling onto the mattress and settling between her thighs. Her left leg falls, and I catch it in the crook of my elbow as I line my cock up with her pussy. Slowly teasing it through her slick folds, the taunt of what to come has a growl bubbling from my lips.

Her eyes find mine, and the looks she gives me strangle my chest, clutching my black heart until the only thing it beats for is Saoirse Ryan.

Finally, when I can no longer be anywhere but inside her, I push forward, easing my cock into her inch after slow and painful inch. Her walls clench around my dick as sparks erupt behind my eyelids. My head falls back, tilting towards the ceiling, as I draw in and out of her in deep, elongated thrusts.

For the first time in my life, I'm not rushing my release. Instead, I savour every fucking moan she gives me.

Gripping her hip with my free hand, my fingers sink into her soft flesh as I feed off every curse I draw from her lips.

"Rohan." My name is a pleading whisper as she relishes the build-up. Needing her lips on mine, I push forward. "Raise your hands above your head, love."

She does as I ask, and I capture her wrists with one hand, pushing them into the mattress as I grind my hips forward, hitting her right where she needs me.

"Good girl," I praise before claiming her mouth. This kiss starts out slow and demanding, matching the rhythm of my thrusts.

Her eyes hold my gaze as I tell her all the things I can't

find the words to say. I'm lost in her. I'm gone for her. She is mine.

Overcome by a magnitude of the emotions, I tear my eyes from hers and pull out of her before flipping her onto her front. My fingers tighten around her hips, and I pull her arse up as she rises to her elbows before peering back at me over her shoulder. "Fuck me like you mean it, King."

Capturing her hair with my hand, I gather it into a ponytail held together by my fist before tugging on it. Her head falls back and her back concaves beneath my hand as I spear my cock into her cunt with a forceful thrust. With my free hand, I grip her breast, holding her steady as I pound into her tight pussy, over and over.

"Rohan, yes…Oh, God. Right there, my king."

Six letters and I'm a fucking goner. My pace picks up as I chase those letters around my head, silently begging her to call me her king again.

Releasing her breast, I guide my hand down her rib cage, past her slightly curved stomach, until finally, the pads of my fingers are writing my name on her clit.

Her breaths deepen as she matches me thrust for thrust until together, we both fall victim to our release.

We collapse onto the bed in a tangle of limbs, both panting and utterly spent.

Finally, I wrap my arms around her and draw her into my chest.

"Give me ten, and we're doing that again."

Saoirse

My body aches in all the right places as I roll my shoulders back, stretching off my slumber. The weight of heavy lids keeps me from opening my eyes fully as I reach across the mattress, searching for Rohan. Blinking the sleep from my eyes, my lashes finally flutter open when all I find is an empty space next to me, still warm from his body heat.

Rolling onto my back, I shelter my eyes from the morning sun beaming through the floor-to-ceiling window by bringing my forearm to my face. Last night was the best night's sleep I've had in weeks.

Once we finally made our way up the stairs and into the main bedroom, Rohan spent the night exploring every inch of my body with his tongue before flipping me over and filling me with his cock. I can't even remember how many times he pushed me off the desire's cliff last night and again in the early morning hours, but if the aches exhausting my muscles are anything to go by, it was a lot.

Love drunk and utterly satiated, I rise from the bed, taking the top sheet with me. Then, tucking the sheet beneath my armpits, I shield my body from the cool air and head for the door, allowing the white sheet to billow behind me with every step.

Finally, I step out into the long, wide landing and take my time scanning the artwork decorating the walls. The art history fanatic inside me squeals with glee when I recognise some convincing replicas of my favourite pieces.

Finally, my gallery tour ends when I reach the top of the most exquisite stairs I've ever seen. The granite imperial is something out of a fantasy novel, held high by three stone-faced archways.

Holding onto the wrought-iron rail, I feel like a noble queen descending as I slowly ease down the steep steps.

When I reach the bottom, I peer around the expansive hallway, taking in the timeless architecture that constructs the open hallway, a blend of Gothic and medieval design that's nothing short of breathtaking.

When we arrived yesterday, I didn't allow myself to wander or explore, too caught up in the thoughts clouding my head. Making a mental note, I promise myself that

later today, I will explore every nook and cranny of the
property that is now my home.

That thought strikes me in my gut. I'm still trying to
process everything Rohan and I discussed last night. Even
though I know we've barely tipped the iceberg of secrets,
he still has more to reveal. But he's winning me over, one
piece of information at a time.

Finally, after I push through the archways that lead
towards the kitchen, Rohan's deep, husky morning voice
echoes through the air, leading me forward. I come to a
halt when I find him leaning against a huge breakfast
island. His back is to me as he gazes out the double doors
into the walled garden as he holds his phone to his ear.

Leaning against the counter, I eavesdrop on the one-
sided conversation. "Better than I thought…Yeah…I don't
want to leave her on her own…Right, fuck." Finally, as
though he feels me leering at his bare, tattoo-covered back
with my greedy eyes, he turns and flashes me his devilish
grin.

With the phone still clutched to the side of his face, he
stalks towards me, intent beaming from his hungry eyes.
"Okay, I'll be there." He closes the distance between us,
lowering his mouth to my neck and nibbling on my skin,
sending shivers down my spine. I remain quiet, muffling
my moan with clenched lips. Finally, he pulls back,
mouthing *good morning* before replying to whoever is on

the other end of his call. "Give me an hour…Okay, that will do. See you then, boss man."

Pulling the phone from his ear, he disconnects the call before dropping it onto the side cabinet right inside the doorway.

His arms circle my waist in the next breath, drawing me into his chest before he plants his lips on mine, stealing my greeting with a soul-touching kiss. When he pulls back, the smile on his face knocks every ounce of sense from my head. "Good morning, mo bhanríon álainn." *My beautiful queen.* "Did you sleep well?"

"Amazing, thank you." My eyes flick towards the phone. "Was that?" I hesitate, not knowing how to finish that sentence.

Rohan's shoulders rise with his intake of breath before finally, he replies, "It was your dad. There's been some development since last night. He needs me to meet him so we can go over our plan of attack. Strike when the iron is hot."

I nod, not knowing how to continue. Deep down, I know I'm not ready to face the man who created me, so instead, I avoid the questions in Rohan's eyes and push past him to get a glass of water, but his fingers curl around my elbow, drawing me back.

"Hey, don't shut down on me. If you don't want to talk about him yet, we don't have to, okay?"

"Okay."

His gaze drops to the sheet wrapped around my body and then back again. I shake my head at the mischievous grin in his eyes. He's trying to distract me, and it's working.

Finally, he grasps my waist in his palms, then he bends at the knee and picks me off the floor. Within seconds, he has me laid across the breakfast bar, the bed sheet piled in a crumpled heap on the floor, leaving me in all my naked glory. Then, with his hands on my knees, he spreads my legs open while he trails his tongue along his lower lip. "A breakfast fit for a king."

"Oh, God." My back arches off the counter when his mouth connects with my cunt. My hands grip the back of his head, holding him in place as he sucks hard on my clit. Lapping at me like a starved man as I writhe against the marble countertop. My fingers bury themselves into his messy morning hair as my hips buck against his tongue. He's relentless with his strokes, teasing me by sucking on my clit, and when he pushes two fingers inside of me, curling them against my G-spot, I almost bound off the counter as my moans bounce off the stone walls.

"Yes," I cry out as he spears his fingers into me with deep, torturous thrusts. "Fuck, Rohan. Right there."

I'm so close.

My hips race against his tongue as the pressure builds beneath my skin, rattling every cell in my body.

"That's it, mo bhanríon. Fuck my face with your cunt."

"Jesus, Rohan." My body ignites.

"I want to taste you on my tongue for the rest of the day. Give it to me, love. This pussy is mine."

Fireworks explode behind my eyes as my cum coats Rohan's lips and tongue. I lie there panting, my body spent from the pressure of my release. Finally, he steadies me on my feet, leaving me craving for more. "As much as I'd love to bend you over this countertop and fuck you from behind, I need to get going." He leans forward, claiming my mouth with my cum still glistening on his lips.

Eventually, he pulls back, and instantly, I miss him. Then, as if the reality of what he has to do next hits him, his hand settles on his neck as he rubs his nerves away. I know he's struggling with leaving me here by myself with everything going on, but honestly, I'm looking forward to the alone time, so I can gather my thoughts.

"I'll be fine, Rohan."

"I'll only be a few hours, tops."

"And I'll be right here when you get back."

I can see his thoughts as they dance across his face, then suddenly, he's taking my hand and pulling me out of the kitchen and down the long hallway. Finally, he halts in front of a large painting, then drops my hand as he tugs the right side and opens it like a door. A gasp leaves my mouth when I see the large black safe nestled seamlessly into the wall. Standing by, I watch as Rohan punches a code into the keypad before twisting the dial. The click of the lock floods the air, and then Rohan pulls the safe open, showcasing a mirage of firearms.

My eyes widen as shock settles tiny goosebumps along my skin. He reaches in, pulling out not one but two handguns. I watch him with a mixture of awe and terror as he does whatever checks people do with guns, and then he shoves the first one into the waistband at the back of his suit pants.

With the second gun in hand, he pulls me into his body until my back meets his front. He then reaches around and places the gun in my hands. "Wrap your hands around the grip," he demands, placing his chin on my shoulder. His hot breath brushes along my neck as I swallow back the fear, and do as he asks.

"When holding a handgun, your grip should be high and tight, meaning there should be no spaces between your flesh and the gun." I follow his instructions, ignoring the rapid rhythm of my heart as it tries to escape my rib cage.

"Now, can you see that vase by the door?" he whispers against my neck, and I nod my reply. "That's your target. Don't look directly at it. You need to line up the front and rear sights." He points to the two little triangles on either end of the barrel. "The front sight should be in clear focus, while the rear sight will be a little fuzzy. Don't pull the trigger until you see both sights aligned."

Peering over my shoulder, he places my arms where he wants them to be. "Now, use the centre of the pad on your index fingertip and the first knuckle joint to press down the trigger."

I line my finger up and draw in a breath.

"Now, shoot."

The force of the bullet leaving the barrel cocks my shoulders back, but Rohan's steady stance behind me keeps me rooted in place.

The vase explodes, spreading several shards of chain shattering through the air. "Good girl," he praises before pressing a kiss on my neck. Finally, he spins me around to face him. "Now, if anyone dares come into this house while I'm gone, shoot first, ask questions later."

"Rohan! I can't shoot someone."

"Sure you can. Just remember what I said. High and tight, line up your sights, and pull the trigger."

"You're insane."

"Only about you." He gives me one last lingering kiss before he leaves me standing in the middle of the hallway, completely naked, and holding a gun.

What the actual fuck?

IT'S BEEN ALMOST THREE HOURS SINCE ROHAN LEFT, AND I can't seem to settle the nervous energy swarming like a colony of angry bees in my stomach. I've done everything I can think of to pass the time, even walking through the beautiful gardens, and picking some flowers from the blossoming camilla rose and lavender bushes. When I can't focus on anything other than where he is and if he's safe, I decide to relieve the tension in my muscles by taking advantage of the large claw bathtub I saw in the master ensuite.

As the water fills the tub, I dissect the flowers I picked from the garden and scatter the petals into the water, perfuming the air. Once the bath is ready, I step in and slide my body underneath the water. Laying my head back against the brass tub, I close my eyes and let the water wash away all my worries.

Beyond relaxed, I bathe in the quiet time, leaving the stress of yesterday behind, and shutting out the world as it turns around me.

Suddenly, a tight grip clasps my neck, and my eyes spring open. Greeted by a black balaclava, my eyes then connect to penetrating pools of forest green. Everything about this intruder is reminiscent of the very first night Rohan and I collided paths.

The man before me, dressed in black from head to toe, has my heart thundering in my chest as the fear I once felt overrides my senses. It can't be him…no, it can't. "Rohan?" I croak beneath the pressure of his chokehold, begging for him to prove my wild thoughts wrong.

Gone is the desire that danced around those eyes this morning, burnt away by whatever demon blackens his murderous glare.

"Pretty little Saoirse." The words slither from his lips, each syllable wrapped in disgust, seeping into the heart I'd stupidly given him.

"Rohan…please, stop!" Something dark crosses his eyes as I plead his name, but he doesn't loosen his hold. The bathwater splashes as I tear at his wrist, fighting to free myself, but it's useless.

Through the slight cut out of his mask, I watch in fear as a slow, toxic smile creeps across his face. "Did you really believe *I* could love you?"

Tears pool in my eyes as fear clogs my throat. "I thought…" My eyes close as I replay all the moments we shared in the past twenty-four hours. Images of us dancing, of him carrying me up the steps as though I was the most precious thing he ever held, flashes of our tangled limbs as he whispered pretty Irish words in my ear—all a lie.

Mustering up every ounce of strength I have left, my

eyes shoot open, and I pull against his grasp with defiance as my heart shatters under his hand. "Go on," I rasp. My nostrils widen as I suck in as much air as I can. "Kill me."

There is no remorse in his eyes, no hesitation, no fucking love.

I was an idiot to believe otherwise.

His hand tightens around my neck, pushing against the lump in my throat, choking me with my own tongue.

I should have seen this coming. He was *never* my hero. Stupidly, I neglected all the red flags and disregarded all warning signs. I willingly gave him my heart. I knew loving a man like Rohan King would kill me, and I dug my own grave.

In the next breath, my head is under the water and fluid rushes up my nose as I struggle against the heavy-weight holding me under. His reflection blurs into a shapeless figure, but I continue to fight, splashing through the water as my arms fail me. And then my body stills. All I can see are the broken petals of camilla roses and lavender floating above me like lost clouds.

My demise wasn't his fault. It was mine, for believing every delectable lie he told me.

His words are distant, but I feel them reverberate through me. "Lies, Saoirse. It was all lies."

TO BE CONTINUED...

ACKNOWLEDGMENTS

Imposter syndrome…haha, fuck you!

The Ma, for the endless phone calls we had while you helped me work out my plot, the northern slang words, and the Belfast impressions that had me rolling. If only everyone had a mammy like you.

Mr Shauna, you kept me going when I was so close to giving up. You always find a way to make me laugh so hard I almost pee my pants. Also, thank you for that one word, in that one sentence…without you, this book would be incomplete. (He made me say that.)

My boys, J & B, for all those oven pizzas and quick dinners you endured while I was lost in the world of Killybegs… Ice cream is on me! Love you lots!

My sister Emma, thank you for always hyping me up, and helping me finalise this book. You are my biggest fan, and I love you for it!

Leila James, my work-wife! Without your help, I never would have finished this book. Thank you for all the early morning to late night sprints, and the daily chats that kept me motivated. You the real MVP! (Shameless plug, go check out Leila's books because THEY ARE AWESOME!)

My editor Zainab (Heart Full of Reads), thank you for making my words shine, and for the endless SHOUTY CAPS and awesome gifs and memes. You had faith in me from the beginning.

My alpha team, Carrie, Gina, Michelle, and Natalie. You girls give me life. You cheered so hard for Saoirse, Rohan, and Liam, and I am so thankful for each and every one of you.

My beta crew, Elle, Traci, and Ashley. You girls ate this book up, and provided me with amazing feedback. I loved your comments and encouragement. You're all amazing, and I am so happy to call you girls my friends.

All my lovely arc readers and street team members, thank you so much for helping me get Rohan and Saoirse out into the book world! You're all amazing! So much love for each and every one of you.

Finally, to everyone who picked this book up and got lost in between the pages. I hope you enjoyed the first instalment of the Kings of Killybegs series.

ABOUT THE AUTHOR

Creating worlds so the lost souls have somewhere to escape to.

Shauna Mairéad, AKA, alter ego to Shauna McDonnell, is a dark romance author from Dublin, Ireland. She enjoys crafting three-dimensional worlds and memorable characters with redeemable villains and the women who bring them to their knees.

Her writing journey began in December 2019, when she released her first contemporary novel, Luck, 4Clover series. Now, she's bringing out her dark side with her debut dark romance **Delectable Lies** *(Book One in the Kings of Killybegs Series)*

Sign up for Shauna Mairéad's Newsletter

Check out all the Kings of Killybegs Merchandise

♪ a g

Secrets, lies, and larger threats are lurking...

Find out what happens next in the next instalment to Rohan and Saoirse's story.

DESTRUCTIVE TRUTHS

Coming soon!

Follow me on social media to stay up-to-date with all things KINGS OF KILLYBEGS.

Printed in Great Britain
by Amazon